A WICKED KISS

"Lady, you are a menace," Ram growled. "An uptight prude who needs a little loosening up. And after the abuse you've heaped on me the past two days I feel justified in being the one who sets you straight."

Hannah's breath escaped in tiny bursts of fear as she struggled against his hold. "Let me go."

"You truly despise whiskey?" he asked.

"I do."

"And you know this from experience?"

"I don't need . . ."

"Have you ever had a drink before?"

"I wouldn't . . ."

"If you're going to condemn something, you ought to at least know what you're talking about, don't you think?"

"I know enough . . ."

"I don't think you do. I think you need to actually taste some."

"Never . . ." she cried, but it was too late. He'd lowered his head toward her and she could see the amber drops clinging to his lips. He brought his mouth down on hers, open and demanding, and the drops poured onto her lips. She tasted a mixture of warm, sweet maleness along with the bite of the liquor. She thought surely the drops had already infected her, for she felt drunk and dizzy. She couldn't push him away, didn't want to.

SUPER ROMANCE

BOOK YOUR PLACE ON OUR WEBSITE
AND MAKE THE
READING CONNECTION!

We've created a customized website just for our very special readers, where you can get the inside scoop on everything that's going on with Zebra, Pinnacle and Kensington books.

When you come online, you'll have the exciting opportunity to:

- View covers of upcoming books
- Read sample chapters
- Learn about our future publishing schedule (listed by publication month *and author*)
- Find out when your favorite authors will be visiting a city near you
- Search for and order backlist books from our online catalog
- Check out author bios and background information
- Send e-mail to your favorite authors
- Meet the Kensington staff online
- Join us in weekly chats with authors, readers and other guests
- Get writing guidelines
- AND MUCH MORE!

Visit our website at
http://www.zebrabooks.com

SINFUL

Marti Jones

Zebra Books
Kensington Publishing Corp.

http://www.zebrabooks.com

This book is dedicated to Rob Cohen and John Scogna-miglio, for their belief in me. And to all the fans who kept in touch, encouraging me with their letters and cards while we waited for this day.

ZEBRA BOOKS are published by

Kensington Publishing Corp.
850 Third Avenue
New York, NY 10022

Copyright © 1999 by Marti Jones

First Printing: August, 1999
10 9 8 7 6 5 4 3 2 1

Printed in the United States of America

Chapter One

Southern Oklahoma—1889

"Oh, baby, that's right. Yes, there; touch me there."

Fumbling with the ties on the front of the woman's worn dress, Ramsey Kellogg didn't even flinch when they tore. He was too eager, too hard, and he knew the cost of the dress wouldn't be more than a silver dollar. The sound of fabric ripping only enflamed his lust.

"I'll throw in an extra five spot to cover the dress," he said, his words mumbled as he sucked the soft flesh of her neck. "It'll be worth it." He grasped the front placket and tore it open down to her navel. As he'd suspected, she wore nothing beneath the cheap garment, and her ample breasts tumbled out into his eager hands.

His offer pleased her and she wiggled out of her clothes, shimmying her hips and licking her lips. Naked, she came back to him and began to unbutton his shirt. She drew out the process until Ram was tempted to rip his own clothing from his body. She tossed the shirt onto the end of the iron-railed bed. It fell to the floor and she bent to pick it up, her round, voluptuous bottom tipped up at him invitingly. He grabbed her hips and shoved her nude derriere against the throbbing mass straining the front of his trousers.

It had been a long time since he'd made love to a woman, his last case being longer and more hellish than he'd expected, and this woman knew how to wring every pounding emotion out of a man. She was good, touching him until he ached for release.

Convincingly playing the eager lover instead of the bored whore.

She moved her bottom up and down until Ram could hold out no longer. He spun her around and drew her close, fumbling with the buttons on his trousers. She shoved them down around his ankles, and when he took a step toward the bed he realized he hadn't removed his boots.

He waddled to the mattress and plopped down to discard the bothersome footwear.

Sounds of singing rose from the saloon below, accompanied by the sudden crash of breaking glass, but Ram ignored it all as he struggled with the tight leather encasing his feet.

The whore was now as aroused as he was and she impatiently grabbed his boot and brought it up between her hard, muscled thighs.

When the first boot came loose she lost her balance and staggered forward, giggling as her breasts swung side to side like erotic pendulums.

"Like a tight fit, do ya?" she asked, tossing the boot to one side.

"You know it, darlin'," he told her, grabbing her waist and dragging her toward the bed.

"One more." She backed up and took his other foot in her hands as the strains of the song from below grew louder and louder. Ram tried to focus on the vise her thighs made as she clutched his leg. He imagined them clutching his hips, his waist, his neck. . . .

"What the hell is that racket?" he yelled when he realized he was humming a familiar hymn. The religious doxology wrenched him from the present and thrust him into a maelstrom of bitter memories from his past. This particular song evoked thoughts of punishings, scoldings, hysterical rantings and blood. So much blood.

"Damn," he said, shaking off the painful memories. His anger only increased as he realized his ardor had died. He glanced around, as if to find some way to block out the noise. "How the hell am I supposed to do *this* with *that* blaring all around me?"

He jerked his foot out of the woman's grasp and hobbled to the door. Yanking up his trousers, he opened the door and stuck his head out, peering over the banister.

The woman came up behind him, still naked, and looked down in resignation.

"Fortune's version of Carry Nation," she mumbled, sidling up beside him on the landing. "And getting an early start, too." She glanced at the sun streaming through the small window on the upper landing.

Ram glared down at the ruckus going on in the saloon. A pack of women dressed in ugly gray and brown dresses with bonnets big enough to boil a goat in circled the tables, singing and brandishing their Bibles above their heads. The one in the lead was screaming condemnations on the evils of liquor, and saloons in general, her voice grating sharply above the catcalls and whistles of the rowdy patrons, who'd obviously seen the display before.

"Don't pay 'em no mind," his companion said, reaching around the front of his pants and frowning when she realized his interest had wilted. As she slid her hand beneath the coarse fabric and loosened buttons, the woman below chanced to glance up.

Ram couldn't see her face beneath the enormous brim of her bonnet, but he saw her freeze, as though she'd been glued to the floor. Several women behind her bumped into her back as she stood staring upward. The other women followed her gaze, and he heard a collective gasp echo in the sudden silence.

Only then did he realize he stood in the open with a naked whore whose hand happened to be down his pants.

He couldn't be sure from such a distance, but it appeared the woman in front shuddered all over as she lowered her head and drew her Bible tight against her chest. Then her voice rang out, loud and decidedly off-key. She hoisted the good book at him like a weapon and raised her face to the ceiling.

He recognized this hymn as well and fought to keep the memories from washing over him again. But the festering bitterness he was usually able to keep at bay crawled out from its hiding place, leaving a black trail of disgust as it filled him.

"Save it for church, sweetheart," he called down to the woman.

Several men stopped to look up, calling out encouragement to him or roaring with bawdy laughter. Ram felt the woman's eyes on him, though he could see nothing beneath the bonnet, and he pulled Sally in front of him and gave her bare buttocks a teasing smack.

The woman sang louder, and her cohorts quickly recovered their voices and joined in. Ram turned and went back into the room with his companion.

"They've been goin' at it like that for nearly two weeks," she explained. "I swear, old Martin is about ready to strangle that Sullivan broad."

Ram didn't feel like talking—not about the women downstairs or anything else. But he knew sex with Sally was out of the question with the familiar strains of religious hymns ringing in his ears.

He grabbed his shirt off the bedpost, muttering, "It's like trying to get a poke backstage at a tent revival."

He jabbed his arms into the sleeves and tugged on his other boot.

"What are you doing? Where are you going?"

"Anywhere but here, lady," he said, tossing the promised five spot onto the bed.

She snatched it up, then pouted. "What about the other?"

"There isn't going to be any other. Not in here with that going on downstairs."

"No use goin' to another saloon. It'll be the same at all of 'em."

Ram muttered another expletive and set his hat on his head. "Then there's nothing in this town for me," he told her.

He left her sitting on the bed and headed for the stairs. The women were still downstairs, singing and preaching. The owner had grasped the leader of the group around the waist and was trying to forcibly remove her from the room, but she'd dug her heels in. The man was making little progress, other than to provide his customers with a comedic sideshow while they drank their booze.

As Ram approached the bottom stair, one of the patrons, a dusty, trail-worn wrangler by the looks of him, decided to join in the fun. He grabbed one of the group and swung her into his arms, pinching her bottom and planting a wet, sloppy kiss on her lips.

The woman screamed so loud, Ram's hat nearly blew off, and another patron—a farmer who must have known the woman—jumped up and attacked the man from behind. The woman flew forward under the impact and landed in the lap of an elderly gentleman, who gave her another pinch. She slapped him, but he only grinned a toothless grin and drooled down the front of her tobacco-brown dress.

Shrieking, she shot off the man's lap and headed for the door, never looking back. Apparently, some of the other patrons could see the advantage of scaring the women off once and for all, and a free-for-all broke out. The wranglers tried to accost the women, while the locals belatedly made an attempt to defend them.

"Shit," Ram mumbled, tucking his head and heading for the bat-wing doors. The last thing he needed or wanted to do was get into a fight over something he had no interest in one way or the other.

Halfway to the doors he heard a terrified cry. He stopped, shook his head and headed for the stream of sunlight guiding him out of the melee. He wasn't about to defend some pious, uptight Holy Roller who'd do better to use her brains than her Bible as a shield.

Another cry sounded directly behind him, and he glanced back briefly. The rowdy wrangler had tossed the leader of the religious group over his shoulder and was heading up the stairs. The whore he'd left upstairs was standing at the top, egging the man on.

"Bring her up, mister; we'll have a party. She'll be singing in tune in no time."

The man laughed, the woman screamed and the whore looked down at Ram with a challenge. No doubt she saw a chance to pay back the woman for ruining her business and costing her much-needed money.

"Damn it all to hell," Ram cursed, glancing around at the full-scale brawl.

Everyone was busy busting tables or heads, and no one else seemed to have noticed the woman's predicament.

He reached the foot of the stairs as the wrangler and his package hit the narrow turn halfway up. The woman grabbed the banister with both hands, surprising her attacker and nearly knocking the man off balance. He tottered, hefted her higher and took another step. But she refused to let go, and Ram had to smile as she violently kicked the man's legs.

Just as Ram reached the pair, she landed a lucky blow to the man's groin with her knee and the wrangler bent double, dropping the woman right into Ram's outstretched arms. He clutched her to him, knocked off balance by the sudden shift of weight.

He intended to set her on her feet with another snide remark about her efforts, but as she slid slowly down the front of his body he felt himself grow hard again. His frustrated member was making it known that at this point it'd take whatever it could get. And a nice, slow rub of friction was enough to get it interested.

Ram's arms tightened as he fought to rein in the unconscious reaction. He moved back and felt nothing but air as he missed a step and lunged forward in an attempt to keep from careening backwards down the stairs.

His sudden movements propelled them both into the wall and he braced his arms to keep from smashing her. But once more his body thrust against hers, and this time their positions weren't so subtle. Her legs were sprawled, his thighs between them, and his hand had landed right on her left breast. His erection was nestled in the pillow of her mound and needles of sexual awareness zinged through his nerve endings, making all the hair on his body stand up.

He tried to look into her eyes but could see nothing past the hideous bonnet, except for a slash of mouth, nose and a long tendril of flaming red hair.

"Miss, I'm . . ."

Before he could get the words out, she snapped her knee up into his groin, and Ram tumbled down the stairs with a roar. The wrangler took advantage of his position and leaped on his back, pummeling him with angry fists. Ram saw a pair of black kid-leather boots scurry past his nose, and he cursed the little prude for all he was worth. The wrangler pounded him one more time, and Ram raised up with an animal howl, shaking the man off. He spun around, landing one solid blow that broke the man's jaw and rendered him unconscious.

With his nether areas lodged in his throat, Ram staggered forward and took out his rage on the remaining wranglers. Within minutes the men were lying prone on the floor and only Ram, the owner and a few of the locals remained standing.

Walking funny and holding his crotch, Ram went to the bar and poured himself a half glass of whiskey. He downed it in one gulp, poured another and drank it. After the third whiskey he could finally breathe without feeling as though he'd pass out from the pain.

"Nice going," the owner said, shoving broken glass to the floor as he cleared the bar. He poured Ram another drink as the locals hauled the wranglers into the street. "Pull up a stool, if you can find one that ain't broke, and have a sit. All the whiskey you want is on the house."

"I think I'll stand, if it's all the same to you," Ram muttered, loosening his trousers in front as normal feeling came back to the area.

The man chuckled and shook his head. "Nailed your willy a good one, did she? I'm not surprised. She's a true ball-buster, that one. Been bustin' mine, so to speak, for damn near two weeks. Ever since the news came down from Kansas that that bluestocking bloomer Carry Nation was at it again. All that woman needs is a good . . ."

"Carry Nation?" Ram cut in sharply, vaguely remembering the whore mentioning something similar. "What's she done now?"

"That milksop preacher husband of hers couldn't stir the people to close down the saloons, so she's taken to invading them with hordes of her followers to raise a ruckus and disturb the patrons. Hopes to drive off business with their preaching and hymn singing."

Ram thought of how fast his lust had died beneath the assault and acknowledged that the women were probably on to something.

"And this is just the beginning," the old man lamented, refilling Ram's glass. "Wait'll they get a hold of this," he said, pulling a folded newspaper from beneath the counter. He spread it open to the front page, and Ram skimmed the headline. Dated five days earlier, the article told how Carry Nation had been forcibly removed from a saloon by the proprietor. When onlookers rallied in support of Mrs. Nation, the city officials ordered the saloon closed. The defeated saloonkeeper was last seen on his way out of town.

"I'd say you've got a problem on your hands, mister." Ram shook his head with empathy, but he was already planning the quickest route out of Fortune. No booze and no women meant no good for his purposes.

"Yep, and it's the same everywhere for a forty-mile radius. That damn Sullivan woman has organized WCTU groups in every town."

"WCTU?"

"Woman's Christian Temperance Union. Bunch of tee-totaling . . ."

"Forty miles!" Ram snapped, becoming aware of what the man had said. "One woman is responsible for rallying women for forty miles?"

"You got it. Started out with a simple little sermon by our own candy-assed preacher. For some reason Hannah Sullivan took to the cause like stink to dung, and she's spent every minute since causing grief. And it don't look like she's about to quit anytime soon. I'm telling you, she needs to be good and proper la . . ."

"Well, good luck to you, mister. Sounds like you're going to need it."

Ram emptied his glass and turned from the bar. The remaining locals had set the unbroken tables and chairs upright and were nursing glasses of whiskey along with their wounds.

A lost cause, Ram thought. The womenfolk causing the trouble were their wives, sisters and mothers. And they'd proved they wouldn't allow the women to be mistreated, no matter how much they hated what they were doing.

When he had to go home to a furious female every night, even the most stubborn man would find his mind being changed pretty quick.

Yep, Fortune had seen the beginning of the end for the saloons, Ram was certain.

That thought riled him. For years he'd watched self-righteous, hypocritical do-gooders trying to force their opinions on others. Even now, a simple hymn could stir up the pain and torment they'd caused him. The sooner he shook off the dust of Fortune the better, he thought, once more tamping down futile emotions.

"Hey, drifter," the saloonkeeper called after him. "You handled yourself pretty good tonight. How'd you like a job?"

Ram started to tell the man he wasn't a drifter—he was a bona fide investigator on hiatus between cases—but then he thought, what the hell. Explanations weren't worth his time.

"No thanks," he mumbled, starting for the door again.

"Wait up a second," the man said, skirting the bar and knocking broken pieces of furniture out of his way. "Think about it, why don't'cha? You'd be perfect for the job. You can step right in and take control; you just proved that. And unlike some of the others who've tried to help, the sheriff included, you've got no connection to the women-folk, and no connection to the wranglers and cowboys that come through. You could keep those women out and the men peaceable.''

Ram shook his head, but the man continued, undaunted. "Look at this place. I can't afford any more trouble like we had here tonight. And there're four other saloons in this town alone. You'd be handsomely rewarded if you could put down Hannah Sullivan and her group. You'd leave Fortune a rich man.''

Ram could have told the man he had more than enough money already. But the idea was starting to appeal to him. Although not for any reason this man would understand. It *would* be downright pleasurable to put the Bible-thumpers in their place. And maybe it would score a few points against the demons that had plagued him for too many years. For damn sure it'd make him feel better to win, just once, over the holier-than-thou attitudes that had made his life a living hell for so long.

Still, the small amount of pleasure he'd find in winning would hardly be worth the trouble.

"No. No, thanks," he said, tossing the idea aside. He searched the floor for his hat, which he'd only just realized he'd lost in the scuffle, and spotted it by the stairs. He went to get it, the owner hot on his heels.

"Just stay the night and think it over. Got an empty room upstairs you can have, no cost, as long as you want. And Sally, too.''

"What?" Ram turned on the man, angry that he'd offer up the woman like a free lunch. But the owner misread his reaction and, thinking he'd gotten Ram's attention, plowed on.

"Sure. Plus a sizable fee. I speak for all the saloons in

town, I guarantee. The future of our livelihoods is at stake here, mister. I'm not stretching the tale. If we don't stop that Sullivan bitch pretty soon, a man won't be able to get a drink or a poke anywhere in the whole West territory. I'm appealing to you for men everywhere. You're a whiskey drinker, right? And you can appreciate the need for Sally and her kind. Why, what'll the country be like without the refuge of the saloons?''

'''Just slow down, old timer,'' Ram said, wrinkling his nose in disgust as a sliver of spittle ran down the corner of the man's mouth. He was practically frothing.

Ram wasn't sure he liked the man at all, but he had to admit he had a point. Several good ones, in fact. He'd seen religious zealots whip a crowd into a frenzied mob, crying and screaming and falling out in ''spells.''

He could easily imagine a wave of righteousness sweeping the nation, outlawing booze, whores and even establishments where men came just to have a cigar and a quiet moment away from their daily strife. It galled him that the efforts of so few could affect so many, but he'd seen it happen too many times. He'd felt its effects on his own life and still had the scars to prove it.

He was a free agent since leaving the Pinkerton detectives, and he didn't have a current case pending. He needed a break anyway, a rest after the horrors of his last manhunt. The faces of the farmer, his wife and their four little children, all butchered by a drifter for fun and a few bucks, haunted him, even though he'd taken pleasure in personally sending the killer to hell.

A tussle with a pack of Bible-toting bloomers might just be the diversion he needed to put him back on track. Besides, he thought with a wicked grin, it would be fun to see this Sullivan woman put soundly in her place. She was probably some homely female who couldn't give it away, jealous of women like Sally that men were willing to pay money for.

And he owed her one for trying to emasculate him when he'd come to her aid.

"I'll take the room for the night, and I'll consider the job," he told the man, picking up his crushed hat with a muttered oath. "But if I want Sally," he added with a hard look, "I'll pay just like everyone else."

Chapter Two

"Oh, Francis, it was dreadful. The worst encounter to date. Mary Beth was assaulted, and her husband has a broken nose. I don't know how that marriage will survive; it seems doomed for certain."

Hannah Sullivan paced to the parlor window of the parsonage and stood fingering the frayed corner of her Bible. The name SARAH HEALY was inscribed in gold lettering in the corner, a constant reminder that even the Bible she carried was a hand-me-down of the minister's former wife.

"I'll set up council with the Grays as soon as possible," Reverend Healy said, his bespectacled eyes never rising from the scrawled words of the sermon he was laboring over. "But if Rupert Gray can't keep from bending his elbow at that saloon, I don't see there's much I can do for them."

"Oh, but Mary Beth is such a sweet, dear woman. And

Rupert isn't bad, not really. I mean, he doesn't beat her, or starve her, or even go upstairs when he's at the saloon. . . ."

"Hannah!"

Hannah jumped, startled by the harsh rebuke in the reverend's tone. Then, realizing how inappropriate her words had been, she flushed. "I'm sorry, Francis. That just sort of fell out."

"We've spoken about your tendency to loose words, Hannah. Really, it's not at all the proper thing for a minister's wife to speak about."

"No, of course not, Francis. But, just between us—I mean, we are engaged."

"Yes, and if you think I will ever long to kiss lips that have harbored such swill, you don't know much about a decent man's expectations."

The setdown stung, and she fought against her natural instinct to react with anger. After all, she reminded herself, she was the one in the wrong. Francis certainly knew more about being respectable and godly than she did.

And that was what Hannah wanted to be, more than anything else in the world.

Above her desire to be Francis's wife, or even the leader of Fortune's chapter of the WCTU, Hannah needed to be respectable and righteous.

"I'm sorry," she whispered.

"I'm very busy, Hannah. Not that I don't enjoy your company, but don't you have things you should be doing for the union? Plans to be made for future rallies?"

"That's just the thing, Francis. I think it might be getting too dangerous to continue. Someone could have been seriously hurt this afternoon. As it was, Doc Snell's been busy all day patching up that group of wranglers. And some of our own men were injured, as well as . . ."

Reverend Healy removed his spectacles and glanced up

at Hannah with disappointment. She stammered to a halt
as he polished the lenses with his handkerchief.

"God's work isn't always easy, Hannah, or pleasant. You
undertook this mission to rid Fortune, and indeed this
country, from the evils of drink, did you not?"

"Yes, of course . . ."

"And does Fortune still have four of those dens of
depravity stealing hard-earned money from our weak-
minded menfolk?"

Francis's questioning made Hannah feel personally
responsible for the fact that the establishments were still
in operation. She cringed as she admitted sadly, "Yes,
Francis."

"And are those painted harlots still luring unfortunate
husbands into their webs?"

Hannah briefly considered chastising the minister for
his own terminology, then was horrified by her thought.
Who was she to judge right from wrong? Certainly if Francis
said it, it must be acceptable language for a man in his
position.

"Yes, Francis, I'm sure they are. In fact," she said, eager
to tell him what she'd witnessed in the upstairs hall of the
saloon, now that he'd opened the door to this discussion,
"I saw one of them this afternoon. She was totally nude,
Francis. I mean, without a stitch on. And she was with a
man. I didn't recognize him; he must have been passing
through. I don't think he was with the wranglers, since I
saw him beat one of them nearly senseless, but he wasn't
from around here, of that I'm sure. He was very tall and
had a huge muscular chest and the longest legs I've ever
seen. And his hair was longish blond, and sort of tousled.
But I suppose that could have been from the activity he'd
been engaged in before . . ."

"Hannah!"

The minister shifted uncomfortably in his chair and

adjusted the papers before him. Hannah bit her tongue and started to apologize again. But something kept her from actually uttering the words. Maybe it was her new ideas about women's equality, or the new pride she'd found in her work. Whatever it was, she found she wasn't so eager to humble herself before anyone, not even Francis.

He raised a brow, obviously expecting the flood of apologies that usually followed one of Hannah's slips. She bit her lip and shrugged her shoulders. "You brought the matter up, Francis. I was just commenting on it."

"Injudiciously, as usual." He sighed and rubbed a ha over his thin brown hair. "Really, Hannah, I don't see I'll ever turn you into a proper minister's wife. Or what made me think I could, knowing your background."

Hannah flushed with suppressed anger that he would bring *that* up now.

Francis loved her, she was sure. Although he was seldom verbal on the subject. And he was the most righteous man she'd ever met. But sometimes his barbs stung, and she had to wonder if he intended to hurt her with the words or merely help her, as he insisted.

He must have noticed the crimson fury staining her cheeks then. He laid his glasses aside and came to her, taking her hands.

"No one blames you for your mother's sins, dear. Least of all me. I chose you to be my wife, my helpmate. But you must truly leave that part of yourself behind if you ever hope to be a respected servant of God in this community, Hannah. That is what you want, isn't it?"

She softened at his words. "Of course, Francis."

"That's my girl," he said, patting her hand. "Now, why don't you go and gather your flock and prepare for tonight's rally?"

"But, Francis, there's something else I need to tell you. . . ."

"Later, dear. I have to finish this sermon, and I haven't made any headway at all this afternoon. We'll talk more tomorrow. Why don't you bring lunch and we can spend a half hour or so together? Mrs. Halliday will be here, so it will be all nice and proper."

Unlike this meeting, she thought belatedly. Francis had told her not to come to the parsonage except when Mrs. Halliday was there to chaperone, but Hannah was always doing things without thinking. No wonder he sometimes lost his temper and grew short with her. He was a saint to put up with her, especially since he, unlike the other people in Fortune, knew the truth about her past.

"All right," she said, clutching her Bible close and offering him a smile.

How could she have thought such mean-spirited things about Francis? He'd been so good to her, so kind. He never condemned her for the way she'd lived before coming to Fortune. He never uttered a word to anyone about the horrors she'd confided to him. Even the clothes on her back and the Bible in her hand had come from Francis.

"Give those devils a good licking," he said, squeezing her shoulder as he walked with her to the door. "You're a soldier for God now, Hannah. Go forth and do battle and you shall be rewarded."

"Good-bye, Francis," she said, turning to face him. She leaned close, hoping he would finally kiss her, finally show some outward sign of the feelings he professed for her. But he simply led her down the porch steps into the fading dusk. Then he turned and went back into the rectory, closing the door behind him.

Hannah stood there staring at the fading copper fireball of the sun as it ebbed beneath the horizon. She felt a wave of shame crash over her and tears stung the backs of her eyes. Why was she forever giving in to the needs of the flesh? Did she take after her mother?

She craved the feel of a man's lips on hers, the touch of his hand, the strength of his arms around her. These were all things that were only considered proper and right when they occurred behind closed doors between a man and his wife. It wasn't something she should long for on the porch of the parsonage with a man of God she'd not yet wed.

"I'll never be good enough for Francis," she muttered. "I'll never be rid of the stain of my past."

But she could try, she thought. She'd work harder than ever to do God's work and to make herself into someone Francis could be proud to introduce as his wife. And once they were married, her needs would be met, and this gnawing hunger she felt constantly riding the pit of her stomach would turn into a heart filled with love for her husband.

"But not yet," she said, her spine stiffening with resolve as she watched the men on the streets heading for the various saloons. "Not until I've done this one thing for Francis, and for God."

Hannah marched down the street with her bonneted head held high. No one knew the shame she carried inside. If she could shut down the saloons of Fortune and the surrounding territory, no one would ever suspect that Hannah Sullivan, the preacher's soon-to-be wife and leader of the Southern Oklahoma chapter of the Woman's Christian Temperance Union, was a drunken whore's daughter.

"It's a bloomer costume, Nan," Hannah explained once more. "Sarah Pellet wore them all the time in her war against liquor in California in the '50s. It's become a symbol of our fight and victory over drink. Besides, Margaret went to all the trouble to sew them for us."

"But it's pants, Hannah," the older woman argued, tugging on the bottom of the short skirt. Her limbs were well

covered in the loose-fitting trousers, which ballooned out
beneath the skirt and gathered at the ankles. The short
jacket buttoned to the neck, the very picture of propriety.

"It's a badge of honor for our cause," Tabby Reid cut
in, snatching up one of the odd suits. "I can't wait to see
Daniel Dowd's face when he locks eyes on me in this."

"It's not meant to entice sinful thoughts," Agnes Pearl
snapped, holding her own costume up in front of her.

"So call it an extra added bonus," Tabby shot back,
sticking her tongue out at Agnes.

"Oooohhh," Nan cried, tugging off the jacket. "I can't.
I believe in the cause, Hannah; you know I do. But I'm
not one of those feminists who thinks men and women
ought to be equal. I don't want to vote, nor do I want to
go to work. I like staying home with my babies, and Howard'll have a conniption fit if I parade down the streets of
town in that outfit. As it is, he's tried everything short of
beating me to get me to stop protesting in the saloons."

"Nan, your husband doesn't even drink," Tabby said.
"Why should he care if we shut down the saloons?"

"Those men are his friends and customers at the bank.
They don't like what we're doing and they've been putting
pressure on him to make me stop."

"Well, it isn't as if you're leading the group," Agnes
said, squeezing her flabby buttocks into one of the costumes. The material strained over her ample thighs, and
Hannah stared in shock at the details outlined by the skin-
tight trousers. She shot Margaret a desperate look. The
seamstress huffed in disgust and handed Agnes another
pair of the odd-looking pants. She shimmied out of the
snug ones and Margaret handed them to the much thinner
Tabby, who giggled and went behind the screen to dress.

"You don't have to wear them if you don't want to,
Nan," Hannah said soothingly. "No one wants to make
you uncomfortable. We're here to help women—and men,

for that matter—by outlawing alcohol and shutting down the saloons that keep men away from home at night and contribute to their drinking and womanizing. It doesn't matter how we dress, just as long as we get the job done."

"Of course, it'll be a sight easier to convince Daniel Dowd to come see me at night instead of visiting that old Sally when I'm wearing this," Tabby said, parading out in the fetching getup.

Hannah had to admit the woman looked sinful, even in such a modest outfit. Of course Tabby, with her generous bosom, narrow waist, full hips and pouty lips, not to mention her streaming blond locks and sky-blue eyes, would look gorgeous in a burlap flour sack.

"Oooohhh, my," Nan said, cringing at the beautiful Tabby. "Howard's gonna kill me for sure."

"Oh, hush," Agnes snapped, finally getting into her own costume. "Howard can't blame you for the way Tabby looks. Now get your gear on and let's get moving. I gotta be back by two-thirty to get the beans on, or they'll never be ready by the time Ed gets home at six."

Hannah decided to let Nan alone to decide for herself what she'd wear. She couldn't push the women into doing things that would disrupt their home lives. The havoc they were wreaking on the men was trouble enough.

After donning her own outfit, she put her bonnet on over her upswept hair. The tangled mass of red curls was another legacy from her mother, and Hannah regarded it as one more unruly trait to be harnessed and tamed. Like the unfulfilled desires that had kept her awake long into the night after her meeting with the reverend. And the sinful images she kept seeing of the stranger from the saloon.

She saw him again in her mind's eye and felt a subtle tug in her stomach. Pressing a hand to her middle, she forced her mind back to her present task.

"The whiskey seller's wagon will be here at noon. He always parks in the alley behind the Double Eagle," Hannah told the group. "He goes to Josey's café for dinner and he's gone at least an hour before coming back to unload the first shipment. The whiskey sits there unattended for sixty minutes. That's plenty of time for what we've planned."

"But Hannah," Nan whined, "can't we get into trouble for this? I mean, that whiskey doesn't belong to us. We can't just . . ."

"Yes, we can, too," Agnes announced, slapping her big straw hat down on her head and tying the ridiculously large bow beneath her chins. "What're they gonna do, arrest us? Not likely, if they want their suppers cooked and their beds warmed."

"Oh, my!" Nan fluttered off behind the screen, twin flags of color riding high on her cheeks. Tabby giggled and Hannah had to smile, though she knew Francis wouldn't approve of the woman's sharp tongue. She sometimes wondered why Agnes wasn't the leader of their little group. She had more spunk than Hannah and was a true feminist. She carried membership cards for not only the WCTU, but organizations for women's suffrage and Indian rights, as well.

Hannah knew Francis disdained Agnes as a sharp-tongued, loudly outspoken, quarrelsome radical. But deep down in her heart, Hannah admired Agnes, and wished she'd been raised by someone with so generous a nature and open a mind.

"Come along, ladies," Agnes said, flashing Hannah a rare, winsome smile. "We're burning daylight."

They left Hannah's little house at the edge of town and marched proudly down Main Street in their bloomer costumes, Nan included, though she kept to the middle and occasionally ducked her head. Several women gasped or pointed, and more than one man burst out laughing at the sight, but the women marched on. Daniel Dowd reacted with a loud whistle, and Tabby stopped long enough to grace him with a beaming smile before Agnes tugged her back into the throng.

They made directly for the back alley adjacent to the Double Eagle Saloon owned by Martin Pollack. It was the largest and most prosperous saloon, and the first on their list to be shut down. It was also the place where Hannah had had the encounter with the stranger the day before.

As she made her way down the dusty road, she couldn't help thinking about the astonishing sight that had met her eyes when she'd happened to glance up while picketing the saloon. She hadn't even noticed the woman at first, though nudity wasn't something she came across every day.

It was the man who'd drawn her gaze. He'd been so big and muscular, his upper body bare and tanned, not like the few pale-chested farmers she'd seen shirtless in her life.

Unfortunately, she was more familiar with a man's physique than she'd have liked because of her mother, and she knew this man was unusual. He'd stood there glaring like some Greek god of mythology, his arms gleaming and his features seemingly cast from stone, and Hannah had felt something wicked and hot shift inside her. Breathless, her heart racing, she'd stood paralyzed by his mere presence.

And then she'd seen movement, and that's when she noticed the naked whore. Hannah would never forget the feelings that coursed through her when she followed the pale, slim arm to where the woman's hand disappeared beneath the man's trousers.

She'd felt shock and anger, and something more. She'd been suffused with an emotion she didn't recognize but suspected was closely related to jealousy.

But how could that be? she wondered. She loved Francis. And she was going to marry him one day, when she'd proven herself worthy. And even if she never did, even if there was no Francis, a whiskey-drinking womanizer was certainly not the fate she'd choose for herself.

Even she deserved better than that.

Chapter Three

No one attempted to stop the women as they entered the back alley and gathered around the flatbed wagon parked by the rear door of the saloon. A swarm of lead-winged butterflies took flight in Hannah's stomach, but she smiled nervously at the women and pressed on.

The others hung back, apprehensive now that the moment was at hand. Hannah cleared her dry throat, rubbed her moist palms on the billowing folds of her short skirt and took a step forward.

It took her a moment to figure out how to break the seal on the first bottle, but it soon snapped beneath her hand, and she smelled the strong, familiar odor of the liquor as fumes escaped. She tamped down the memories the smell evoked, knowing they would consume her if she let her guard slip.

Her knuckles were white where she clasped the neck of the bottle, her hands trembling from remembered anger, fear and humiliation.

So harmless-looking, she thought, staring at the warm amber liquid. Yet so lethal.

She tipped the bottle upside down and let each slow glug, glug, drown her doubts. When the bottle was empty she released a heavy breath and reached for another. By the third bottle the other women had joined in, and a puddle formed in the alley and ran in a stream toward the street, the heavy odor filling her nose.

The women had emptied two cases and were working on a third when Hannah heard a window on the second floor slide open. She glanced up sharply and saw the startled face of the whore from yesterday.

The woman blinked in dazed bewilderment, or maybe it was the effect of the strong sun in her eyes after the dark interior of the saloon. Either way, it took a few seconds for her to register what the women in the alley were doing. When realization dawned she hefted the bowl she carried and rained the contents down over them.

Hannah barely had time to sound a warning before the soapy water splattered around them, dousing their legs and feet as they scampered away from the wagon. Nan shrieked as her back took most of the deluge.

"Quit your caterwauling," Agnes said, brushing pellets of cloudy spray from her shoulders. "At least it wasn't her chamber pot."

This set off new cries from Nan, and Hannah waved her off with Mary Beth to get out of the damp clothes. Tabby fluffed a curl on her forehead and reached for another bottle.

"Better get a move on," Agnes told Hannah, brushing past her on her way to the wagon bed. "She'll no doubt send up the alarm. We don't have much time now."

Hannah knew this was true and could see their plan coming to an end even before it had started. She glanced around the alley, looking for something that would speed up their destruction.

A broken crate lay to one side of the back door and she raced over and grabbed up two of the wooden slats that had come loose. Heavy square nails still jutted out on one end of the boards. With a wicked grin, she handed one to Agnes and, wielding the other like a baseball bat, took out four bottles at once.

Tabby laughed with glee and began lifting bottles from the remaining crates, lining them up along the side of the wagon as Hannah and Agnes crashed bottle after bottle.

A pack of men rounded the side of the saloon just as the back door flew open and the stranger stepped into the alley, followed by the saloon owner, whose face was mottled with rage. The stranger held up his arm to keep the man from charging the women.

Hannah knew real fear as she saw the owner shake with undiluted fury. But she hid her panic and met his angry gaze with her chin tipped up. They'd had less than two minutes after being spotted, but she knew the damage they'd done was extensive nonetheless.

Stepping forward, the stranger grabbed the board and wrestled it out of Agnes's hand. Looming over Tabby, he shouted, "Get out of here."

The girl shot Hannah a terrified look before turning to race out of the alley. The other men surged forward, surrounding Hannah and Agnes. Agnes gave one of them a shove when he got too close.

"What do you think you're doing?" the stranger asked Hannah, reaching for her weapon. She turned swiftly, avoiding his reach and managing to get her back against the wagon. She felt safer somehow, but acknowledged that she was now well and truly trapped.

"I'm preventing the rum-suckers in these parts from leading our good men and boys astray," she pronounced loudly to the mob in general. "And fighting God's war against the demon alcohol."

Agnes pushed her way up to the wagon and harrumphed her agreement.

"You're destroying property that doesn't belong to you, and that's against the law," the man countered, again reaching for the stick, which Hannah continued to hold beyond his reach.

"Man's law, perhaps, but not God's. He has given me a mission. I am acting on his behalf."

"Yeah? Well, I've got news for you, lady. God ain't the one the sheriff's going to arrest when he arrives in a few minutes. It'll be you."

"Your threats don't scare me," Hannah told him boldly, stiffening her spine. "Ephesians, Chapter Five, Verse Thirteen, says, *'Be not drunk with spirits, wherein lies excess; but be filled with the Spirit.'* " Pointing her finger to Heaven, she stared him down.

A slow, wicked smile spread across his full lips, and he took a step closer to Hannah. She gripped the board in her hand but knew it would do her no good. He was too close; she couldn't get it up to hit him if he tried to hurt her.

Agnes huddled close, peering intently over Hannah's shoulder at the advancing stranger. The other men shuffled nervously, uncertain of the man's intentions.

Hannah smelled an intoxicating blend of soap and cologne as he leaned in close. She saw sparks of amber in his brown eyes as they flashed down at her. Swallowing hard, she wished she had not backed herself against the wagon. The hard, unyielding planks of the wagon's sides cut into her back.

" *'Drink thy wine with a merry heart,'* " the man said, a hint of whiskey on his breath.

Hannah gasped and pressed her hand to her heart.

"Ecclesiastes, Chapter Nine, Verse Seven," he announced to the group.

A stunned silence filled the alley. Hannah was furious, the men confused. They turned to one another with furrowed brows and questions in their eyes. Finally, one young man stepped forward from the mob and scratched his head.

"Is that true, Miss Hannah? Does it really say that in the Bible?"

Hannah flushed and felt a lump choke off her breath. She'd never read the scripture he'd referred to, and she wasn't totally confident in her Christian infancy to challenge him, though she had to wonder if such a verse even existed. After all, what would a whiskey-loving womanizer know of scripture?

Then she saw Agnes's lowered head out of the corner of her eye, and Hannah realized he must be right. Her anger boiled as she sought a suitable retort.

"I don't see any wine in this wagon," she said to the group. Then, turning to her nemesis, she pretended to sniff daintily. "And I don't believe that's wine I smell on your breath either," she countered.

He shrugged and laughed in her face, and Hannah noticed the odor wasn't the same sour smell she remembered from her mother's breath. This scent was honeyed and almost pleasant.

Reaching behind her, he picked up one of the few undamaged bottles. Twisting the top off easily, he brought the bottle to his lips and drank deep.

" *'Give strong drink unto him that is ready to perish,'* " he quoted, holding the bottle out to Hannah.

She slapped his hand away.

"Proverbs Thirty-one and Six," he added triumphantly. "I don't know about these men, but when I woke up this morning I was feeling mighty close to that state myself."

He drank some more and lifted the bottle toward Hannah's lips. She tried to pull away, but she had backed up as far as she could go and his hand was still ascending. His heat reached out to her and she had to crane her neck to keep her lips from touching the bottle.

"*'I have come into my garden, my sister, my spouse,'*" he continued in a whisper, his breath warm on her cheek. "*'I have drunk my wine with my milk: eat O friends; drink abundantly, O beloved.'*"

Hannah couldn't breathe; she couldn't move. His words were like a caress, his nearness a seduction of her senses. He was quoting scripture to her and she was melting beneath the tender words he spoke, as though they were a sonnet he'd written for her alone.

Another quiet lull followed, this one shorter. Then a smile broke across the face of the saloon owner, who had looked ready to commit murder up to that point. One of the other men had taken up guarding him when the stranger approached Hannah; now he shook the man off and took a step forward, bending double as great laughs shook him.

"I think I'll make a banner using some of them fancy words and hang it over the front doors, boys. What do you think? I don't believe I've ever heard that windbag Reverend Healy preach a better sermon, nor hold an audience for so long. Have any of you?"

The men began to laugh, and soon the alley was filled with the sound. Hannah even heard a snicker come from Agnes's direction. She fumed. What had happened? How had he so mesmerized her? He surely must be the devil, drawing her out of herself in such a way that she'd forgotten the other men in the alley. She'd even forgotten Francis, and her pending engagement, until his name was mentioned.

"Don't call him that," she snapped, pushing forward.

"And if you've never heard Francis preach those verses . . . well, it's probably because this—this man, has quoted them erroneously," she cried.

But no one was listening to her. The group had found an ally in this tall, handsome stranger, and they were congratulating themselves on setting Hannah and her union down a mighty peg. With a few sentences, he'd not only undone two weeks' worth of work on her part, he'd given the men strong ammunition to use against her in the future.

She could see her plans for a saloon-free Fortune blow away like dust on Main Street, along with her hopes for a speedy engagement, and something in her snapped. How could this horrible, awful man justify what he and the others were doing inside those saloons? And how dare he use the Lord's words to do it?

She'd lived with the side effects of alcoholic indulgence all her life. She'd watched the degrading things her mother did for a bottle.

Her last night in her mother's house flashed through her mind, burning away the protective veneer she'd spent years developing. The hurt and rage spilled forth, finding release after being constrained so long to the bowels of Hannah's soul.

The feelings hadn't diminished at all during their hibernation; they'd grown stronger, their roots deeper.

She lashed out with her hand, intending to slap the smirk off the man's face. But in her fury she'd forgotten the board she still clutched. As it whipped toward his head, she saw his smile die.

In a flash he grabbed her arm, jerking the board free. Hannah struggled against his hold, but he was so big and strong, her efforts were no more than an annoyance to him. Her bonnet tumbled off, settling against her back, and her hair fell free, cascading around her face and shoulders.

For a moment Hannah felt the man's grip loosen. His eyes widened in surprise and his hold changed. Now the arms encased her, seeking out the curves and planes of her body. The fingers reached out, touching, grasping. The way she'd longed for Francis to hold her, touch her.

Frightened by her thoughts and the wave of longing that swept through her, she kicked out with her feet to break the contact and end the agonizing moment.

Again he was swifter, sweeping his leg behind her, trapping her limbs between his. Scared and angry, she tried to raise her knee. He read her intentions and brought his foot forward, collapsing her legs beneath her.

Hannah sank to the ground and he let her drop, right on her bottom. She cried out and glared up at him as she felt hot flags of color blaze across her cheeks.

"Uh, uh," he said. "I'm rather fond of my jewels, lady, and if you try to nail them again, I just might make you kiss it all better."

Agnes gasped and the men laughed, but Hannah was too stunned to even move. She'd only thought she'd faced humiliation and shame before, but it was nothing compared to this. Never had she met anyone so truly wicked, so vile!

Struggling to her feet, she felt Agnes reach out for her. The stranger made no attempt to help her up, and she could see he was furious. His eyes blazed and there was a thin white line circling his lips.

What did he have to be angry about? She was the one who'd been insulted and dropped on her bottom. She was the one who'd suffered the greatest embarrassment of her life. Seeking to salvage some measure of pride and dignity, she snatched the bottle from his hand. He blinked in surprise as she lifted it toward her face. The men fell silent, and she paused until she knew every eye was on her.

"You really like this stuff that much?" she said, appearing to study the drink with interest. He quirked one chestnut-brown eyebrow at her but remained silent.

Someone in the crowd shouted encouragement for her to take a drink, and Hannah watched as the stranger's eyes were diverted for a split second. She took full advantage of his brief inattention.

"Then bathe in it," she said, turning it over onto his head and watching in satisfaction as the liquor rained down his shocked features.

Smugly satisfied with her success, she clasped Agnes's hand and tried to force her way past the man. But again his arm snaked out and grabbed her. He spun her into his arms, loosening her grip on Agnes and slamming her body against his.

"Lady, you are a menace," he growled. "An uptight prude who needs a little loosening up. And after the abuse you've heaped on me the past two days I feel justified in being the one who sets you straight."

Hannah's breath escaped in tiny bursts of fear as she struggled against his hold. Agnes looked ready to pounce should the stranger attempt to actually harm her, but Hannah could see the apprehension in the older woman's eyes.

"Let me go."

"You truly despise whiskey?" he asked.

"I do."

"And you know this from experience?"

"I don't need . . ."

"Have you ever had a drink before?"

"I wouldn't . . ."

"If you're going to condemn something, you ought to at least know what you're talking about, don't you think?"

"I know enough . . ."

"I don't think you do. I think you need to actually taste some."

"Never . . ." she cried, but it was too late. He'd lowered

his head toward her and she could see the amber drops clinging to his lips, his chin, even the tip of his nose. He brought his mouth down on hers, open and demanding, and the drops poured onto her lips. She tried to force him away, but his grasp tightened. He lifted his mouth and she gulped air, but it was only a short reprieve. He rubbed his cheek over her lips and they stung from the coarse growth of beard on his face.

Again he forced his mouth over hers, and this time she tasted a mixture of warm, sweet maleness along with the bite of the liquor. She thought surely the drops had already infected her, for she felt drunk and dizzy. She couldn't push him away, didn't want to. She clung to his neck, trying to keep from falling as her knees went weak beneath her.

He lifted his head, his glance caught by something just over her shoulder. With a little push, he thrust her out of his arms, snapping her mind back to the reality of her situation.

"Today's just full of new experiences for you, lady," he said with a wicked grin. "Your first drink and your first night in jail."

Hannah gasped as he spun her around, right into the hands of the waiting sheriff.

Chapter Four

Hannah opened the door to her house and stepped inside, leaning back with a heavy sigh. She'd never been so glad to get home.

She sat on the cream-colored divan and began unlacing her boots. Her feet hurt, her head ached and even the fact that she was at home instead of in jail couldn't erase the horrible experiences she'd had that day.

The sheriff had hauled them to jail like common criminals, stopping just short of herding them into the cell. Hannah probably would have gone quietly, she'd been so disturbed by her encounter with the stranger.

Thankfully, Agnes had raised a ruckus and demanded her husband be sent for immediately.

Sheriff Dobson complied, and Ed Pearl arrived within the half hour. He'd been furious at Hannah for dragging his wife into such a fracas, she could tell, but he'd been polite and authoritative, as usual. He'd insisted that the women be let off with a warning, and the sheriff, having no experience in such matters, agreed. Martin Pollock had demanded that Ed Pearl pay restitution for the lost whiskey, but Agnes had forbidden her husband to give the whiskey-seller a penny.

"I'd rather spend the night in jail," she'd stubbornly insisted.

In the end the sheriff had no choice but to let the women go. The whiskey-seller, a short, odd little man, had been grousing about his losses to Martin Pollock as Ed escorted Agnes and Hannah out into the streets, where a crowd of women had gathered bearing signs demanding their release.

It was a rather grandiose gesture, considering they'd been held for less than an hour, but Hannah was grateful for the unified show of support after her humiliation at the hands of the stranger.

Ramsey Kellogg, she thought with a pang of remembered fear, a huge dose of renewed embarrassment and a strange wash of heat in her midsection that she couldn't identify.

She'd learned the stranger's name during the course of the sheriff's questioning, and it had stuck in her brain. Who was the blasted man? And what was his connection to Martin Pollock and the Double Eagle Saloon?

Yesterday she'd thought him no more than a drifter, a stranger in search of liquor and feminine companionship, like so many other men she'd seen pass through Fortune on their way to parts farther west.

Martin had spoken of Ramsey Kellogg like a friend and an ally, though. She wondered if it was possible the saloon owner had gone so far as to send for outside reinforcements to help eradicate the WCTU.

In a way, that would be an encouraging and rather flattering thought, for it meant Martin saw her and her group as a real threat. A serious opponent to the saloons in Fortune.

But Hannah couldn't help feeling a bit intimidated, too. She could finesse her way around the men of Fortune. Most of them had been friends and acquaintances of hers for the two years she'd lived there, not to mention husbands and brothers of most of the women in her group.

But this stranger, Ramsey Kellogg, was an unknown element, a wild card she didn't know how to play. He'd already shown her he could be cruel and insulting. He'd manhandled her in a way none of the townsfolk would have dared. And he obviously was completely without scruples, she thought, remembering the scene in the upstairs hall of the saloon, and the way he'd chugged the whiskey in the alley.

But he quoted scripture like a man of God. And when he touched her, he evoked fires of longing and passions she'd tried to suppress.

A whiskey-lover, she thought with disgust, rubbing her forehead. A womanizing rum-sucker. And he stirred to life feelings she'd hoped were buried deep and well. Emotions she'd put down to her mother's influence.

One touch and she forgot everything she'd been running away from. One tender phrase and she was ready to follow in her mother's sinful footsteps.

Good Lord, she'd even forgotten Francis and her love for him!

"Francis!" she cried, clasping her hand over her mouth. What would he do when he heard what had happened? Would he call off the engagement?

It was very possible, she realized, her heart sinking like a stone to the hollow pit of her stomach.

"No, no," she whispered, shaking her head. "That can't happen. I won't allow it. I've come so far. Too far to let that—that *man* ruin it all now."

She had to see Francis. She must talk to him and make

him see that this was just another test of their determination and commitment to do the Lord's work together.

They had declared war on Satan in Fortune, and he'd retaliated tenfold in the form of a handsome, devilish rake by the name of Ramsey Kellogg.

"Kissed you? Full on the mouth? In view of half the town?" Francis roared, his voice sounding every bit as though he was casting out demons from his pulpit on Sunday morning. Hannah could smell the fire and brimstone, feel the heat of hell under the soles of her feet.

"Francis, I tried to defy him," she said, her cheeks flushed scarlet from the renewed humiliation and the tiny twinge of guilt she felt that her statement wasn't entirely true. But she'd never confess that to a living soul, especially not this most righteous man of God.

"He took my words and twisted them until I didn't know what I meant to say and what he meant for me to say. I swear, it was as though I was bewitched," she sputtered, and realized *that* at least was true.

A kiss that should have filled her with disgust, or at the very least anger, had instead shaken her to the core and left her trembling with fiery emotion.

"Francis, you can't think that I ever intended or even imagined something like that would happen. We were on a mission to destroy the liquor being delivered to the saloons. To try and stop the sin at its source. I don't know who this man Ramsey Kellogg is, or what he's doing in Fortune. And I vow I can't conceive why he would have assaulted me in such a rude and outrageous manner. I suppose I should consider lodging a complaint of my own with Sheriff Dobson. The man is a scoundrel, and for the safety of our town he should not be allowed to remain in Fortune."

The idea that Ramsey Kellogg might be run out of town and branded a lecherous degenerate was suddenly so overwhelmingly appealing, Hannah felt tears well up in her eyes.

Yes, that was the answer. She'd cry foul until the whole town rose against him, the object of her humiliation cast out of town.

Another twinge of guilt stabbed her heart. He'd embarrassed her, for certain. And there could be no doubt that he'd bedeviled her and dashed her plans. But his kiss had been more an assault on her senses than on her person—and she'd be a liar to swear different.

Hannah was a lot of things, some of them unbecoming, but a liar she was not.

She faced Francis, unprepared to confess the truth but unwilling to stoop to dishonesty to hide her shame.

"We'll speak no more about it," he said, surprising her into silence. "I suppose we were foolish to think we could wallow with pigs without getting a little mud on ourselves. No sense smearing it about any more than necessary. I'll address the subject briefly from the pulpit, denounce the actions of all those present as unneighborly, to say the least, and you and your ladies will be cast in the light of righteousness. For since Abraham and Lot have the righteous suffered for the sins of the unrighteous."

Hannah could barely form a reply. Francis's generosity surprised her and increased her guilt and shame. He believed in her, put his faith in her despite knowing her past. Unlike most of the people who knew her growing up, he refused to paint her with the same brush as her mother, or label her guilty by reason of association.

He truly was a good man.

Too good for her, she thought, cursing herself for having inherited the sins of her mother. For surely she had not rebuffed the stranger's kiss, or fought to remove his arms when they slipped around her and cradled her in their warm, strong embrace. Even now she could feel the heat of longing in her own limbs, crying out for human contact. She wanted to be held, touched, loved. She wanted to know intimacy.

Without thinking, she threw herself into Francis's arms, pressing her cheek to the soft wool of his sweater and breathing in the scent of starch in his shirt.

"Oh, Francis, I do care for you so. And you've been kind beyond words. I'm so lucky you rescued me from myself."

"Nonsense," he murmured, touching her hair in a rare display of affection. "I'm the lucky one. What man could hope for such a dedicated and prudent helpmate? You will make a fine minister's wife one day."

"One day soon, Francis?" she asked, looking up into his narrow eyes. Eyes the color of cold spring water.

"Soon enough, Hannah," he told her. "When the time is right."

Hannah didn't know why the time wasn't right now. She'd waited nearly a year for Francis to propose, and almost another since then for him to suggest a wedding date. But he always put her off, claiming this thing or that needed to be done before they could settle into any kind of life together. Hannah didn't see why the trials and travails that arose couldn't be handled as easily if they were married, but she'd stopped pushing the issue months ago when Francis refused to be swayed.

She'd thought this final battle, this call to arms against the ever-increasing popularity of whiskey and saloons that was pervading the West, would prove once and for all that she would make a good minister's wife. But first she had to win—not only the battle, but the war. Her future happiness as Francis's wife and helpmate depended on her success.

Hannah shivered as she remembered Ramsey Kellogg's hot lips and whiskey-dark eyes. Yes, her future was dependent on her victory in this latest crusade. And she knew she'd never faced a more daunting opponent.

"Now, what is your next plan of action?" Francis asked, setting her away from him as though the close moment had been no more than a wisp of a dream. Hannah felt the chill of rejection where his warm body had been and wanted to press her body close to his again, feel his heat and her own melding.

"I wanted to speak to you about that, Francis," she said, resisting the urge and stepping a chaste distance away. "There has been a—a development."

He went to stand behind his desk, putting physical distance between them equal to the emotional chasm he'd created. He shuffled his papers, and she could tell that his mind had already returned to whatever he'd been working on when she'd arrived.

"What's that?"

"A letter, Francis. I received a letter. Two actually, over the past week."

He gathered a pile of papers and straightened it into a neat stack by tapping the edges on the desk.

"That's nice," he murmured, frowning at something his eye caught on the top sheet.

"No, Francis," she said, stepping closer and clutching her hands at her waist. "They weren't nice. Not at all."

He licked the end of a pencil and made a brief note on the page; then his gaze drifted up to her face.

"What did you say?"

"The letters," she told him, impatience now clear in her tone. "They weren't friendly correspondence. They were more like . . . threats."

"Threats?" He blinked and shook his head, and for the first time Hannah noticed how thin his hair had become on top. Such a ridiculous thing to notice at a time like this, but there it was. The strands were so sparse when he looked down, exposing his pate, you could see the pink of his skin shining through.

"Yes. Oh, are you paying any attention to what I'm saying? I have been receiving threats, slipped under my door. And just the other day I went out to get my stepladder, the one I use to prune the roses on my trellis, and one of the rungs was cut clean through. If I hadn't noticed before I climbed onto it, I would have taken a nasty fall."

"Cut?" he scoffed. "Are you quite sure? Couldn't it have snapped the last time you used it and you just didn't notice it then? Really, Hannah, who would want to threaten you?"

"Well, I think that would be obvious," she said, one hand going indignantly to her hip. "It must be one of the saloon owners. They don't like me trying to interfere with their business."

"I wouldn't worry too much about it. I'm sure it was nothing more than a cowardly, even childish prank. Those men might be saloon owners, but they're also businessmen, and almost certainly beyond anything so puerile. It was probably some young pup who thought he'd make a name for himself with the men holding up the bar in his favorite saloon.

"Now, scoot on home and let me get back to work. I'm sure you and your ladies must be as busy as bees in springtime, hatching new campaigns for your next confrontation. You've got them on the run, Hannah. Now's the time to keep the flame high under the town's outrage."

"I suppose you're right, Francis," she said hesitantly. "We can't just give up when we've come so far. Besides, I refuse to cease my efforts on behalf of the misguided men of this town. They've got to be made to see that only wickedness and grief come out of the bottle."

"That's a girl. Why, you'll be replacing Carry Nation

on the front pages of the newspapers before long if you continue crusading so stringently.''

"I don't know about that. But I appreciate your confidence. You must know your support means a great deal to me.''

"Of course, darling," he said, smiling at her across the wide blackened oak of the old desk.

Hannah knew not to expect any parting touch or romantic farewell; it just wasn't Francis's way. It saddened her a little, but she told herself that romance was for fools and things like dependability and a sterling reputation more than made up for the slight lack. She smiled and nodded awkwardly, then turned to leave.

"Oh, Hannah . . ." he added, stopping her.

She spun around, hoping he would do something just a little romantic and impractical, her rational assurances to the contrary.

"Try to avoid any more ignoble displays with that vulgar stranger. The people of Fortune think rather highly of you right now. But we both know that's because I've kept the truth of your arrival here and the details of your past a secret. I don't imagine they would hold you in such high esteem if the truth should come out.''

Hannah winced as the sting of his rebuke whipped across her unguarded heart. Why did he have to bring up her past at a time like this, when he'd been praising her?

Or had he?

Somehow Francis's accolades seemed to hide snapping teeth that nipped at her hard-won confidence and dragged down her already meager feelings of self-worth. And this time he'd gone a shade too far for her to disregard it as unconscious insensitivity.

"That was cruel and uncalled for, Francis. My encounter with Ramsey Kellogg had nothing to do with my mother, my father or my unfortunate past. He'd have done the same to anyone in my position, trying to thwart his debauchery. I did not signal him in any way that I might be interested in his attentions. Indeed, his actions were meant to demean me in the worst possible way. And I thought he had succeeded, for that was the most degraded I'd ever felt in my life. Until now.''

She didn't wait to see how her words affected Francis. She hadn't said them to provoke an apology or even a twinge of remorse in him. In that moment she couldn't have cared less how he felt. He'd wounded her, and she was both angry and confused by the mixed signals he sometimes sent her.

Hannah's hand closed around the porcelain doorknob as Francis called out to her in a voice edged with condescension. Her shoulders stiffened, but she refused to turn around and hear the apology she knew would be half-hearted at best and lacking in sincerity. Instead, she decided it might go a long way toward expressing her displeasure if she just ignored his attempt to cajole.

She turned the knob, swung the door open wide and slammed it behind her with a resounding, and satisfying, bang.

Hannah's anger lasted almost until she'd reached her tiny house four streets west of the parsonage. She entered through the rear door leading into the kitchen, the screen slamming behind her echoing her frustrated departure from Francis.

Maybe he was right. Had he merely been trying to warn her to be careful to keep her past closely under wraps? It was certainly true that the town would reject and scorn her if they knew where and what she came from, or how she'd come to live in Fortune.

No one, least of all the women she called friends, would consider having anything to do with her.

She liked being part of this town. Growing up an outcast, she'd never been allowed to associate with the other children—the ones from *good* families.

But sometimes she would sneak up where they were having an ice cream social or a birthday party and, hiding behind a tree or nearby building, watch them having fun. How she'd wished to be part of the group, laughing, chasing and playing croquet.

Tiffany Grace Menwell had a miniature china tea set and she would invite all the other girls over for glorious tea parties where her mama would bake tiny little sweet cakes and they'd use real linen napkins with elaborate embroidery.

Once, Tiffany Grace had caught Hannah peering from behind the huge oak in her backyard. She whispered something to the other girls, and they'd all watched wide-eyed as Tiffany Grace marched to the tree and, after calling Hannah a name too foul to repeat, spit on her.

Hannah had seen Mrs. Menwell come running and thought she might be saved further humiliation, but the woman had not chastised her rude daughter. She'd swept her behind her skirts as though she was afraid the girl would catch something from Hannah; then she'd stiffly ordered Hannah to go home.

The giggles of the other children had echoed in Hannah's dreams for a long time. The painful memory still crept up on her at times, and her heart would grow heavy as she pictured the perfectly painted roses on the dainty china cups. Never before had she seen anything so beautiful. Or suffered a humiliation quite so complete.

Francis's words paled beside the bitter memories, as did Ramsey Kellogg's brutal setdown. Two years of living a seemingly settled and acceptable life had almost made her forget how tough she truly was. A possible slight was nothing in comparison to some of the things she'd endured.

Especially in light of all Francis had done for her over the past two years. He was a good, decent man who treated her with respect and kindness, although he was occasionally thoughtless and sometimes unintentionally cruel.

It was probably only her own sensitivity to the truth of her past that made it sting so.

And so what if Ramsey Kellogg had wounded her pride? She hadn't thought her mission to close the saloons of Fortune would be a pleasurable chore. She'd known the fight could get ugly. She'd never been one to run and hide just because her feelings were hurt.

Indeed, she'd grown a tough hide the day of Tiffany Grace Menwell's tea party and it had served her well in the years since.

Ramsey Kellogg might think he'd subdued her with his punishing kiss and embarrassing setdown, but she wasn't beaten yet. Not by a long shot.

She held fast in her belief that liquor caused the ruination of individuals and families. She'd lived firsthand with the horrors most of her life. And no hard-drinking booze advocate with loose morals and fewer manners was going to bring her down that easily.

No matter that he was the most handsome man she'd ever seen, and that his kiss still burned on her lips.

Chapter Five

"We can stand in front of the doors and bar the entrance," Agnes said. "I dare any of them wet-behind-the-ears roughnecks to try and move my person."

She thrust out her extensive bosom, planted her hands on her ample hips and parted her feet, practicing what she must have thought to be a firm stance. Hannah covered a smile with a shy cough and simply nodded.

"Yes, that might be a good idea. Less combative, but no less effective. We certainly don't want to cause another brawl like the one the other night, where the men we are trying to save end up in harm's way. However, we all agree we're not ready to abandon our cause just because things have gotten a little heated, right?"

She glanced around as everyone nodded and tried not to notice that one of their flock was no longer among them. Apparently Mary Beth couldn't face the thought of possible arrest or worse—that she might be the next one

subjected to the kind of treatment Hannah had endured
at the hands of Ramsey Kellogg.

The whole town was talking about the scandalous
encounter between Hannah and the stranger, and opinions ranged from outrage to amusement, depending
largely on who was doing the telling.

Hannah forced herself to ignore the hushed voices
behind her pew at church and the subtle stares she drew
as she walked through town.

And try as she might, she couldn't ignore the wild, lustful
dreams she'd begun having about the man. She'd even
tried praying to stave off the unsettling images each night,
but every time she closed her eyes she could still see the
man's honey-eyed stare and taste the dizzying blend of
whiskey and desire. Several times she'd awakened drenched
with sweat, her breathing labored.

For nearly a week she'd carefully avoided another confrontation with him by holding meetings at the church
and passing out circulars to people on the street. She'd
reread every morsel of information she'd collected about
the crusading editor William Jennings Demorest, one of
the first to promote the idea of prohibition, and Frances
Willard, leader of the praying-in-saloons crusade of '73 and
'74, and one of the original founders of the Woman's
Christian Temperance Union.

Without a doubt these two were among the first great
initiators of the temperance movement for both economic
and social reasons.

Demorest believed liquor destroyed lives, promoted
crime and poverty and even corrupted the judiciary. He
had run for mayor of New York on the temperance ticket.

Willard fought more for the protection of the home and
the Christian way of life. She, even more than Carry Nation,
was Hannah's idol, a woman of good family background,

above reproach, who could recognize the evils of drink and the demoralization it caused.

How wonderful it must be to be as strong, as brave as Frances Willard, and to fight for a cause for no other reason than because you believed in it and felt it was important.

"Well, I agree with Agnes," she said, being careful not to look too closely at her own reasons for taking up this particular battle. "We'll hand out circulars to the men attempting to enter the saloons, and we'll warn them of the staggering statistics of wife-beaters, thieves and murderers produced by the consumption of alcohol. We'll plead and pray and persuade the customers away. Then the saloons will have no choice but to close their doors forever."

"Here, here," Margaret cried, brandishing her stack of leaflets. "You all know my Slack won't lift a hand less it's got a drink in it, but at least if the saloons are closed he'll have to do his drinking at home. And that's what he can hide under the hay in the barn loft, 'cause all I find in the house I dump out the back door. I swear, I got the happiest rose bed in the whole county."

The other women laughed, and Hannah smiled as she slowly looked around the room at the eager faces. She *was* doing a good thing; they all were. Each of them was united in a common goal for very different reasons.

Margaret's husband, called Slack because of his penchant for avoiding work whenever possible, would have put them in the poor house long ago with his own drinking if it weren't for Margaret's talent with a needle.

Tabby went along because crusading was considered popular in far-off places she thought of as exotic, like St. Louis and New York.

Nan was an avid prohibitionist because she'd been raised in a strict Southern Baptist church, where any imbibing was considered a sin.

And then there was Hannah. Hannah took up the cause

because of her mother, and the love of a man she could
never hope to be good enough for.

"All right, then," she said, brushing off the troubling
thoughts. "If we're all ready, let's go. The sooner we get
in front of the saloons, the more men we'll encounter and,
hopefully, turn away."

They made their way toward the Paper Pony, a saloon
on the east end. Although slightly smaller than the Double
Eagle, it was just as popular. They had several faro tables
and a running game of chuck-a-luck in the back room.
Men who weren't favored by Lady Luck at cards could bet
on the outcome of three thrown dice.

Hannah had chosen this particular place because she'd
heard from Francis that Mary Beth's husband had lost over
twenty acres of prime farmland the past weekend betting
against the house.

And, also, because she didn't want another run-in with
Ramsey Kellogg, who, she'd learned, was residing at the
Double Eagle.

Blast the man anyway; why didn't he just leave? He had
no family in Fortune—she knew that for a fact. He hadn't
been seen with anyone who might be considered a long-
standing acquaintance, and anyone who happened to mention him within her hearing seemed as baffled by his presence as she was.

All she knew for sure was, he'd quickly become her
nemesis. A living, breathing example of all the things she
most feared and detested. And if his actions both in the
saloon and in the back alley were any indication, a shining
example of the debauchery saloons encouraged.

At least if he was having a high time at the Double Eagle,
she could relax, knowing he wouldn't be antagonizing her
and her group at the Paper Pony.

As the saloon came into view, they could see several men
lounging around the walkway out front, slouched against

posts, feet crossed at the ankles or resting on the railing. Smoke haloed them all as they puffed away on hand-rolled cigarettes and fat, stinking cigars. Above the half doors, Hannah could see puffs of smoke dancing around the flickering chandeliers hanging over several tables.

The men spotted the group and straightened up with a lot of chuckling and elbow nudging. A few were locals Hannah knew from the general store, the café and town meetings. The others were strangers and, judging by their clothing, either miners on their way out west or day laborers.

Hannah winced at the presence of the latter, since everybody knew day laborers were not as well respected as full-time hands, with good reason.

These nomadic men had a reputation for being wild and rambunctious. They were a rowdy, reckless group who sought boisterous entertainment that often ended with bouts of fighting, cussing and shooting.

She groaned and slowed her steps.

"The Paper Pony may not have been the best choice for our demonstration, ladies," she said.

Nan held back, and even Tabby looked slightly intimidated, but Agnes just harrumphed. "Nonsense. It's roadhouses like this that bring those kind of troublemakers into Fortune. Why, it was one of them fancy-dudded fellows what stole that twenty acres from Mary Beth's old man. Now he's living off her hard work and toil while she tries to put up enough from the crops that're left to see her family through winter. It's a sin and a crime of nature."

Hannah hadn't considered that it might be the strain of losing that much land and crops that had kept Mary Beth away tonight. She'd assumed it was the fear of being accosted, or possibly shame at what Ramsey Kellogg had done to Hannah. But now that she thought about it, she wondered how Mary Beth and her children would survive without the much-needed food and income from that land.

A wave of sick panic hit her as she recalled the many nights she'd gone to bed hungry because her mother had drunk the last of the money she'd hid for food. Toward the end, she'd begun to hide the day-old bread the baker would sell her cheap just so she'd have something to fill her stomach after her mother passed out.

Hannah vowed to go the very next morning to check on Mary Beth and see if there was anything she could do for the woman's family.

"Gambling is the devil's work, no doubt about that," Nan whispered, shaking her head. "Why, I remember how Brother Hargrove raved against those Catholics holding raffles on Saturday nights back home. Absolutely sinful," she added, her eyes wide with shock at the memory.

Agnes puffed out her cheeks and blew a disgusted breath. "Ain't nothing wrong with a little game of chance now and again, especially if it's for a good cause. I've been thinking we could add a cakewalk to the annual church bazaar, drum up some extra money for the new building fund."

"A cakewalk! Why, Agnes, I'm just surprised at you," Nan sputtered. "What's wrong with the bake sale we have every year? It's always been a good draw."

"But most folks can bake for themselves, or they have wives who can. We usually sit there half the day, then end up buying each other's goods just so we don't have to be seen taking our own stuff home again. A cakewalk would add excitement, and people would be drawn just to see if they could win. And we'd sell tickets, so each cake would bring in more than just selling it outright. Especially Winfred Gallows's awful fruitcake à la prunes."

Nan moaned beneath her breath. She was dead set against any game of chance, but since she'd been the one whose turn it had been to buy Winfred's fruitcake last fall, the memory was still sharp in her mind.

"How did we get on the subject of that brick laxative Winfred foists off every year?" Tabby asked, fanning herself with her leaflets. "I thought we came here to stir things up and meet some men."

Agnes glared at her and Nan gasped in shock.

"I meant, to meet them going into the saloon and head them off," Tabby added, smiling slyly.

"Yes," Hannah said, amused by the girl's flirtatious manner despite herself. "We seem to have gotten off the subject. We're here to do a job and there's no point in putting it off any longer."

"No point a'tall," Agnes readily agreed.

"I'm ready to face the lion in his den," Nan added.

A picture of long blond hair and eyes the color of goldstone flashed across Hannah's mind. *Eyes the color of a lion's,* she thought. How appropriate. She hadn't made the connection before, but she knew she'd never see eyes that color again without thinking of this night and her own battles. Both internal and external.

"Up with the home—down with the saloon!" the women cried as they tried to poke their tracts into each man's hand. Some politely refused; some accepted them, then dropped them to the ground to be trampled beneath passing boots. One man generously took one, then loudly blew his nose into the paper and handed it back to Nan.

"Ooooohhh," she shrieked, holding the offending wad out by the edge. "Take it, take it, take it," she said, dangling it out to each woman who, in turn, shied away.

"Stop that caterwauling." Agnes snatched the paper from her hand and dropped it into the spittoon by the saloon door. "And let's get on with this thing. Ain't one of those men even looked at those handbills we're doling out. We need to do something to get their attention."

"Agnes is right," Tabby whined, patting the back of her upswept hair. "This is getting tiresome."

"I say we kneel right here on these steps and pray those men out of that saloon," Nan said.

"Say that again?" Agnes eyed her as if she'd gone around the bend.

"Prayer, Agnes. You do know what it is, don't you? Or do you go to church every Sunday just to show off your ready-mades from the mail-order catalogue?"

"Now just you watch your tongue, Nan . . ."

"Come now, ladies, we're all in this together," Hannah soothed. "I'm as discouraged as you all are, but we've got to have faith."

"Well, don't *you* think we ought to pray, Hannah?" Nan asked, pinning her with a hard stare.

Hannah swallowed and thought for a minute. The idea of kneeling on the steps of a saloon was distasteful to her, and more than a little disconcerting. But she wanted to be the preacher's wife, after all, so she supposed she should set an example.

"I—um, I read that it was very effective for Frances Willard back in the seventies," she admitted. "I don't suppose it would hurt."

She glanced imploringly at Agnes.

"All right," the older woman conceded grudgingly. "But you all don't have the stiffness in your joints like I do. I probably won't be able to get up at all after this fine spectacle."

The women knelt and smoothed their skirts around them. They'd given in to Nan's pleas and foregone the bloomer costumes this time. They bowed their heads and Nan began a loud and fervent prayer for the souls of the men "drowning in their own weakness and depravity," as she put it. Hannah's mind wandered and she couldn't seem to focus on the impassioned pleas Nan shouted heavenward. What kind of minister's wife would she make if she felt awkward and conspicuous kneeling in prayer? She wasn't suited to the position by virtue of her upbringing; that went without saying.

Only her actions could justify such a union. Hannah had known that for some time, and she'd tried to be a good and loyal servant of the Lord and a hard worker for the church. But she wondered now if she did it so she'd be deserving of a man like Francis, or if she wanted a man like Francis so she'd feel deserving.

As her gaze drifted around the walkway, she noticed one man dart into the saloon, while several more peered over the bat-wing doors. She could feel a sudden tension in the air as the fine hairs along her arms stood up. She reached over and touched Agnes on the arm and the woman nodded in understanding.

"Something . . ."

"Yeah, and by the grins on the faces of those swanky dudes, I'd say it was something big."

Hannah heard the heavy boots draw near to the doorway and her eyes locked on the tips of a pair of expensive Justins, the brown leather worn soft. Heavy cotton twill jeans dyed the color of butternut rode close to the longest legs Hannah had ever seen. Or maybe it just seemed that way, since she'd never observed a man's legs from this angle.

She couldn't miss the elaborately carved gunbelt or the steel-handled pistols he wore low at his hips, but she passed right over his checked chambray shirt on her way to those inevitable amber eyes.

"Oh, no," she whispered, squeezing her eyes shut and finding no difficulty murmuring a prayer of her own at that moment. When she opened her eyes again, he stood with his arms outflung as he held the louvered doors open.

"Well, now. What have we here?"

The men standing around the walkway snickered and punched one another in anticipation of another run-in between Hannah and this bedeviling newcomer. But when Kellogg turned to glare at them, their humor wilted.

"We stood right here, Ram," one of the men said, puffing out his chest and thumbing his suspenders. "Kept 'em from going in just like you said."

"I see that. But it seems they've gotten around us just the same. No one can concentrate on their gaming, what with this revival going on outside the door. It seems to be causing a streak of bad luck."

"Hallelujah," Nan sang out, clasping her hands and raising them above her head.

Hannah noticed the woman's reaction seemed to cause a tightening in Mr. Kellogg's jaw muscles, and a twitch started in his cheek.

"Maybe the men should just go on home if their luck has run out," she said, smiling softly as she rose to her feet. She fussed with the folds of her skirt to hide the tremor of fear that shook her.

"Maybe you should go on home and their luck will return."

"I have no intention of doing that. And this is a public walkway, so don't even think about trying anything to force us off."

"I rarely have to use force," he told her, his words all the more threatening because they were spoken so low. "And never on women."

"Well, given that and your obvious lack of charm, I can see why you'd need the services of a place like this."

The twitch in his cheek disappeared and the hint of a smile snuck across his wide, full lips. The gold in his eyes flashed brilliant as he quirked his brows together and pretended to study her.

"My, my. You do know how to use that mouth of yours,"

he said, stepping closer and letting the doors swing shut behind him. "In more ways than one."

Out of the corner of her eye, Hannah could see Nan hauling Agnes to her feet. Tabby was striking what she obviously thought was a seductive pose against the nearest post. Margaret had taken a nervous step back.

"I'll say it again, Mr. Kellogg: This is a public walkway and we have every right to be here."

"So, you know my name. Should I be flattered you went to the trouble of asking around?"

"Certainly not. I simply wanted to make sure I had it right when I filed the assault complaint against you with Sheriff Dobson."

"I was just doing my job, lady. Like I'm doing now. So I'll ask you one more time to take your friends and go on home where you all belong."

"There is sin and corruption going on in that saloon," she said, pointing behind him. "And as concerned members of the Woman's Christian Temperance Union, I'd say that this *is* exactly where we belong."

"You're not going to accomplish anything by squatting out here singing hymns and shouting sermons. If these men wanted to hear that, they'd go to church. And since the saloons aren't even open on Sundays, you certainly can't claim unfair competition."

"Maybe these men would attend church on Sunday if they weren't so hungover from visiting the saloons on Saturday night."

"That's not my concern. I've been hired to make sure these men have a pleasant and relaxing experience in a place with a comfortable atmosphere. And you all are just putting a real damper on the whole thing."

"Good. Then I'd say we've done what we set out to do and I see no reason to stop now."

"How about this for a reason? In about thirty seconds

a whole barrel of beer is going to flow right over these steps and onto anything that gets in its way. That's the only warning you're going to get, so I suggest you move along."

"You don't frighten me, Mr. Kellogg," she lied, grateful her shaking knees were concealed.

"Then that makes you not so bright, Miss Sullivan," he said, raising his hand and crooking two fingers forward. The doors opened, and as Ram stepped to one side, two men struggled forward with a cask of beer. They tipped it, and the frothy brew rained down on the planks of the walkway, splashing everyone within a three-foot radius.

The women shrieked and rushed out into the street as the beer sloshed against the bottom rail, where it became trapped and formed a puddle some two inches deep.

"Care to kneel in that, Miss Sullivan?"

"There are other saloons in this town," she said, angrily shaking the foam from the hem of her dress as the heavy odor of malt and brewed yeast filled the night air. She couldn't care less about her clothes, but once more this man had embarrassed and bested her and she was fighting mad.

He nodded. "And you'll find the same reception at each of them. I told you, I've been hired to keep your bunch from harassing the men coming into the Double Eagle, the Paper Pony and every other saloon in this town. It's my job and I take my work very seriously."

"You may keep us from kneeling on the walkway outside the saloons, but you cannot keep us from doing whatever is necessary to put these wretched places out of business. I will not stop until I have seen the last door closed on this type of establishment in Fortune," she told him, bristling with determination.

"Then you've got a fight on your hands, lady," he

warned her, "because I intend to see that they remain open and prosper."

"Why do you care what happens in this town? We live here," she said, motioning toward the women clustered around her. "You have no connection to Fortune in any way. In time you'll be gone, and you probably won't even remember the name."

"The name isn't important. This could be any of a hundred small towns strung out all over the country. Each with a group of frustrated, uptight prudes who wouldn't know a good time if it jumped up and bit them on the ass, trying to make sure no one else is having any fun, either. You might say I'm a fun-loving guy, just trying to see you don't succeed in sucking every ounce of pleasure out of a man's life."

"That's absurd," Hannah said, stung by his insults and surprised that his opinion should matter a whit to her. "And just the sort of cheap shot I'd expect from a fi'penny hustler like yourself. Come along, ladies."

Hannah fumed. The lowlife, womanizing, good-for-nothing drifter probably hadn't done an honest day's work in his life and wouldn't know how to treat a decent woman. So what if he was handsome; he was a toad in every other way. A slug who saw a way to make a few bucks by doing the dirty work the saloon owners hadn't had the guts to do on their own.

Francis was right: None of the saloon owners had the nerve to actually do anything to stop her and the other ladies from closing them down. Instead they'd hired this scoundrel with the morals of an alley cat. She certainly would have believed him capable of sending the threats she'd received, and even of seeing them through. But since she knew exactly when he'd arrived in town, and it had been weeks after the ominous notes had begun arriving, Hannah found herself in a most incredible position.

This man, who she could easily loathe and who had touched her as no man ever had, even before she knew his name, was also the only man she was sure *hadn't* sent the disturbing warnings.

Chapter Six

Ram handed each of the four day laborers a Liberty half-dollar and pushed open the doors to the Paper Pony with a flourish. "Drinks are on the house for the rest of the night, fellows, compliments of a grateful management."

The men piled up to the bar, leaving Ram alone on the deserted walkway. The sounds from the crowded saloon faded behind him as his gaze followed the rigid back of the Sullivan woman leading her brood away.

He'd accused her of being not too bright, a fact he knew to be untrue, just to see her get her Irish up again.

For some perverse reason he got more pleasure out of watching her get riled than in anything he'd done in a long while. She had spunk and incredible passion. Ram admired that. Mostly because he couldn't remember having ever felt that passionate about anything in his life.

And she had guts. That was one thing he hadn't found in many of the women he'd come across.

If only she weren't so blame puritanical. Lord only knew

he wanted no part of any holier-than-thou woman trying to save his soul while she drove him out of his mind with her constant nagging and harping and Bible thumping.

"From bluestockings, bloomers and strong-minded she-males in general, Good Lord deliver us," Ram quoted, remembering something he'd read in the paper Pollack had shown him. The editor's words struck a familiar chord with Ram; he knew better than most the damage a woman could do in the name of religion.

"What trick of nature gave that woman looks and a body like that, then went and ruined it all by dousing her with an overabundance of misguided morals?"

That wild red hair made his fingers ache to run through the silky, corkscrew strands. Her mouth was just made for kissing, and he wanted to do just that. Again and again, until he got his fill.

He shook his head as her little band disappeared out of sight; then he strode down the walkway toward the next saloon. He might as well call off the rest of the men he'd set to watch. It seemed Miss Hannah Sullivan was wisely packing it in for the night.

Ram wandered from one saloon to the next, accepting congratulations on having gotten the best of Hannah once more. His plan had been simple, really. He couldn't be everywhere at once, so he hired lookouts to watch the front and back entrances of the saloons and fetch him if the women showed. In a matter of minutes he could be at any one of the four saloons, ready to send the trouble-makers on their way.

But to Sullivan and her group, it would seem he was everywhere at once. And that was exactly what he intended. She'd soon learn she couldn't get around him, or through him, and she'd go on back to her sewing circles or hen parties. Then he could collect his money and be on his way.

The sooner the better, he thought as he stepped out of
the last saloon. He hadn't been able to get that kiss out
of his mind. It was branded there, along with the smell of
her hair and the feel of her curves pressed against his
body. He wanted her, in a way he hadn't wanted a woman
in a long time. Not a nice friendly little poke between
strangers, but a soul-deep, all-night, every-man's-fantasy
kind of ride.

The kind he knew Hannah Sullivan had in her, if she
wasn't so all-fired determined to smother it in scripture
and drown it in hymns.

He'd had his fill of that kind of thing, and trying to love
a woman who only wanted to love God. How could any
man compete with that?

Well, he didn't intend to. Not again. Ram had learned
his lesson the hard way, and he wouldn't stick his head
out only to have it chopped off. No, sir, the sooner he put
Hannah Sullivan in her place and the dust of Fortune
behind him, the better he'd like it.

Of course, that wasn't going to be any time soon unless
he took the initiative and made her see, once and for all,
that he wasn't going to back down or give up. They could
play this cat-and-mouse game for months, with neither
making any significant headway. Or he could go to hell
across lots and end this foolishness tonight.

Action had always appealed to Ram more than idleness,
and the direct approach more than the subtle. Besides, he
wasn't enjoying this assignment as much as he thought he
would, and his wanderlust was acting up of late.

Making up his mind, he crossed the street, turned up a
side alley and made for the west part of town and the little
yellow-and-white cottage he knew belonged to Hannah.
He'd asked around some himself.

Not that it had done him any good. If he didn't know
better, he'd swear Hannah Sullivan was running from

something. No one seemed to know where she came from, how she came to be in Fortune or how she paid for her house and her necessities, for that matter.

She piqued his curiosity and teased his detective's instincts, and Ram pledged to find out her secrets before leaving Fortune for good.

As he approached the house, he could see a blaze of light from the front room, so he figured she must still be up. Pushing open the waist-high iron gate, he let himself into the front yard. He could make out the area well thanks to the full moon and the gaslights set at the end of each street. There was a nicely tended flower bed on either side of the brick steps and a rose-covered lattice trellis running up between the two front windows.

Something in Ram stirred to life, a dream long dead and buried deep. A tiny house, the sound of a baby softly cooing, a beautiful woman welcoming him home with eyes full of love and a kiss just for him.

He stepped onto the porch and rapped on the door. His dream faded as he waited, but he could still feel the wisps of longing it left behind. He cursed his weakness and brief, foolish flight of fancy.

Several minutes passed and still there was no answer. He rapped again and waited. Had she gone to bed and left a lamp burning? It seemed unlikely.

He decided to go around back and check the kitchen. Maybe she was in the rear of the house or making noise and couldn't hear him knocking.

As he rounded the corner of the house he could see the windows in back were lit up as well. The woman must have more money than the First Families of Virginia, to burn oil like it was well water.

He put his boot on the first step and froze. A well-tended house, lovingly cared for, wouldn't have a broken window marring the beauty.

So why did this one?

A chill black silence surrounded him and suddenly he could feel the tension. No crickets chirped, no night birds called out to nearby mates. Even the breeze seemed to have stopped, and Ram felt the hairs stand up on his neck like they did when he was about to get the drop on someone he'd been trailing. He reached for his pistol.

Fear for Hannah's safety made him want to burst through the door shouting her name, and only his natural instincts kept him pressed against the wall of her house. Ram didn't take time to wonder why he suddenly cared so much about the vexatious woman. He'd think about that later.

He leaned in close and carefully peered through the hole in the glass, straining to see through the lace curtain filtering his view.

"Hannah?" he called softly, raising the pistol. "Miss Sullivan? It's Ram Kellogg; I'm coming in. Don't be frightened."

He turned the knob and was surprised to find it locked. Reaching slowly through the breach in the window, he twisted the bolt.

The kitchen was bright and cheery, with white cupboards and canary walls. The broken shards crunching beneath his feet seemed even more incongruous.

Ram stepped softly through the house. With the lamps blazing he could easily scan each room and see they were vacant. A short hall branched off from the front parlor and he could make out two closed doors, one on either side. He went to the first and gripped the knob, his heart pounding in his ears and his palms sweating.

He'd tracked killers, bank robbers, even the most notorious gunfighters. But he'd never been as nervous about his own safety as he was about Hannah's at that moment.

Hot on the heels of his fear came righteous anger. Anger

that she had pushed someone to violence with her overzealous meddling. Anger with himself that he should care so much about what happened to her and why.

"Miss Sullivan?" he called softly, slowly turning the knob and inching the door inward. "Are you in there? Are you all right?"

A shot rang out, deafening him momentarily, and he felt the bullet whiz by his ear and explode into the doorframe. Splinters of wood flew by him as he dropped to the floor and rolled against the wall, his gun instantly cocked and aimed at the huddled figure on the bed.

His finger twitched and then fell still on the trigger as he realized who it was a split second before he shot Hannah Sullivan.

"Holy shit, lady, you nearly blew my frigging head off," he shouted. "And I just about repaid you in kind." As he rolled to his feet he saw her trembling hands lift the gun again, as though taking aim. With another muttered curse he dove across the bed, smashing her into the mattress and knocking the gun from her hand.

A scream ripped through his eardrum and pierced his brain, and he winced as he clapped a hand over her mouth.

"What in hell is wrong with you? Have you gone completely mad?"

A watery whimper escaped from her and only then did it register to Ram that the bedroom was not lit by a lamp, but only by the light flowing in through the opened door.

Hannah had been sitting in the dark, a gun in her hand, obviously expecting someone. The same someone who had broken her window. When he opened the door, she couldn't have known it was him; all she'd have seen was the silhouette of a man.

Damn! He'd probably just scared her gray.

"Hey, Hannah," he whispered, rolling to one side as he scooted up in the bed, taking her trembling body with him. He cradled her in strong but tender arms. "Hannah, it's me, Ram Kellogg. I'm not going to hurt you. I didn't mean to frighten you. I knocked, but you must not have heard me."

"So you just thought you'd let yourself in," she snapped, her voice weak but with a hint of her usual rancor.

Ram nearly smiled to see her spirit returning so quickly. He started to release her, then thought better of the idea and continued to hold her.

"Yeah, well, you'd know better than most that I don't hold much with the niceties."

"I'll say."

Another tremor shook her, and Ram thought he felt her snuggle closer to his chest. He closed his eyes and absorbed the feel of her in his arms. Her skin where he touched it was soft, her body well rounded but firm.

"You can release me now. I'm not going to try to shoot you again."

"That's true," he said, reluctantly releasing her before tossing his legs over the side of the bed. "Because I'm not stupid enough to let you get your hands on that peashooter again."

"That's a Colt Dragoon," she informed him, as though his remark had insulted her personally. "Used in the Civil War. And if I'd have wanted you dead, Mr. Kellogg, you'd be pleading with St. Peter right now."

Ram heard the scratch of friction and smelled the sulfur as Hannah lit a candle on the table next to her bed. She replaced the matches in a small silver box, then turned to look at him. He could see her face was devoid of color. Her bright green eyes stood out like emeralds on a bed of cotton; her lips were a pale slash. She was acting cool, but he could see she'd been terrified.

"I fired a warning shot," she told him, rising from the bed despite the fact that she was wearing nothing but a thin white nightgown. She walked unself-consciously to a nearby chair and picked up a nappy robe that looked as if it was made from one of his mama's old bedspreads and put it on, tying it tight at her waist.

Ram frowned at the oddly conflicting sides to Hannah Sullivan. So uptight and rigid in town and on the streets, but not batting an eye now that he was in her bedroom watching her don her wrapper.

And it wasn't just the aftermath of fear that made her forget she was unclothed. She truly didn't seem to be made uncomfortable by what most people would consider, at the very least, an awkward situation.

It was as though this woman of casual mores was the real Hannah, and the prim zealot was a carefully studied portrait of what Hannah Sullivan considered a proper lady.

Another puzzle, Ram thought.

He picked up the gun—which, he noticed, was indeed a circa 1860s Colt Dragoon—and tucked it safely into his waistband, out of her reach.

"I'm not the one who broke your window," he said.

"I know."

She briefly inspected the hole in her otherwise pristine white doorframe and muttered in dismay.

Ram frowned. "How could you know that?"

She turned to him and her gaze went to the gun stuck in the front of his trousers. "Because whoever broke my window has been harrassing me for several weeks. Before you ever arrived in Fortune."

She reached toward the placket of his pants and Ram felt the air rush out of his lungs.

His first reaction was to stop her, prevent her from getting the weapon until he'd had time to sort out all that had happened. But it was her gun, her house, and he knew she was still frightened, despite her brave front.

As her hand closed over the grip of the pistol, her knuckles brushed his stomach and the washboard muscles jumped and twitched.

"I'll take this back now," she said, carefully placing the Colt in a drawer in the bedside table. "It belonged to my grandfather and was the only thing my mother didn't manage to sell off after he died."

Before Ram could question her about the odd comment, and the hint of sadness and disgust he detected in her voice, she turned toward him and held her hand out toward the bedroom door.

"I think we should continue this in the kitchen, unless you have some objection."

"Not at all."

She led the way down the hall to the kitchen, still bright and oddly cheerful despite the curtains fluttering over the broken window and the glass on the floor.

"Coffee?"

"If you don't mind," he said, finding it difficult to believe she was being hospitable to him, but curious enough to stay as long as she'd let him.

"I suppose it's the least I can do. After all, it would seem your timely approach scared away whoever broke my window before he could let himself in and do—whatever it was he intended to do," she told him, shuddering. Her voice quivered, and Ram realized her courage was mostly bravado.

"And who would that be exactly?" he asked, vowing to find the man and make him suffer for what he'd put Hannah through tonight.

She shrugged. "I don't know. He doesn't sign his name to the notes he leaves, and tonight is the closest I've come to actually meeting him."

She spooned coffee beans from a metal canister into a grinder and cranked the handle a few times, weighing the grounds that fell into the tin scoop. After filling the pot with water from a bucket by her sink, she lit the stove and put the coffee on to boil.

Ram had noticed a broom in the corner and, as she worked, he swept the shards of glass up and dumped them into a bin by the back door.

"Thank you," she whispered, pulling out a chair and collapsing into it.

Ram went to replace the broom and noticed a heavy rock lying by the linen chest in the corner. He picked it up and unwrapped the piece of paper bunched around the stone.

Scanning the note, Ram knew it wasn't the first threat Hannah had received. And if the others were anything like this one, he was amazed at the true depth of courage it took for her to continue with her quest. Silently she reached for the note and the rock, and Ram handed them over.

She briefly scanned the note, then glanced up. "Well, he's gotten more colorful in his descriptions, but I can't say more imaginative."

Her hands trembled and she clenched them together, but the tremors soon racked her whole body. Ram wanted to go to her and hold her close once more, but he knew she was trying not to give in to the terror and he didn't want to break the tenuous threads holding her together.

"If the situation has deteriorated to this, why don't you stop harrassing the saloon owners?"

"Because I'm not a quitter and because I believe in what I'm doing. And that's why, Mr. Kellogg, I'm going to win."

"It's my job to see that you don't."

She took a deep breath, and he noticed that the banter was quickly dousing the fear and shock that had momentarily gripped her. He pressed on.

"My job and my pleasure," he added. "I'm sorry you were frightened tonight," he said, playing down the rage and terror he himself had experienced, "but I can't say

I'm surprised. If you fan the flames of discontent, you can't expect not to get burned. This person," he said, waving at the note sitting ominously between them, "is obviously disturbed and very dangerous. You can't just ignore his threats and hope he'll go away."

"On the contrary, Mr. Kellogg," she said, picking up the note and the rock and dropping them both in the bin. "That's exactly what I intend to do. If you've realized nothing else since you arrived in Fortune, you should have realized one thing: I'm determined in my plan to close down every saloon in and around Fortune, and no rock-lofting coward hiding behind the dark of night is about to scare me off. And, for that matter, neither are you."

"I'm not trying to scare you, Hannah. That isn't my way. Usually I'm a man of reason and logic. And you've got to be reasonable and see that there's no possible way you can ever make Fortune, let alone this country, dry. Logically it wouldn't work anyway. If liquor was outlawed, men would still make their own and sell it to their neighbors. Folks've been hawking shinny since this country was born. You can tax it and regulate it to death, but it won't make a bit of difference. In the end men will have their spirits. And there's nothing wrong with that."

"How can you say there's nothing wrong with it?" she exclaimed. "When men drink away their money and their farms and leave hungry children and bitter, desperate wives? Men—and women—who drink are more likely to mistreat their families or run off and desert them completely. Lives are ruined every day by liquor and you not only defend it, you accept money to protect it."

"Weaknesses in human beings like cowardice, greed and plain meanness are what ruin lives. Anyone who mistreats his family would do it whether he was drunk or not. Same goes for those who steal, lie and cheat at cards. Liquor doesn't make people do bad things; it's just a fact of human nature."

"And that's just about the sort of hogwash I'd expect from someone who has whiskey for breakfast," she snapped. "Besides, you aren't exactly impartial on the issue, now are you, Mr. Kellogg?"

"No, and neither are you, Miss Sullivan," he shot back, his own ire building now that he'd gotten started. "Quite the contrary, in fact. And I for one am mightily curious to know why that is. Was your daddy especially fond of the sauce and quick with the strap? Or maybe you're one of those bitter and desperate wives you spoke so earnestly about. But, no, you're not wearing a ring, so I guess that's not it. Unless—I've got it," he said, snapping his fingers. "Your drunken husband sold it for whiskey and then ran off."

Ram had only been goading Hannah to make her see how absurd her prejudice was toward drinking, and to get her mind off the evening's disturbing events. But as he watched, her face paled, haunted by some awful memory, and a shiver went through her. He'd hit a nerve. A raw, bleeding, exposed nerve, and he wished he could withdraw the barb.

He stood without thinking and went to her side. Kneeling beside her chair, he reached for her hand and found it astonishingly cold and clammy.

"What is it, Hannah? I meant to bait you into a discussion so we could resolve this ridiculous feud, but I didn't mean to upset you so."

Snatching her hand out of his grip, she turned blazing eyes on him. "You can't upset me," she lied, her voice as cold as her fingers had been moments before. "You don't have that kind of power over me and you never will. And spare me the mocking concern. If you cared so much about my feelings and my welfare, you wouldn't be working for

the very men who've been sending those awful notes and
who broke my window tonight."

She pushed away from the table and went to the back
door, opening it on a night suddenly moonless and dark.
"No, Mr. Kellogg, you and I have nothing to discuss. We
are on opposing sides in this and, I'm certain, every other
issue of any importance. And that will never change."

"Never is a long time, Hannah," he taunted her, passing
closer to her than was necessary in the sizable room.

"I must insist you address me as Miss Sullivan," she said,
the stiff-necked prig carefully back in control now. "That
is, if you *must* address me at all."

"Miss Sullivan," Ram drawled, suddenly angry with this
sourpuss who'd chased away the spirited, confident woman
he'd watched don her robe without so much as a blush.
"I'm sure our paths will cross again very soon."

"I look forward to it," she snapped, slamming the door
behind him hard enough to free the remaining glass in
the pane and send it raining to the floor.

Chapter Seven

Hannah stood in the front pew, her hands gently clasping the hymn book, her voice raised in song. Francis used to tell her all the time how much he liked the sound of her voice. He didn't mention it anymore, but Hannah always found herself taking special care with each verse.

Again the thought came to her that she should be singing for the pleasure of the Lord and herself, not Francis. It had begun to bother her of late that she cared so much what the man thought.

She'd been especially plagued with worry that he would learn about Ram's disturbing visit to her house the night before. In fact, she'd been so afraid of Francis finding out that she hadn't even told him about the broken window. She'd found a scrap of wood and nailed it over the missing pane and hadn't mentioned it to a soul.

If she truly loved Francis, why did she fear being honest with him? Was she ashamed of the way she had behaved with Ram Kellogg?

That was ridiculous; she had done nothing of which to be ashamed. But Francis knew the truth about her mother, and because of that she knew how it would sound to him to hear that a man had been in her bedroom.

Actually, Hannah corrected herself, her bed.

When she closed her eyes, she could still feel the weight of Ram's body pressing her into the mattress, smell the scent of his hair and the freshly laundered cotton shirt he'd worn. It had been dark and she'd been terrified, so her senses were heightened.

Every detail was embedded on her brain. The way his rough, callused hands had lovingly caressed her bare arm, his warm breath washing over the sensitive lobe of her ear as he whispered soothing reassurances.

The way she had been irrationally comforted when she realized it was Ram in her room.

She felt safe in his arms, secure. And she'd trembled uncontrollably when she thought how close she'd come to killing him.

"Get thee behind me, Satan," she sang, and she snapped back to herself so suddenly that she hit a sour note. She could see Francis wince behind the pulpit. She cleared her throat and sang softly.

Why, oh why, did Ram Kellogg vex her so? He stood for everything she loathed most in the world. He purposely taunted her and had set his mind on single-handedly seeing her plans for a liquor-free Fortune put down. He drank like a fish, cussed like a Singapore sailor and enjoyed the company of whores. The man didn't have one redeeming quality.

And yet Hannah couldn't forget how he'd come to her rescue. An imposing figure silhouetted in her doorway.

He is my tribulation, Hannah thought. *A test to see how steadfast I can be against adversity. How strong my will to resist temptation is.*

And how tempted she had been to stay in Ram's arms and let him chase her demons away, instead of fighting them alone, on her own, as she'd always had to do before.

Finally the sermon ended, and Hannah found to her dismay that she couldn't remember a word of what Francis had preached. Several members of the congregation commented on his "inspired" oration.

Hannah just smiled and agreed and wondered what she had missed by daydreaming.

It was the second Sunday of the month and everyone gathered on the grounds, weather permitting, for dinner. Today the sun was bright and huge; cottony clouds sailed through a sky the color of a robin's egg.

Hannah spread a snowy tablecloth over two sawhorses covered with a board as women began unloading food from the wagons clustered around.

The children ran about, tagging each other and shrieking with glee, and sweethearts found quiet spots beneath trees to whisper words only they could hear.

Hannah thought she had never seen a more perfect setting. Her heart ached with happiness that she was part of such a serene moment. She'd never felt so content, and she never wanted the feeling to end. Once she married Francis it would never have to.

As her gaze swept the group of people gathered around the reverend she spotted Mary Beth and Rupert Gray. Some of Hannah's joy in the day subsided as she saw the beaten, haggard look on Rupert's face. She noticed a few new lines around Mary Beth's eyes as well.

The couple had had a hard time of late, and by all indications it was about to get a lot worse. But at least Rupert had shown the decency to accompany Mary Beth to church this morning. He hadn't been in years, and his presence would go a long way toward diverting the gossip about his scandalous loss of the twenty acres.

A small price, most would say, if it brought him back into the fold.

"Pride goeth before a fall," Winfred Gallows whispered, coming up behind Hannah. She had a look of unsuppressed glee as she nodded toward Rupert.

Winfred had been one of the most outspoken of the group when they'd discussed starting a chapter of the WCTU in Fortune. But somehow she always managed to have another, more urgent commitment whenever the group had a march or demonstration planned. Hannah tried to be a good Christian and find something good in everyone, but Winfred had been a real challenge in that area.

"It's pride goeth before destruction," she corrected, glaring at the woman. "And a haughty spirit before a fall," she added pointedly.

Winfred waved her hand, ignoring—or ignorant of—Hannah's implication. "You get my meaning. Now that he's gambled and drunk away everything they had, he comes crawling back to the church hoping for charity."

"Well, then, he's come to the right place, hasn't he?"

"How's that?" Winfred asked, frowning as she eyed the couple, now standing off to one side, alone. No doubt she'd soon take note of the fact that they hadn't brought a covered dish like everyone else.

"It's our duty to our fellow man to show kindness," Hannah remarked sharply. "And especially Christian charity in a time of need."

She strode off, hoping Winfred, though notoriously dense, had gotten *her* meaning.

Hannah had borrowed Francis's buggy to transport her contribution to the day's fare, since she'd prepared several dishes and hadn't been able to carry them all. Luckily, the buggy was close to the Grays', and as she swept toward them, she planted a smile on her face. No use letting Winfred's nastiness ruin the day.

"Rupert, it's so good to have you back with us. I know Mary Beth must be pleased, too." She gave her friend a reassuring hug. "I hate to bother you both, but I could sure use some help carrying food to the tables."

"Sure, Hannah," Rupert said, quickly returning to his usual good-natured self. Mary Beth, seeing through Hannah's ploy, smiled sadly. But Hannah just smiled back obliviously, pretending her request hid no secret motive. They each carried a platter of food to the table and no one else was aware that the food hadn't been brought by Mary Beth.

Pride might not be the most honorable trait a man possessed, but sometimes it was all he had left. A woman, too, for that matter.

Hannah enjoyed herself the rest of the day, and her contentment went a long way toward diluting the memory of the intruder. But as she approached her house, she remembered the broken window and knew she would have to do something about having it repaired.

She had chosen to walk home rather than ask Francis to drive her, since she had only one small skillet to carry. The rest of her pans still contained food, and she'd insisted that Mary Beth take it all home for the family's supper that night.

As she let herself into the small yard, she could hear noises from the back of her house, and she instantly regretted her decision to return home alone.

Had the intruder come back, this time to carry out the threats he'd made in his notes? The thought shattered the beauty of the day. The sun went behind a cloud and a cold wind crept over her.

But it was still broad daylight. Surely no one would

attempt to harm her when people were still out walking on the streets.

Although, ironically, no one seemed to be walking down her street at that moment, Hannah noticed. And her house was set back a good distance from the others on her road. Her neighbors weren't near enough to hear a scream, even if they happened to be at home with their windows open.

She gripped the iron skillet by the handle, deciding it would make a serviceable weapon, especially if she could sneak up on the villain. She crept around the side of the house and saw the man squatting by her back door. His head was lowered, his hat hiding his features, and Hannah felt satisfied that he hadn't heard her approach.

But as she tiptoed up behind the hunched figure, he turned on her, his gun drawn, and she realized he'd known she was there all along. He'd only been waiting for her to get close enough to spring.

"What are you doing here?" she snapped as Ram replaced his gun in his holster.

"About to get clobbered, it looks like," he said, eyeing the raised skillet.

Hannah flushed and lowered the pan, tucking it nervously behind her back. "I heard noises back here. I guess I'm a little jumpy."

He nodded. "You've got reason to be."

"What were you doing here before almost getting clobbered?" she asked, taking another step toward him.

Ram leaned to the side and Hannah saw the new glass in her windowpane. She felt ridiculously pleased and a grin struggled to her face. Fighting back the warm feelings he seemed to bring out in her, she tried to looked annoyed.

"You didn't have to do that," she told him.

"I know I didn't have to. But I figured I would worry less knowing it had been done."

Another wave of pleasure coursed through Hannah, and

this time she couldn't hide her smile. She knew she was being foolhardy, but she couldn't help it. She felt special suddenly, because this man cared enough to fix her broken window.

Of course, he would probably do the same for any woman in a similar situation. It was nothing to do with her personally, she tried to tell her foolish heart. But she couldn't ignore the twinge of joy his protectiveness gave her. No one had ever felt the need to look after her before, and it was a strange and wonderful sensation.

"Thank you," she murmured, suddenly shy. She eased forward, pretending to inspect his handiwork in order to avoid his penetrating gaze. "Nice job."

"Thanks."

"I—um, baked some pies yesterday for the church dinner. I kept one for myself, though. Would you care to come in and have a piece? It's the least I can do to thank you for the window, and I still owe you a cup of coffee from last night," she said, embarrassed that she had thrown him out before the pot had finished boiling.

"Sounds good." He nodded and wiped his hands on the sides of his denims. "I could take a look at that doorframe, too, while I'm at it."

"That would be right neighborly." She nodded back, feeling more foolish by the minute but not certain what to do about the awkwardness between them. Finally she cleared her throat and went past him into the house.

Hannah put coffee on, removed the pie from the pie safe and cut two slices while Ram took the bucket of putty into the bedroom.

She tidied her hair, smoothed her skirt and wiped the table. Twice. Then she realized what she was doing.

Why was she acting so ridiculous? He was a whiskeylover. And everything she did not want to be attracted to in a man, she reminded herself.

It didn't help calm her.

He was some kind of easy on the eyes, she had to admit. And, contrary to what she'd thought, he must have some decency in him to show up and repair her window for no other reason than concern for her safety.

Unless he did have another reason.

Was this just a ploy to win her over and get her to back down in her fight against the saloons? Could he be that deceptive?

Hannah made a disgusted noise, frustrated with herself and her silly notions.

Of course he could be deceiving her. He could be any number of things, she thought. What did she know about him, after all? What did any of them know about him? Nothing more than his name, if Ramsey Kellogg was even his real name.

"All it needs is a little sanding and a coat of paint," he said, startling Hannah out of her musings. "I'll come by tomorrow and finish it up."

"That's not necessary, Mr. Kellogg." Nervousness made her voice sharper than she'd intended, and she saw his eyebrows draw together the way she'd come to notice they did when something perplexed him. She tried to sound more natural but still determined. She had to set things straight between them right away.

"I hope you don't think your coming here like this will change my mind about the temperance struggle. I mean, I appreciate all you've done, but it won't influence my opinion about the saloons."

He shook his head, a frown now marring his handsome features. "I never thought it would."

She glanced around anxiously. "Good. Then that's settled. Coffee's almost ready. Here, I hope you like apple," she said, poking the saucer of pie at him.

He stared at her for a moment, then set the saucer down.

"That's all right. I really should be getting back to work anyway."

He headed for the door, then turned suddenly, catching Hannah close behind him. She took a quick step back and nearly stumbled.

"I suppose I'll see you around?" he said, asking as though it was a question he already knew the answer to.

Hannah shrugged and tipped her head to one side. "If you hang around the saloons, you're bound to."

Ram chuckled at the incongruity of that statement. He collected his bucket of putty and his screwdriver and left without saying good-bye.

Hannah tossed both slices of pie into the bin at the back door, her appetite suddenly lacking. Had she insulted the man by questioning his motives? It seemed only sensible when she spoke, although she could see how it might have been a bit untimely, considering the job he'd just done for her.

No matter. She wouldn't have him thinking he could set her off course with a few friendly gestures.

She *would* see the saloons in Fortune closed. Afterwards . . . well, that was up to Francis.

If he didn't make up his mind soon to go forward with their wedding plans, Hannah had been thinking she might see about joining up with Carry Nation, traveling around the country closing saloons, lecturing on the temperance issue and organizing more chapters of the WCTU.

This mission had been born in her because of her mother, and that motivation kept her going. Francis's praise warmed and encouraged her, but she now knew she would continue the effort even without his support. She had to, to keep her own demons at bay.

But she'd digressed from the matter at hand. The matter being Ramsey Kellogg.

He'd done a fine job repairing her window. And she

knew it couldn't have been easy for him to get a pane of real glass on such short notice. In fact, she wasn't sure how he had managed the feat. She knew Moffett's General Store didn't carry luxuries like that. And he hadn't had time to get it from the mail-order catalogue.

Puzzled, and still a little flattered, despite his questionable motives, she swept aside the curtain to have another look at his handiwork. A startled scream escaped her lips.

"It's just me, Miss Hannah," Daniel Dowd said, his eyes going wide in his boyish face. He looked as startled as Hannah felt, and she clasped a hand to her pounding heart as she opened the door for him.

"I sure didn't mean to frighten you. I was just about to knock."

"It's all right, Daniel. I didn't realize you were there. What can I do for you?"

"Well, ma'am, I have a telegram and it seemed right urgent, so I brought it on over."

He swept his hat off his white-blond hair and ran nervous fingers through the wavy locks. "I'm sorry, Miss Hannah, but you know I can't help but know what comes over the wire. I have'ta decipher it and all." He thrust a folded piece of paper toward her and stared at the toes of his boots. "I'm just as sorry as I can be, ma'am."

Hannah felt a spark of apprehension flicker through her heart. The paper felt coarse and heavy in her hand and she had to force herself to take a deep breath.

Only one person knew where she was. And only one person would be wiring her here.

"Thank you, Daniel," she said, tucking the paper into her skirt pocket.

She went to the old baking powder tin in which she kept small change and drew out two bits.

"Aren't you even gonna read it, Miss Hannah?" he

asked, accepting the money without looking at it. "It's about your ma. . . ."

"Daniel," she cut in sharply, "since you're the official wire operator I don't have to ask that you keep this confidential. You're doing a good job and I know you'll do your duty."

"Yes, ma'am, I sure enough will. And not a soul'll hear a peep from me. But, Miss Hannah . . ."

"Thank you, Daniel." She opened the back door and offered him a smile forced across numb lips. Her lungs burned from holding her breath, but she didn't trust herself to relax until she was alone once more.

As the door closed behind the youth, Hannah sank weakly into a chair. Otherwise her knees would surely have buckled beneath her. She pressed her sweating palms against her forehead and squeezed her eyes shut.

She'd known this day would come. There had been a time in her life when she'd prayed for it. Now she just wanted to rid herself of the message burning a hole through the striped twill of her skirt. She didn't want to think about what this would mean, didn't want any of *that* life to intrude on the one she'd built for herself here.

The paper seemed to grow as heavy as a brick, weighing her clothes down and refusing to be ignored.

But she would ignore it, she thought, making up her mind at that moment. There was no reason she couldn't.

Hannah pulled out the telegram and dropped it into the trash bin by the door with the discarded pie, the glass from her shattered window and everything else that was no longer any use to her.

Chapter Eight

Hannah tidied the kitchen and changed into her nightgown, then let down her bright auburn tresses and began to brush. As she counted the strokes, she tried not to think about the telegram, Ramsey Kellogg or anything else disturbing.

But as she turned down the covers on her bed and climbed in, she was inundated with memories of the man, lying on the same sheets, holding her as close as a lover. She didn't want to remember his tenderness, or the way she'd felt in his arms. But it was safer to think of him than to dwell on the message calling out from the waste pile in her kitchen, so she let her mind wander to Ram.

Ram. That's what she'd heard the day laborers call him. She whispered the name hesitantly into the dark of her room, feeling shameful but liking the way the name felt on her tongue. She could almost imagine calling out to him.

She repeated it, this time more playfully. *Ram, time for*

supper. He would look up and smile, his golden gaze caressing her face like summer sunshine. *Ram, this pump's not working.* And he'd tease her as he cranked the handle effortlessly, his muscles straining against the fabric of his shirt. *Ram, kiss me again, and this time mean it.*

Wrenching desire shot through Hannah and she felt beads of moisture dotting the bottoms of her feet. She kicked off the covers and lit the lamp, disgusted that she'd let her imaginings go so far.

What utter foolishness. As if she'd let that womanizing rum-sucker within ten feet of her lips again. And how absurd, the thought of a man kissing her making her feet sweat! It was absolutely mortifying, and disgraceful to the chaste, respectable alliance she had with Francis.

Huffing with self-disdain, she made her way to the kitchen for a glass of cool milk. Her stomach was beginning to feel slightly empty and she hadn't been able to go to sleep hungry since . . .

The light from her lamp fell on the wooden bin and she gave in with a feeling of resignation. She'd known, somewhere deep inside, that she couldn't ignore the telegram forever.

Setting the lamp on the table, she retrieved the paper, carefully scraping off chunks of apple and coffee grounds. She wiped it carefully with a dishcloth and spread it open before her.

No surprises here, she thought, reading it the first time without emotion. Just words on a paper, she refused to let them register on her brain. Or on her heart.

She fingered the edge of the coarse page, smoothing a tear, and reread the lines.

What did she feel? So many emotions were struggling to break through her resolve, she felt as though a dam was about to burst.

And if it did, if she let them out, what then? She hadn't

allowed these feelings to follow her to Fortune. Whenever they tried to poke through the walls she'd built around her heart, Hannah would chase them back into the darkest regions of her soul.

Now she'd have to let them out, expose them to the light of day and deal with them once and for all. Could she do it? Was she strong enough? Had age and distance given her the wherewithal to put her past to rest for good?

She didn't feel particularly strong at that moment. In fact, she had the incredible urge to run back to bed and draw the covers over her face and think of something, anything else. Even the horrid fantasies of Ram Kellogg were preferable to facing these nightmares.

But Hannah was no longer a child who could hide out until the ugly and the hurtful went away. She was a grown woman who had fought to leave her past behind. And she'd succeeded. Nothing could change that. This was just the epilogue to a bad story. One last scene she had to play out before she could move on to the happily ever after she'd heard about in fairy tales and dreamed of her whole life.

She read the message one last time, then went to pack her bag and write a note for Francis.

More and more Ram found himself avoiding the things in which he usually found pleasure. He hadn't taken Sally up on her numerous invitations to join her upstairs, even though the woman had made it clear he was welcome to a free ride any time he wanted.

And instead of drinking in the saloons he frequented, he found himself watching for Hannah and her group. Tonight he'd even been disappointed when she didn't show up, and he cursed himself for twenty kinds of a fool.

The woman was a fanatic, one of the narrow-minded,

puritanical zealots who'd made his life hell for over twenty years before he'd forever walked away from anything remotely spiritual.

That had been ten years ago, and Ram hadn't looked back since. Until now. Hannah stirred to life in him things better left alone. Things that were dead and buried, literally as well as figuratively.

He didn't want to revive a single one of those awful, tormenting memories. So why did he constantly allow thoughts of Hannah to invade his heart, worming in and wrapping around it like a serpent? Why was he so consumed with the idea of finding out who had been threatening her?

And why should he feel such unmistakable rage toward the unknown aggressor, when they were presumably on the same side?

He'd eyed every man in every saloon he'd visited tonight, searching for something to indicate who might have sent Hannah the ominous notes. Finally, he couldn't take it anymore. He'd begun to see treachery and deceit in every face, no matter how guileless.

"I just need some air," he said to himself, strolling down the narrow street.

If only he knew more about Hannah Sullivan, he might be able to put the pieces together. But the more he tried to find out about her, the deeper the mystery grew. For a former Pinkerton detective, he'd come up empty on Hannah's background.

Apparently she'd bought the cottage she lived in two years ago after the owner passed away, leaving no heirs. If anyone knew where she came from before settling in Fortune, they weren't talking. And what did she do for money? She had a few chickens, and he'd learned she sold eggs to the general store about once a week, but that would hardly meet all her needs.

It seemed Hannah Sullivan just appeared in Fortune.

Of course, Ram knew there was more to the story than that. And he knew he'd find out the whole truth eventually. But he wasn't a patient man. He wanted to know all there was to know about Hannah, and the sooner the better.

He wasn't surprised when his supposedly aimless walk led him to her street. The gaslights flickered, making the pools of light at their bases waver. It was a nice street, a nice house. And Hannah Sullivan was probably a nice lady underneath her misguided and exasperating zeal.

So why did the woman insist on being such a menace?

Surely the answer to that question lay somewhere in her shadowy past. If—no, *when*—he found out what was at the bottom of her crusade, maybe he could figure out a way to dissuade her from any more nonsense about closing saloons and outlawing liquor.

The very idea! As if any man would stand still for that foolishness. Why, saloons were the only places men could go for solace away from the harping and nagging of women who thought their duty in life was to save the soul of every poor bastard whose path they crossed.

Fresh anger rose up in Ram as he wondered once more what made Hannah Sullivan tick. She was a puzzle, no doubt about that. And if there was one thing he could never walk away from, it was a good perplexity.

A light went on in the house and Ram eased under the branches of a nearby tree, hidden out of sight in the shadows. What was she doing up at this hour? he wondered. Could she be planning another sneak attack like the one in the alley outside the Double Eagle? He'd wondered why she and her band hadn't shown this evening to preach and sing and stir up their usual brand of mischief.

Damn! Here he was, wandering around like a mindless fool, thinking of everything but what he'd been paid to do.

Of course, if she was about to cause trouble, he couldn't have planned his appearance any better. He'd be right behind her, on top of whatever she had in mind.

Ram lit a cigarette and waited. Another light went on, and he was certain Hannah was up to no good.

He glanced at his pocket watch. Two in the morning. The woman certainly had a burr in her butt about drinking. No wonder someone wanted to put a halt to her crusade.

He ought to scare the bejesus out of her and put a stop to this foolishness once and for all. Then he could get the hell out of Fortune and forget about Hannah Sullivan and her flaming hair, glass-green eyes and that body that could make a man drool.

The light in her bedroom went out and Ram tossed aside his cigarette so he wouldn't give away his presence. He waited. Five minutes, six, seven. What was she doing?

The second light went off and he tensed as he slipped deeper into the shadows. He could barely make out her silhouette as she slipped around the corner of the house. She carried something in her hand, and it must have been heavy, because she was listing slightly to one side. He frowned, wondering what manner of deviltry she'd thought up this time.

Of course she had to be smart as well as beautiful. It was always the smart women who gave a man the most trouble.

She unlatched her gate and made straight for the tree where Ram hid. He pressed himself tight against the rough trunk and held his breath. He'd been careless; another mistake. He never should have gotten close enough for her to see him. In his business, mistakes like that could cost him his life.

But Hannah passed by without a sideways glance, and Ram wondered at her preoccupied mood. She should have noticed him; he wasn't that well hidden.

He let her reach the far end of the street before he set out after her, and then he was careful to keep a safe distance so she wouldn't know she was being tailed. She strode hurriedly toward the center of town, her stride purposeful and her head held up, despite the dark path she walked.

Ram noticed with some admiration that she hadn't stumbled or misstepped one time, although it was moonless and the scattered streetlamps put out only a minimum of light.

He trailed her to the Wells Fargo building, where she knocked on the door and, after a moment, was let in.

Damn Hannah Sullivan for a brain teaser, he thought. He couldn't find out so much as a smidgen of gossip about her life prior to her arrival in Fortune two years ago. He hadn't been able to predict her assaults against the saloons, and now he was completely baffled by her early morning sojourn to a supply house.

Could she be having an affair with one of the local men? But what was she carrying and why would she bring something so heavy to a rendezvous? Ram hadn't lived a life of iniquity for ten years without running across a few odd things in his travels, but Hannah Sullivan had him stumped.

"And the only thing worse than a beautiful woman with brains is one cloaked in a mystery," he whispered, finding a shadowy doorway where he could watch for her to come out. "Draws men like flies to dung."

He snorted, disgusted with the tightening of desire he felt in his loins. A knot pulled at the muscles of his abdomen and his thighs tingled with awareness. He didn't know when it had happened, but he'd begun to want Hannah Sullivan badly.

Of course, it could have something to do with bouncing the mattress with her earlier, or the fierce protective urges that the attack on her had stirred in him.

But Ram thought it probably had more to do with her lips, which tasted like the sweetest peach in Georgia, and her breasts, which were just the right size to fit in a man's palm. And all that glorious red hair he could imagine cascading over his bare chest as she rode him.

The sound of a wagon rattling down the street drew Ram out of his fantasy before something embarrassing happened.

He cursed Hannah Sullivan again. She was a prude and a shrew, and he'd do well to remember the way she nearly emasculated him for trying to rescue her that first night in the saloon. What would she do if he tried something even more ribald? Something hot and wild and sexy, like he'd been imagining?

The wagon stopped before the Wells Fargo building and Ram straightened with interest. If Hannah Sullivan was indulging in a secret tryst, her party was about to be interrupted.

He could hear muffled voices, but the wagon had blocked his view of the door. He eased along the walkway, careful to keep his back pressed against the walls of the buildings until he could see more of what was happening in front of the shipping and supply house.

Ram could see the two figures clearly in the pool of light from the opened door. The driver, Ram deduced from the dusty, worn clothes and the fact that he was a stranger, appeared to be arguing with a farmer Ram had met at the Double Eagle. Rufus, Rupert, something like that.

The only reason Ram remembered him at all was that the man had foolishly bet, and lost, part of his farm to one of the day laborers a week ago at the Paper Pony.

Ram disdained fools and folks who gambled what they couldn't afford to lose.

He saw the men nod and shake hands, and then they began to unload several large crates from the wagon and carry them into the supply house. They worked for nearly an hour, hauling stuff into the building, then another or so hauling more crates out and loading them into the wagon.

Ram was wondering what Hannah was doing all this time. Could she really be involved with a two-time loser like that farmer? And hadn't Ram heard the man had a wife? Was the saintly Hannah Sullivan a fornicator and an adultress?

The thought of catching the woman in a compromising position that would forever end her war against the saloons should have thrilled Ram. He ought to be smelling the sweet fragrance of victory. Instead, his stomach turned, and he thought he might be in need of a bicarbonate.

He settled back as the men worked loading the wagon. Dawn was just breaking over the horizon when Ram saw Hannah appear once more from inside the building. He could see now that she carried a valise and was dressed in a heavy gray skirt and traveling jacket. She'd swept up her hair and donned a little three-corner hat that rode at a jaunty angle on her head.

She said a few words to the farmer, then allowed the driver to help her into the interior of the wagon. Ram watched all this with confusion.

It would seem Hannah Sullivan was sneaking out of town under the cover of night, hidden in the bowels of a cargo wagon.

The driver climbed up on top and snapped the reins and they were off.

Before the dust settled back on the road Ram had slipped across the street. The farmer had gone back inside and Ram rapped sharply on the oval glass in the door.

"We won't be open for another hour," a disembodied voice called through the door. "Come back then."

Ram knocked again, harder, and heard heavy footsteps as the man strode closer.

Ram could see his silhouette through the frosted window and knew his was visible as well, but the man couldn't tell who he was.

"I said, we're closed."

"Open up," Ram ordered. "I've got business with you that can't wait."

There was a moment of silence; then the latch shot back and the door opened a few inches.

"Oh, Mr. Kellogg, it's you. What are you doing up and around this time of the morning?"

Ram pushed his way through the door, noticing the look of surprise and immediate apprehension that crossed the other man's face.

"What are you up to, Rufus?" Ram asked, trying to appear only mildly interested. "You haven't been frequenting the saloons. I thought you'd be working what's left of your farm even harder now."

"It's Rupert, Mr. Kellogg. And I am working the farm during the day. But with twenty acres' less crop this year, it just isn't goin' to be enough."

He hung his head slightly and then spoke again, his voice rough with emotion. "Ed Pearl was good enough to hire me on for the night shift here. I get some sleep in between the loads that come in, and the extra money'll help my family out."

Ram closed the door behind him and reached into his pocket for the Liberty half-dollars he carried to pay the scouts he used to watch for Hannah and her group. The women hadn't shown the night before, so he had several coins.

"I'd like to do something to help your family out, too, Rupert," Ram said, taking another step toward the man. Rupert eased back farther, obviously suspicious and a little disconcerted by Ram's demeanor. He eyed the door Ram now blocked with his body.

Pulling the coins from his pocket, Ram held them out to the wide-eyed man. Ram saw him swallow and then slowly lift his hand toward the money.

Just before he snatched the coins away, Ram closed his fist tight.

"But first, I'm going to need a little bit of information from you."

Chapter Nine

As Ram rode out of town on his bay mare, he pondered what Rupert had told him. The man didn't know where Hannah was heading, or why. If he had, Ram was sure he'd have sold the information for the extra money Ram offered. Still, he'd given Ram enough to go on.

Hannah Sullivan had paid passage on the Wells Fargo wagon across the border to Fort Smith, where she planned to catch the Rock Island express.

Ram figured a full day's ride on the supply wagon would put her on the noon train. All he had to do was beat the wagon to Fort Smith. The train would be out of town before she realized he, too, was on it.

It took less than a minute for Ram to decide to follow her. He knew she was up to something, and this was his chance to finally learn more about the mystery that was Hannah Sullivan.

And although he wouldn't be in the saloons nightly, neither would she. Since Hannah was the main reason he'd been hired in the first place, he reasoned it was his job to trail her and find out what manner of mischief she'd gotten in her pretty head to stir up this time.

He also admitted to a healthy dose of plain old curiosity.

It hadn't taken him long to collect a few belongings, and he'd left without waking Martin Pollack to tell the man where he was going and what he was up to. It had been a long time since Ram had answered to anyone for his actions and he wasn't about to start now. Even if the man *was* paying him.

He stopped once to rest and water his horse, but otherwise he made good time. When he reached Fort Smith the place was relatively quiet. He got a meal and a room for the night after ascertaining that the Wells Fargo wagon hadn't arrived and wasn't expected until morning.

The sheets in the run-down hotel were worn soft, but they were clean and smelled as if they'd been hung out in the afternoon sunshine. Ram settled back and decided to get a good night's sleep while he still could.

But every time he closed his eyes he saw Hannah Sullivan. At first he assumed his mind was preoccupied with her because she was his latest assignment and he always became absorbed in every case, no matter the circumstances.

However, as the night wore on and he tossed and turned, he began to wonder what it was about the woman that had him tied in knots.

Hannah did, and didn't, remind him of Doreen. Thoughts of his wife were never pleasant, and he tried to turn them off as he always did. But tonight, for some reason, she wouldn't go easily.

Her religious zeal had been even more fervent than Hannah's, her fanaticism like a fast-spreading disease. It had quickly sapped the vibrance that had first attracted him to her. Soon after the wedding he could barely remember her laugh, or even her smile, for they vanished.

In the end it had destroyed any love he'd had for her. Only guilt remained. And a bitter hatred of anything remotely resembling the spiritual.

Hannah certainly put him in mind of that breed, and in that way she reminded him of his wife.

But that was where the similarity ended. Hannah had an inner flame she couldn't hide, even beneath her cloak of religion. She was passionate, kissing him back though she claimed to loathe him and all he stood for. Hell, she probably hadn't even realized she was doing it, but Ram sure as hell noticed.

Even her enthusiasm for the temperance cause proved she was hot-blooded and tempestuous.

Again Ram found himself drawn to the fire, despite having been badly burned.

Some time in the early morning hours he finally drifted into a fitful sleep, waking just after dawn feeling achy and ill-tempered. He crammed his things back into his saddle-bags and went to find someone to look after his horse while he foolishly chased after a woman who could bring him nothing but grief and aggravation.

"A single ticket to Blue Springs," Hannah said, counting out the coins from the bottom of her reticule.

"Don't get much call for that one anymore," the man said, writing in the destination on a stub. "Fact is, they're taking it off the run in another month." He leaned forward, his eyebrows arched curiously as she reached for the ticket he held just out of reach.

"Is that so?" she said, grabbing the ticket and pushing the money through the half-circle cut out of the window between her and the nosy stranger.

"It is," he told her, taking no offense at her abrupt manner, if he even noticed it.

Good, Hannah thought. That meant the town was even worse off than when she left.

That thought, and the wish that the whole place would just dry up and blow away to dust, almost made her feel better about her trip.

Her back ached from sitting in the cramped interior of the cargo wagon all night, although, surprisingly, she'd been able to sleep for several hours of the journey. Her mind had been in such turmoil at the thought of returning to Blue Springs that she wouldn't have thought sleep possible.

Now that she'd resigned herself to the inevitable, she felt nothing more than a grim determination to get this chapter of her life behind her and put the past to rest for good.

The train was crowded with people and Hannah finally found a seat all the way in the front of the car, next to a woman with a small baby. She smiled and placed her valise in the overhead bin before arranging her skirts and sitting. She adjusted her hat, tucked in a few strands of fiery hair and wished she'd had time to wash up a bit.

Heat swirled around the bodies pressed into the cramped area, and soon Hannah could feel moisture running down her back to settle at her waist. Her face was shiny with perspiration. She glanced out the coal-grimy window and wished they would get underway. The air might still be hot, but at least they would be moving.

The woman seated next to her removed a fan from a carpetbag at her feet and opened it, waving it at the baby, who'd begun to fuss.

Hannah sympathized with the child. She almost felt like whining herself.

There was some delay and Hannah heard, more than saw, other passengers arriving through the rear door. She wondered where they would sit, since she'd hardly been able to find a spot herself.

Finally, the roar of the great coal fire in the engine rumbled through the train and Hannah heard the click-clack of the wheels.

They gained speed, and a brisk breeze started through the opened windows around the car. People grinned and nodded, sharing the small joy.

Hannah tried to relax, but the baby was crying in earnest now and nothing the woman did seemed to pacify it. Not wanting to seem hard, Hannah offered the flustered woman a small, indulgent smile.

"Pardon me, ma'am," a deep voice said from behind Hannah, "but I'd be honored to offer you my seat in the rear of the car."

Hannah thought the man was speaking to her and she turned, a grateful smile on her face. Instantly, the smile died and she gasped.

"You? What are you doing here?"

She realized belatedly that she should have recognized the smooth, seductive voice. It had haunted her dreams enough of late.

But, she told herself, she'd never dreamed *he* would be on this train, or anywhere near Fort Smith.

"Offering this lady my seat," Ram said, nodding to Hannah's seatmate.

Turning to the other woman, he touched his hat and motioned to the rear aisle. "The seats in the last row are larger and offer a bit more privacy, should you need to tend to personal matters," he added.

"Why, that's most gracious of you, sir," the flustered mother cried, snatching her carpetbag and pushing past Hannah in her rush to take Ram up on his offer before he changed this mind. "Most generous," she muttered, hurrying down the aisle toward the empty seat Ram had vacated.

"Hannah," he said, slipping past her knees to take the window seat.

Hannah's mouth dropped open, then closed several times before she could get another word out. When she did, it wasn't exactly profound as she repeated her earlier greeting.

"I asked what you're doing here."

"Isn't that funny, that was the very thing I intended to ask you." He removed his hat and slipped it under his seat, then stretched his booted feet out in front of him.

"None of your business," she snapped, futilely looking around the car for an empty seat. Of course there were none. She huffed and cut him a sharp glance. "You followed me."

"Well, I can't imagine any other reason to go to Blue Springs, Arkansas. God knows the man at the ticket window was astonished to have two passengers heading to 'that dried-up hole in the wall,' I believe was the term he used."

"This is outrageous!" Hannah fumed, shifting in her seat to see if any of the other passengers had overheard their conversation. She realized she should keep her voice down or risk drawing even more unwanted attention. "My whereabouts are none of your concern."

"On the contrary, I've been paid to keep track of that very thing. And when someone I'm being paid to watch sneaks off in the dead of night, I consider it my duty to find out what they're up to."

She glared at him for a full minute; then her face softened and she shook her head.

"You've wasted your time. This has nothing to do with my fight against the saloons. It's a personal matter."

"Care to elaborate?"

She shifted and felt the sweat pool at the small of her back once more. She looked away. "No, I wouldn't."

"Then I'll just have to see for myself, won't I?"

Her head snapped around and she clasped his arm without realizing she'd done it. "You can't. This is none of your business, I tell you. You have no right to intrude on my personal life like this."

"Don't I? Isn't that exactly what you've been doing to the men of Fortune? Intruding on their private lives by trying to close the saloons and ban the liquor they enjoy?"

"No! This isn't the same thing at all," she whispered harshly as he reached down to remove the fingernails that had dug into his muscled forearm. Hannah flushed, realizing she'd been clutching him in a desperate grasp.

"Then tell me what you're up to."

She gripped her hands together in her lap. "No."

Ram shrugged, leaned back and closed his eyes. "Then I'll just have to see for myself," he said, pretending to settle in for a nap.

"You can't accost me in this manner," she told him furiously. "I'll have you thrown off this train before we get anywhere near Blue Springs."

"You do and I'll make sure you're standing right next to me when it pulls away."

Hannah made a rude noise under her breath but didn't say anything more. She knew he'd keep his promise somehow if she raised a fuss over his presence. And she didn't have time to try to find another way to Blue Springs.

She sat next to him, smelling the male scent of leather and bay rum, trembling with rage.

How could he do such a low, despicable thing? And just when she'd begun to think he might actually have a decent streak in him. Boy, had she been wrong. All his attentions had been just his way of keeping track of her every move for the saloon owners he worked for.

And what truly galled her was that she hadn't even realized she'd been followed all the way from Fortune!

After several tense, quiet minutes, she gained control of her emotions and tried to reason with him.

"It's nothing, really. I swear, I'm just going for a visit."

"Uh-huh."

"I have friends there, that's all."

"Yep."

Groaning, she turned away again, feeling the beads of sweat at her temples. She dabbed at them with her handkerchief and decided to remove her hat, hoping it would ease the pressure building in her head.

"Look, they're going to need you in Fortune," she said, glancing longingly at the hatpin and imagining several heinous things she could do to the exasperating man beside her. "I left a detailed plan of harrassment for the ladies to carry out in my absence."

"You don't say?"

"I do." She nodded, and a red curl dropped over her forehead.

Ram peered at the fetching picture through slitted eyes and fought a grin. High color rode her cheeks and she'd gnawed her lip until it was red and sensuously swollen. Her skin glistened and he thought he'd never seen such a beautiful sight. He closed his eyes again, pretending disinterest, though he deeply regretted shutting off the enticing view.

"Well, I dare say you won't have a job when we return to find the saloons have been successfully closed by the WCTU."

"Might not," he said. "Then again, I can't imagine any of those women being very effective without you to lead them. No, they're all followers, and without you I'm sure the town will go back to its usual peaceful cohabitation."

"Oh, you're being so stubborn. What can you possibly gain by following me?"

"Maybe nothing," he said, hiking one shoulder. "Maybe I just get pleasure out of giving you back a little of the aggravation you've given me."

"That's childish," she snapped.

He glanced sideways at her and grinned devilishly. "Yeah, but damned fun."

Hannah twisted sideways, facing toward the aisle. There was no point talking to the man. He was as stubborn as a stump.

What would she do now? She couldn't let him follow her to Blue Springs. Couldn't let him see what she'd left behind, or learn her secrets. A wave of cold fear swept through her at the thought.

No, that must never happen.

She fiddled with her hat and tried to hide her emotions. What would he do if he knew? If he saw the ugly truth? He'd tell everyone in Fortune and she'd be shunned and ridiculed, her dreams for a respectable future shattered.

All the pain of her past rushed forward and she felt desperation grip her. She'd come so far, worked so hard to put all of it behind her and ensure that no one but Francis would ever know.

Francis. What would he do if the whole town found out the truth about her?

She wanted to believe he would stand beside her and go through with their marriage despite the gossip and speculation, but something inside her knew that would never happen. He cared what his parishioners thought about him. He worked hard to earn their respect, and though he'd protected her secret so far, she knew it was as much for his own comfort as for hers.

Anguish filled her. She tried to ignore the man sitting next to her but found she couldn't. She'd threatened and cajoled. The only thing left to do was plead, and she wasn't above begging at this point.

"Mr. Kellogg," she said. "Ram. This *is* a personal matter. I know I've given you some trouble in the past weeks, but I'm asking you to do the honorable thing and leave. Go back to Fortune. I'll be returning in a few days and you can harrass me then until you've had your fill."

"I'm not sure I'll ever get my fill of you, Hannah," he said, straightening with interest at her imploring tone. He started to tease her more, then frowned when he noticed the telltale brightness of her eyes.

"What is it, Hannah? What's really going on here?"

She took a deep breath and blinked away the moisture. "Nothing. I told you, I'm just visiting a friend. But you have no right." Her voice broke on a sob and her eyes widened with horror at the slip. "You have no right to follow me."

The older gentleman behind them leaned forward as he heard the distressed wail, and Ram glared at him until he looked away again.

"Come here," Ram said, putting his arm around Hannah's shoulder and trying to draw her near. She resisted, pushing away.

"Don't touch me," she cried.

The man leaned over the seat again. "Miss, can I be of assistance?"

Hannah jumped, startled, and Ram turned in his seat, glaring.

"No, you can't," he barked. "Now sit back and mind your own business."

"Now see here, young man . . ." the fellow sputtered.

Hannah felt Ram tense beside her, his muscles bunching beneath his shirtsleeves. She quickly wiped away the lone tear that had escaped to run down her face.

"It's all right," she assured the kindly man, "but thank you."

He frowned at Ram and then slowly settled back in his seat.

"Why do you have to be such a bully all the time?" she said, careful to keep her voice low.

"I'm not a bully," he roared, then looked ominously over his shoulder at the intrusive older man. Ram lowered his voice when he saw the man start to rise. "I told you, I'm just doing my job."

"And I told you this has nothing to do with the WCTU or the temperance movement at all."

"Then why don't you tell me what it does have to do with?"

"My mother," she blurted, cursing her slip and wishing she could take back the words. He tipped his head and she saw his eyes soften. There was no turning back now, but maybe she could keep him from following her all the way to Blue Springs and discovering the awful truth. "She's been sick for a long time," Hannah told him.

"I'm sorry to hear that. Has she taken a turn for the worse?"

"She's dead. I received word last night. A telegram from the doctor who'd been treating her."

"This must be a painful journey for you. I'm sorry if I've added to your grief."

"You haven't," she admitted, not sure why she confessed even that much. "It was a long time coming. I'm sure it's for the best."

He looked stunned, but he nodded woodenly. "I suppose that's true more often than not."

She thought she heard a note of something painful in the bizarre comment, but she didn't want to pry into his emotions any more than she wanted him poking around in hers. She'd said what she had to in order to get rid of him; that was as far as it went, and she forced herself to remember how exasperating the man was when he wasn't being kind.

"So you'll get off at the next stop and return to Fortune, then?"

"I don't think it's a good idea for you to travel alone. Especially under the circumstances."

"Nonsense. I'll be fine," she told him, her voice strong, her resolve hardened once more.

"Hannah, let me help you. Just this one time. I know you think you're tough, but it won't make you any less committed to accept a little friendly support."

He reached for her hand, but she jerked away, frustrated and angry. "I don't need your help or your support. We don't even like each other, remember? You're everything I disdain and loathe. Even if I needed a friend right now, which I don't, it certainly wouldn't be you."

Ram tried to hide his shock at her outburst. He kept his face carefully blank and fought the urge to squeeze his hands into fists. "Whatever you say, lady. But you'd better get used to looking over your shoulder because I'll be right behind you until all this temperance horseshit is put down once and for all. I'm gonna be on you like your shadow at high noon. And I don't give a tinker's damn if you like it or not."

Hannah realized too late that she'd pushed the man into a corner. He would never back down now. Her only hope was to try to lose him before they reached Blue Springs.

But what good would that do? It wouldn't be hard for him to find out who she was, or had been. And even if she turned around now and returned to Fortune, there was no guarantee he wouldn't go on without her. And it wouldn't take a detective to learn all he needed to know.

Again she saw her carefully cultivated plans for a decent,

happy life crumbling before her. And again, it was all Ram Kellogg's fault.

Hannah rose and turned to the older man seated behind her, still listening to their conversation.

"Excuse me, could I trouble you to change seats with me? This man is indeed bothering me."

"I can fetch the conductor," the man offered, rising in defiance of Ram's narrow-eyed stare.

"That isn't necessary, I'm sure," she told him. "If I could just exchange seats . . . ?"

"Certainly, miss."

The man collected his bag from the bin over his seat and picked up his hat, placing the bowler on his balding head. As he brushed past Hannah, she caught the heavy odor of sour sweat and bad breath. As she settled into the man's seat she grinned, thinking of the long trip Ram would be enduring beside her malodorous would-be rescuer.

Chapter Ten

By the time Hannah saw the far-off speck of buildings that made up Blue Springs, she'd resigned herself to Ram's presence. She hadn't been able to get another train or sneak away from him long enough to rent a horse and buggy in the one town they'd stopped in.

He'd kept his promise and stayed on her like her shadow.

She still refused to talk to him, but it was just a matter of pride now. Soon he would know the whole truth about her past, and there was nothing she could do about that. Nor did she have any control over what he would do with the information once he had it.

Hannah assumed he'd use it to try to stop her crusade once and for all. After all, that was what she'd do if the shoe were on the other foot.

She'd even begun to wonder if she should return to Fortune at all. There would be nothing there for her if Ram ruined everything by spreading around . . . the truth.

Almost smiling at that thought, Hannah played a little

game she'd always indulged in as a child. She would imagine the worst thing that could possibly happen, and then anything better would seem like a triumph. It was a grim ploy, but still surprisingly effective.

This time she understood only too well the worst that could, and surely would, happen if Ram leaked her secret to the people of Fortune.

First of all, she'd be an outcast. She mentally shrugged. She'd been that for most of her life. The thought no longer stirred fear in her.

Secondly, she'd probably have to sell her house and move away. That image brought a small twinge of pain; she'd come to love her little cottage. But, she reassured herself, she'd find another somewhere, in a town just as nice.

Third, her marriage to Francis would certainly be out of the question.

As the train pulled into the small, run-down station at Blue Springs, Hannah caught Ram's eye.

He rose and turned toward her, his look inquisitive, probing her eyes for the answers she'd refused to give him throughout their trip.

Her blood sped through her veins, her pulse began to pound rapidly against her throat and suddenly she was very warm. And it wasn't just the heat of the crowded car that brought on the disturbing reaction.

She wondered why thoughts of Francis had been the last thing on her mind. And why didn't she feel that all-encompassing panic she'd felt before, when she'd considered the possibility of losing him?

And why, when she'd thought her engagement to Francis ending, had her eyes immediately gone to Ram?

"Will you at least let me accompany you wherever you need to go?" he asked, all his earlier challenge and verbosity subsiding into gentle concern.

Hannah had no more strength to fight him. No doubt she'd need all she had for the coming ordeal.

Besides, at this moment fighting Ram was the last thing she wanted to do. Though it would surely damn her, she wanted someone to lean on. And she wanted that someone to be Ram.

"Yes," she said, bending to collect her valise.

Hannah didn't elaborate, nor did she wait to see what his reaction would be. She simply stepped into the aisle and led the way off the train.

The platform had long since turned gray with age, and several rotting boards had not been replaced. The ticket office was closed, but it hardly mattered. No one, other than Ram and Hannah, got off the train.

This was not a stop where anyone hoped to find a good meal or a few minutes of scenic entertainment.

Blue Springs was practically a ghost town, Hannah thought, scanning the street, which had tufts of grass growing in it and a few locals standing idly on one corner. Even the people looked gray somehow, she thought. No color, no life. Not one ounce of joy in the whole dead place.

"What a cheerful town," Ram said dryly, coming to stand beside her. He tipped back his hat and let his eyes wander aimlessly around the square. He scratched his head and frowned. "Did you really grow up here?"

Hannah nodded. "Yes."

"That explains a lot."

Snapping her head around, Hannah glared at him. "It wasn't like this when I lived here," she told him, not sure why she was defending the place, but stung nevertheless by his less-than-tactful remark. "It was actually quite nice," she admitted, surprising herself.

"I mean, there was a pretty little school just over that hill, and we had a real brass bell. And the teacher would always let me ring everyone in from recess."

Hannah's mind drifted back to those days. None of the other children were allowed to play with her, so she'd always stayed in during recess and washed the blackboards and pounded the erasers.

Thinking back on it, she got a warm feeling when she remembered her teacher, Miss Envel. The woman had treated Hannah like she was special, not dirty and unlovable.

So, growing up in Blue Springs hadn't been all bad. Just 99 percent bad, she thought, coming out of her foolish musings.

"Or maybe it was and I'm just remembering it through a child's eyes."

"Were you a child when you left here?" he asked, stepping so close that his shadow shaded her eyes.

"No," she said bitterly, remembering just how quickly she'd grown up in her last days here. "Not at all."

She could hear the bitterness, the anguish in her voice. But she couldn't hide it. Ram tried to look into her eyes, but she stepped away before he could see her face. Hefting her bag higher, she started across the street.

"The Widow Crumb used to have rooms she'd rent out. Let's see if she's still alive and open for business. I'd like to wash up before . . ."

She stumbled to a halt, took a deep breath and started walking again. Soon enough she would have to face the reason she'd come. And it would no doubt be the hardest thing she'd ever done. But Hannah knew she couldn't face it now, not with so little sleep and on an empty stomach.

As they approached a two-story frame house, Ram frowned. The place didn't look too good to him. The bushes were overgrown and the windows were opaque with dirt. A few shingles were missing, too.

"Is this the best there is?" he asked, feeling foolish when

Hannah shot him a sardonic stare. What had he expected, a classy hotel?

"This isn't exactly St. Louis, you know."

"Yeah, I noticed."

"Nobody asked you to come along," she needlessly reminded him.

"I'm not complaining," he said.

"Sure sounds like it to me," she told him, a knowing smirk on her face.

They proceeded to the door and Hannah set her bag down on the porch. She lifted the tarnished knocker and let it fall back into place with a clatter.

Several long moments passed, and Ram shifted awkwardly on the porch. Why he should feel so uncomfortable, he didn't know. He was only doing his job.

And even if he might argue consolation wasn't in his job description, he couldn't argue the need to keep his eye on Hannah, just in case she was up to something.

The door opened and a short, bent woman peered out. Her gray hair stood out in tufts around her head and her apron was soiled. She squinted to look at them and her upper lip lifted, revealing long, yellowed teeth.

"Who are ya? And what do ya want?"

"We'd like a room," Hannah said, staring at the woman in shock. "If you still rent them out, that is."

The woman blinked watery eyes and leaned closer to stare at Hannah.

"I know you," she announced. "What's your name?"

Ram saw Hannah's obvious hesitation and wondered at the cause. Why would she be shy around some old crone who took in boarders?

"Hannah Sullivan," she said quietly, and her voice sounded small and childlike.

Ram's frown deepened and apprehension gripped him.

"Hah, I knew it," the woman crowed. "I knowed you'd

come back to take your mama's place. And what nerve you've got, too, dragging your fancy man back with you."

Ram blinked, startled. Then he grinned, a little flattered. A fancy man? Is that what he looked like? He started to laugh at Hannah, to share the joke, but he saw her face had gone white and her lips were a pale slash.

"This was a mistake," she said.

"You're darn right it was. Thinking I'd let trash like you in my place." The woman's voice rose and Ram stepped forward, about to speak up and tell the old bat to shut up.

Why didn't Hannah say something? Why would she let the woman talk about her mother in such a disrespectful manner without showing some of the Irish spunk he'd come to expect from her?

Hannah grasped his arm and pulled him away from the door. She staggered down the stairs, clutching him as the woman shook her fist.

"I run a decent place here. I don't allow none of your kind."

Hannah turned and started away quickly, but Ram hung back, confused and more than a little angry. On the porch the woman still stood, sneering at Hannah's retreating back.

"Lady, we don't want to stay in this run-down rattrap you're so proud of," Ram called out, feeling childish but wanting to say something in Hannah's defense. "I'm particular about not sharing my bed with vermin."

"Yeah, you ain't too particular if you'd share it with the likes of that one," she shouted. " 'Course, neither was anyone else around these parts."

Ram actually took a step toward the woman before he stopped. What was he thinking? He couldn't hit her, and she wasn't worth arguing with. Rage shook him and he clenched his fists as he turned away, hurrying to catch up to Hannah.

Why had he felt the murderous need to defend her? he wondered. And what had the old crone been implying with her ribald comments? Could it be Hannah had at one time made her living . . . ?

No, that thought was beyond ridiculous.

"Hannah, slow down. I'm not running a race with you."

His words had little effect as she swept down the street. He could see her chin tremble, but her eyes were dry. The woman had hurt her, and again he was surprised by the anger that caused in him.

"Dammit, Hannah, you're going to fall and break your neck," he snapped, catching her gently by the arm and slowing her flight.

"What's wrong with you? She was a rude old biddy. Why should her meanness upset you?"

"It didn't. I came here to do something and I want to do it and leave, as soon as possible."

"Why? What is it you don't want me to find out? What's here that you're afraid of?"

She snatched her arm out of his grasp and blew a disgusted sigh. "I'm not afraid of anything. I left all this behind, that's all. There's nothing here for me now. There never was. And I want to get back to Fortune and tormenting you," she told him sharply, immediately going on the defensive.

Her words should have made him angry, but he only laughed to see the fire back in her eyes. "That's my girl," he said, grinning. "Where do we go next?"

She paused a moment and took a long breath. A strange expression crossed her face and she stared at him for a long moment. Then she smiled slightly and pointed to a faded blue-washed building at the end of the row.

"Doc Collier's. He's the one who telegraphed me."

"Lead the way," he said, motioning to her to go ahead.

She looked at him for another moment; then they were walking once more.

This building looked little better than the last one, Ram thought, but considerably better than most on the street. Blue Springs was indeed a town on its way out.

Ram had briefly questioned the man at the train station in Fort Smith about Hannah's destination. Although Blue Springs had once been a booming mining town, the coal there had long since been used up. The mine owners and their money had moved on, leaving behind the unlucky few who couldn't—or wouldn't—follow the vein.

But how had Hannah ended up here? he wondered. She looked like a rose among the crabgrass. He wanted to reach out, touch her cheek, look in her eyes and see her smile again. Or yell and sing off-key. Whatever would take away the forlorn look she wore as she waited for yet another door to open.

When it did, Ram felt himself tense against another stinging rebuke. But this time an elderly man wearing spectacles flung the door wide and greeted them both with a smile.

"I knew you'd come, Hannah. You always were such a good girl."

Hannah broke into tears and the man clutched her to his chest and rocked from side to side.

Ram stood back, feeling self-conscious and inept. He tried not to stare, but he couldn't help wondering at two such opposite yet forceful reactions. Who was Hannah Sullivan, he thought, to stir such intense feelings in these two people?

And in him.

"Come in, come in," the man said, removing his spectacles and wiping his moist eyes. "What an old fool I am, making you stand here on the doorstep."

He led Hannah to a worn sofa, motioning for Ram to

follow. They took a few moments to collect themselves; then their host spoke.

"Would you like something? Hot tea, maybe? No, I suppose it's a bit warm for that. How about a nice glass of buttermilk? You always were partial to buttermilk," he said, patting Hannah's hand.

"That would be nice," Hannah said.

"How about you?"

Ram stared at the man aghast. "Me? You've got to be joking. I wouldn't touch the stuff. I'll take something stronger, though."

The doctor blinked at Ram as though he had two heads and then turned to Hannah with a confused look on his face. "I don't understand . . ."

"Whiskey?" Ram explained. "Hell, right now I'd settle for beer."

"I understood what you were asking for," the man told Ram dryly. "What I don't understand . . ."

"Just get him the drink, Doc," Hannah said, waving her hand as she sniffed away the last of her tears. "And don't bother wasting your breath. I assure you it's hopeless."

"Huh." The old man snorted, then shuffled off to the kitchen.

Hannah refused to look at Ram directly. Obviously she was embarrassed by her outburst, her tears, and by Ram's having been witness to the horrible setdown she'd received from the old woman at the boardinghouse.

Ram still didn't understand why she'd hurled such insulting accusations at Hannah, or why Hannah hadn't fought back. But he filed the question away for another time. Hannah wasn't up to an inquisition at the moment.

Still, he knew if she looked at him she would see a million questions in his eyes.

"I've got some sweet corn bread I could crumble in

there if you'd like," the doc said, coming back into the
room and handing Hannah the thick milk.

"No, thank you. This is fine."

Hannah took a sip, remembering the times she'd come
to Doc Collier's when there had been no food in the house
and no money. His wife had been a kind, gentle, childless
woman who would have taken Hannah in in a second and
raised her as her own. They'd fed her, comforted her,
championed her. But she'd always refused to leave her
mother.

Now she wondered why she'd bothered taking care of
the woman all those long, hard years. What had it gotten
her in the end?

Only the worst kind of betrayal, and a shame so deep
she'd fled Blue Springs, never to return. Until now.

She'd had to write the Colliers and tell them where she
was when she settled in Fortune. She hadn't wanted them
to worry. That was how she knew Mrs. Collier had died
two winters ago. And that was how Doc Collier knew where
to contact her with the news of her mother's death.

Hannah repeated the words silently in her head. *Her
mother's death.* She still didn't know what to feel. Relief?
Sadness?

Or, worse yet, nothing at all?

"Where is she?" she blurted out, not realizing the men
hadn't been following her thoughts until she saw the
shocked look on Doc's face.

She glanced at Ram and noticed that a glass was poised
halfway to his lips. She quickly drew her eyes away from
his mouth, not wanting to remember how it had felt against
her own.

"Um, at the undertaker's. Stan Bose took over when his
daddy passed last year. Runs the place now, though he
don't have much business anymore."

Hannah nodded. She remembered Stan Bose Sr. He'd

been a strange, lanky man with dark emotionless eyes. She also remembered Stan Jr. He'd been sweet on her when they were both eight years old, before the other kids realized what her mother was and stopped talking to Hannah.

She couldn't picture Stan Jr. doing what his father had done for a living. She couldn't picture his eyes, bright blue and always filled with mischief, as cold and empty as his father's had been.

"Well, I guess I should go over and speak to him about arrangements, or whatever."

"I've already done that," Collier told her, a bit chagrined. "I wasn't sure you'd come, though I thought you might. Fact is, everything was set for tomorrow, whether you showed up or not. Afraid with the weather warming up the way it is, we couldn't wait too long. The regular week was stretching it even."

"Good," Hannah said with a brisk nod. "Thank you. I appreciate everything you've done." She hesitated, and some of the starch left her voice. She gazed at Collier with warm, soft eyes. "I mean that, Doc. Everything you've done for me over the years. And all you did for my . . . for her, too."

Ram set his drink on the table, looking ill at ease. Hannah thought it served him right for following her and poking his nose into things that didn't concern him. But she couldn't be sorry he was there with her, even if it meant her secret would soon be exposed.

She appreciated the way he'd come to her defense with the Widow Crumb. In fact, that had been the reason for her tears, more than the old woman's stinging insults. What was it about the man that he'd bedevil her on his own but was forever coming to her rescue against anyone else who might hurt her?

He was a riddle, and he'd gotten to her. Now she was

as curious about him as he seemed to be about every detail of her life.

The trouble was, though he'd soon know all her secrets, he was still a complete puzzle.

"Shall we just wait until tomorrow, then? Or would you like to go over to the Bose place now and pay your respects?"

Hannah faced Doc, then shook her head. "Tomorrow's soon enough," she said. Her words said she was sure it would be too soon. "Right now I've got to figure out where we're going to stay the night."

"Why, you'll stay right here," Collier said, slapping his palms on his knees. "The two of you can take mine and Martha's old room and I'll settle here on the sofa."

Hannah stared in stunned silence for a moment, her jaw, nearly hanging loose. "What? No! You don't understand . . ."

"Nonsense," he cut in. "I haven't been able to get a good night's sleep in that room since Martha passed anyway. You and your husband might as well make good use of it."

"My what?"

"Who?"

She and Ram exclaimed at the exact same moment, and then their eyes met. She saw the horror reflected in the whiskey-brown orbs glaring at her and felt ridiculously slighted. Why was *he* so appalled? She was the one who should be, who *was*, disgusted by the very idea.

Wasn't she?

Why, then, did she feel the slightest twinge of excitement to think Doc Collier had assumed they were married? That Ram was her husband?

"I'm sorry," she mumbled, flustered and disturbed by her own thoughts. "I should have introduced you both when we first arrived. I was just so overcome, I didn't think."

"What Hannah is trying to say, and not doing too well, I'm afraid, is that we're not . . ."

"Don't tell me I'm not doing this well. I wouldn't have to do it at all if you hadn't followed me on this trip. Which you had no right to do."

"Hannah, why are you angry with the boy?" Doc cut in, smoothing his gray hair. "A husband's place is by his wife's side at a time like this."

"But that's what I'm trying to tell you, Doc. This man isn't my husband."

Ram had reached for his drink, obviously needing strength to get over the shock of being mistaken for Hannah's husband.

A look of surprise was quickly followed by an expression of deep concern and, finally, grave disappointment on the doctor's face. He shook his head and stood stiffly.

"Hannah, how could you do it? Didn't being raised by that woman teach you anything? How could you follow your mama's ways and take up with this man, with any man, in such a sinful manner?"

As the doctor's question reverberated through the room, Ram gulped hard and began to choke.

Chapter Eleven

"Dammit, I've had just about enough of this," Ram bellowed, shaking off the doctor's attempts to pat his back. Hannah stood by the sofa looking dazed and embarrassed.

"If this is the kind of friend you've been surrounded by your whole life, it's no wonder you latched on to a group of radicals and that sissy preacher. Why, friends like this would make a person glad to be alone."

"Ram, you don't understand."

"Now just a minute, you rascal. I ain't the one taking advantage of this poor child."

"I haven't taken anything," Ram snapped, stepping toward Collier ominously. "And if you say one more word it had better be an apology. Hannah has just lost her mother and I won't have anyone blackening the woman's name, or Hannah's either."

"I ain't done no such a thing," the doc exclaimed.

"Ram, you don't understand."

"I said apologize!"

"Ram!" Hannah shouted, smacking his forearm and forcing him to look at her instead of bearing down on Doc Collier like a mad bear.

He grasped her hand and a shot of electricity zipped through her body. She hated to tell him the truth, to see the look that would replace the indignant anger he now wore on his handsome face.

But at the same time she couldn't let him throttle her friend in some misguided attempt to defend her mother's lost reputation.

"He isn't saying anything about my mother that I didn't know to be the truth from the time I was ten years old. Don't you understand, Ram?" she asked, licking lips gone suddenly dry.

She closed her eyes and took a steadying breath. "My mother was a prostitute."

"What? What are you saying?"

"Don't ask me to say it again. Now can we just settle down for a minute, all of us, and maybe I can explain this whole mess."

The two men looked at each other, still distrustful but thoroughly admonished by Hannah's authoritative tone. They nodded and sat on opposite ends of the sofa.

"Dr. Collier, this is Ram Kellogg. He's been hired to keep an eye on me by the saloon owners in Fortune whom I have been protesting against as part of the Woman's Temperance League. He takes his job very seriously, as you can see, since he followed me across the border from Oklahoma."

She saw a frown crease the doctor's forehead. He eyed Ram with distrust, then opened his mouth to question her further. Hannah cut him off before he could.

"Ram, this is my very good friend, Dr. Cyrus Collier. He knows more about me than anyone and would never say anything to hurt me, though I admit it may have sounded that way a moment ago."

Both men must have realized they'd spoken out of turn, possibly hurting Hannah in some mistaken effort to defend her. Both seemed equally chastened as they let her continue uninterrupted.

"Ram, I appreciate your attempt to defend me and my mother. I assure you, though, that you need never do that against Doc. And Doc, I understand you were trying to save me from possibly turning out like my mother, but I assure you that will *never* happen."

"Hannah, I still don't understand . . ." Ram started.

"I have to admit, neither do I," Doc said.

"Well, I've said all I'm going to about it. This has been a long and trying day," she told them sharply, eyeing each of the men who had, however inadvertently, made her situation more difficult. "I need some fresh air and, frankly, a little peace. I'm going for a walk," Hannah told them, shaking her head. "Alone."

Giving them both a weary look, she left them sitting in the small parlor, astonished.

She hadn't wanted Ram to find out about her past, but she'd known it was inevitable.

It pained her that Doc Collier could think for a moment she would turn out like her mother. And that she'd bring it to his door, even if she had.

Was there no one in this world who really understood her? Ram knew nothing about her past, but he'd known enough to see she was hurt by Doc's accusation.

Doc knew all about her past but knew nothing of the woman she'd become.

Was Ram right? She'd had no real friends growing up except the Colliers, who were more like substitute parents. Was that the reason she'd jumped at the chance to lead the Temperance League? And what about her engagement to Francis, which she'd begun to have doubts about? Was she just trying to make herself a part of something? Was that the reason she'd gone to Fortune in the first place—so she'd finally feel she belonged somewhere?

She remembered another telegram, and the last time she'd seen her mother. It was not a pleasant memory and Hannah pushed it aside, not ready to face it again just yet.

Tomorrow she would see her mother again, for the last time. She would have to confront the pain of her past once more. And then she'd return to Fortune, truly free at last.

"Hannah, wait," she heard Ram call out behind her.

She slowed her steps but continued to stroll down the sagging walkway. He caught up to her and clutched her arm, turning her to face him.

"You forgot your bag," he said, and she noticed he'd draped his saddlebag over one shoulder and carried her valise in the other hand. She reached for it, but he held on until she gave up and started to walk away.

"How could you just leave me with that old man?" he asked, annoyed. "The goat tried to drill me about our *relationship*. I told him we didn't have a relationship, but he kept staring at me like I'd kicked his dog."

"Doc Collier is a good man," she told him, taking another step. Over her shoulder, she added, "Stands to reason you two wouldn't get along."

"Ah," he said, smiling as he turned to walk beside her. "There's that sassy mouth I've come to know so well."

"Yes, I haven't lost all the starch in my sails. Sorry if that disappoints you."

"Not at all. I'm glad to see it. I wouldn't like to see you completely beaten, Hannah."

"No?"

"No."

He took her arm as they stepped off the walkway at the

end of the street. As they moved on, he didn't release her, and Hannah didn't draw away.

"Just when it comes to the saloons?" she asked, tipping her head to meet his gaze.

"Well, there is still that," he admitted wryly, realizing he would miss their banter when that issue was finally settled. Hannah was a formidable opponent. Once he'd thought that a nuisance; now he found he admired her for it. It wasn't easy to find anyone, let alone a woman, who stood so soundly by her convictions.

"So, where are we heading?"

"Well, we still need a place to stay the night. It doesn't look as though we're going to find one in town."

Ram had no answer for that. It was true that the place hadn't exactly welcomed Hannah back with open arms. And Ram sensed that she wasn't up to any more questions about the cold reception. Though it went against his nature, he decided to follow silently for a little while and see where she led.

Sometimes you could learn a lot just by keeping your mouth shut.

They walked on for a few blocks, past where the sidewalk ended. The overgrown shrubs and weeds were even more in evidence here. They passed what might have been a side street at one time, but dense foliage had quickly reclaimed the spot, leaving it little more than a trail.

Hannah didn't speak a word as she made her way out of town. Ram had a million questions he wanted to ask, not the least of which was where they were going, but he continued to hold his silence.

The little he'd learned about Hannah and her mother since their arrival in Blue Springs had only increased his curiosity about this intriguing woman. He vowed to find out the answer to the mystery of Hannah Sullivan soon, before they returned to Fortune.

For purely business reasons, he assured himself. It paid to know your opponent in any fight.

His boots were getting tight on his heels and Ram figured they'd walked at least a mile outside the town limits. The countryside was beautiful here, the trees blooming and the birds singing in the warm afternoon sunshine.

But he knew it would soon be dark and he still didn't know where they were headed. His shoulder ached from carrying his saddlebag and his palm was sweating where the handle of Hannah's valise was clutched.

His decision to follow Hannah without question didn't seem like such a good idea anymore.

"Hannah, where are we going? It's starting to look deserted out here and it'll be dark soon."

"Scared of the dark?" she teased, not slowing her pace. He noticed she didn't even seem winded by the walk, then consoled himself with the knowledge that he carried both their belongings.

"Don't be ridiculous. It's just that when you mentioned finding us a place to stay the night, I thought you might have had a plan in mind. A plan that included a roof and maybe some walls."

"A roof, yes. And walls too. But I don't promise much else."

"Then we *are* going somewhere, not just wandering aimlessly?"

She gave him a look that said she liked it better when he was quiet. She'd said she needed some peace. Ram decided he could wait to learn their destination.

Her eyes were focused and bright, he noticed, her stride purposeful. She'd drawn on some inner strength to get her through this ordeal, and again he was amazed and a little impressed with the never-ending supply of tenacity she seemed to possess.

Eventually the trail widened a bit, and Ram noticed fresh

wagon marks where the tufts of weeds were beaten down. Someone had passed this way recently. That thought made him feel better somehow.

Until they reached the end of the trail, where a small, wretched tarpaper shack sat, tilting to one side. The front door was askew and the windows were covered with planks, haphazardly nailed in place. The roof, such as it was, looked as if it should have caved in years ago.

"You know," he said, pushing his hat back for a better look, then regretting it, "I'm kinda partial to sleeping out under the stars myself. What do you say we set up camp somewhere nearby and just . . ."

"You go ahead."

Ram noticed she didn't look at him, just continued toward the shack. He took a deep breath and followed her onto the porch. He thought he saw something slither off into a nearby bush as they approached the door and wondered why Hannah seemed so unaffected by the appalling surroundings.

She reached through a hole next to the door and drew out a frazzled rope. When she pulled it the door swung open and she disappeared into the dark interior. Ram followed more slowly, giving his eyes time to adjust to the darkness of the shuttered room.

He could see Hannah moving confidently through the cluttered place, her steps sure, and he knew she'd walked the same path many times. The smell of old dust and stale air hit him, and he longed to throw the boards off the windows and let in some fresh air.

Hannah read his thoughts, or had the same ones herself. She disappeared into the back of the house, and soon Ram could see a triangle of light inching toward him. He followed it and found Hannah in a bedroom, the shutters thrown wide on the single window.

"It's the only one not nailed shut," she said, twisting

the rusted latch and finally releasing the lock. She pulled the chain hanging through the looped latch and the window lifted up and out. She hooked one link of the chain over a bent nail and the window remained open.

"There. At least we'll get some air in here, and a little light, as long as it lasts."

She turned to look at the room and a frown drew her eyebrows together.

"Maybe this wasn't such a good idea."

Ram surveyed the bare room, the small sagging bed, the tattered blanket. It was worse than anything he'd seen in all his travels. He couldn't imagine anyone actually living in the place. Not lately, anyway.

The thought crossed his mind that this might have been Hannah's home at one time, but he quickly pushed that disturbing notion away. Surely no one would raise a child in such surroundings, even someone of questionable morals.

Why, then, would Hannah have brought him here? Could this place be some secret hideout from her less-than-happy childhood?

Yes, that must be what it was. When viewed through that probability, he could see its appeal to a curious and unhappy little girl. But he still didn't understand her need to come here now, after all this time. Especially when the place looked like it might actually be dangerous.

But he'd vowed to hold back his questions for a time.

"It's only for one night. I'm sure we can make do that long." He tried to sound reassuring. "A roof and walls, right?"

"A roof and walls," she repeated, nodding. Her gaze drifted over the newspaper stuck into the cracks in the outer walls and the dirt creeping up through the planked floor. "I suppose that's all it is now. All it ever was, really."

She went back into the front room and found a lantern hanging on the one support pole in the center of the room. She found her valise where he'd set it by the front door and rummaged inside.

"Here, let me," he said, reaching into his shirt pocket for a box of matches. He lit the wick and turned it up high, trying to dispel the gloom of the place. He felt as if he was in a large coffin, nailed shut. A shudder shook him. Then he glanced around, and the feeling of unease grew.

"God almighty," he exclaimed, seeing the mattress tossed in one corner, the sheets brown with age and too few washings. A chair, the wicker seat torn in the center, sat across the room by a makeshift kitchen set up around a blackened fireplace.

The stench from the bedding and some old grease left in a pot over the hearth was overpowering.

"Let me toss out some of this refuse and it won't be so bad," Ram said, moving toward the mattress.

"No, leave it. We won't be staying anyway. It was a bad idea."

Ram could see that Hannah's face was pale, her eyes moist and troubled.

"It's only for one night," he said. "We can stay in the other room. It wasn't so bad."

She glanced up at him and her eyes focused on his face for a moment. Then she slowly shook her head. "No, it's not so bad in there," she agreed, though her words sounded hollow.

Ram carried their belongings into the other room and set them on the floor. Hannah appeared with a folded blanket she'd found somewhere.

"You can always go back to town," she told him, removing the old bedding and spreading the blanket on top of the thin mattress. "I'm sure you could charm the Widow Crumb into giving you a room for the night, even though you were seen with me."

"No, this'll be fine. If you don't object to me staying here with you, that is."

She shook her head. "Maybe I should, but I don't. In fact, I'm not sure I'd have had the courage to come alone," she said frankly.

"Why did you come here, Hannah? You could have stayed with Collier. He would have welcomed you once he understood the true circumstances of our situation."

She smiled humorlessly. "No, I couldn't have. I see now that this is what I came back to do. It's the reason I didn't want you following me, although now I'm rather glad you did. I know I couldn't have faced this place alone, or even with Doc beside me."

Ram felt enormously pleased that Hannah seemed to need him. That she somehow felt she could trust him enough to share with him this place from her past.

He didn't try to understand why she would do that, or why it should gratify him, but it did.

"I'd like to help you through this if I can, Hannah," he told her, genuinely eager to ease her burden. "But I think you'd better tell me why we came here in the first place, and what you hope to accomplish by staying in this run-down old hideout."

As she gazed at him, a small smile tugged one corner of her mouth. It was a sad smile, and the sadness reached into her eyes and touched his soul.

"Hideout?"

"Isn't that what this is? Some old place you used to hide away from your troubles in."

She laughed dryly and looked around the room with fresh eyes. "Ah, I see what you must have thought. No," she told him, going to the bed and touching the worn blanket. "This isn't the place I went to hide. This is the place I hid from. Up until two years ago, Ram, this was my home. The only one I'd ever had."

Ram stared at the dark rooms, wads of newspaper the only thing between them and the outside in some places, and a new understanding rocked him.

This was where Hannah came from. This was what she was trying to hide from him, from all the people in Fortune. This place, where up until a few days ago her own mother had still lived in filth and squalor.

The questions he'd been holding in raced to the tip of his tongue, followed by new and more troubling ones. He knew he could wait no longer. He had to have the answers. Now.

But first he had to get Hannah out of this miserable place.

Chapter Twelve

"You must be hungry," Ram said. "I have some food in my saddlebag. Why don't we find a nice spot, outside somewhere, and have a picnic before it gets dark?"

She didn't answer him, merely tilting her head questioningly to one side.

"You must know a good spot, somewhere pretty and shaded," he prompted, his tone almost pleading.

Hannah shook off the strange lethargy that seemed to cloak her. Coming here hadn't been such a good idea, she conceded. Certainly bringing Ram here had been a mistake.

Nodding, she took his hand. "Yes, I know a much more pleasant spot nearby."

"Good," he said, sounding relieved. Taking the lead, he nearly dragged her through the depressing room into the fading light of day. He'd tossed his saddlebag over his shoulder and Hannah picked up her valise.

She didn't fight his proprietary attitude. She found it

rather comforting, in fact. But as they walked away from the shack, Ram realized he didn't know where they were going.

Reading his dilemma, she smiled.

"This way," she said, nodding east. Still holding his hand, she led him through the narrow trail she'd followed so often in her life. She knew where the path turned, where the dead oak lay across the track, the holes that could trip you up.

Not much had changed, she thought, feeling the memories closing in on her again. Not nearly enough.

"There's a spring just down the hill a ways," she told him over her shoulder. "Lots of them around here."

"I guess that's where the place got its name?"

"Oh, no. There was a hot spring here some years ago, drew folks from all around. But it dried up before I was born. It's nothing but a grassy valley now."

"That sounds interesting."

Hannah almost smiled. She could see he was struggling to make small talk, to try and get her mind off the place they'd left behind. His thoughtfulness touched her.

"I suppose," she said, forcing a measure of lightness into her tone.

She was thankful when the path finally opened up and she could see the blue water of the small lake. At one end a rock shelf made a small waterfall where the spring flowed south, and she could hear the gentle bubbling of the water as it cascaded down.

"This is really something," Ram said.

Hannah could see he was as mesmerized by the deep turquoise water rushing up to meet the emerald grass growing on the bank as she'd always been.

"Now this is a hideout," she told him, crooking her hand in a motion meant for him to follow.

She eased behind the rock shelf and heard Ram draw

in his breath. The water had washed away a section of the
rock, making a tiny alcove that jutted out over the small
falls. It was at least ten degrees cooler in the recess, and
secluded, and had always been Hannah's secret place.

Maybe this was where she'd been coming all along, she
thought. This haven from her past. Certainly she felt more
at peace here than she had at that awful shack.

Pushing away the troubling image, she concentrated on
opening her valise and taking out a small blanket, along
with a package wrapped in butcher's paper.

"You're not the only one who came prepared," she said.

Ram offered her a smile full of reassurance as he drew
his own offering out of his saddlebag.

Together they had some soda crackers, a small portion
of cheese, two apples and several licorice whips that Ram
had purchased on a whim at Fort Smith.

"A veritable feast," he said, smiling as he cut the cheese
with his pocket knife.

"And the best icy spring water in all of Arkansas." Hannah beamed, leaning over to scoop water into his canteen.
She'd seen the pint bottle of whiskey in his saddlebag, but
he hadn't taken it out so she saw no reason to mention it.

Ram accepted the canteen, took a long sip and sighed.
"Wonderful."

As he handed it back she eyed the place where his lips
had been. A strange feeling settled over her and she wondered suddenly what she was doing sharing this special
place with a man she barely knew and supposedly loathed.
A man, the bottle of whiskey reminded her, whose very
nature she detested.

She almost felt as though she was coming out of a daze
and realized that was more true than she'd like to admit.
She had been moving automatically since reading the telegram from Doc and deciding to come to Blue Springs. It

had been easier to follow through with her plan if she didn't think too much about what lay before her.

But somehow the cold snap of the water had awakened her, like the princess in a child's tale.

Now her eyes took in every detail of Ram's face, so close to hers in the small hollow, and her heart raced. For two days she'd moved toward this moment without thought, without emotion. Now everything seemed brighter, louder, clearer.

Hannah wasn't sure she was ready to face it all, even with Ram beside her. At that moment she wanted desperately to return to the cocoon of distance in which she'd wrapped herself.

"Hannah, I wanted to ask you . . ."

"Don't. Not now," she said, setting aside the cheese and cracker she'd been about to eat. Suddenly her appetite disappeared.

"All right. We'll save that for later," he agreed, obviously sensing her shifting mood. "Do you want to go back now?" He set aside his own food, inching closer to her in the small space.

His body, so close to hers, seemed to calm some of the anxiety that had abruptly overtaken her. But she still felt the awful sense of dismay at having come back to this place. She shook her head.

"I don't want to go back, ever. It was all a terrible mistake. I shouldn't have gone there."

"It's just a house, Hannah," he said, his voice so calm, so reassuring.

"No, it isn't even that. It's just some boards and tarpaper. But I still shouldn't have gone. And I don't want to go back. Not tonight. Not ever."

"What about tomorrow? The funeral?"

"I'll face it when the time comes. Tonight I just want to forget all the bad memories. I spent some terrible nights in that place, Ram," she admitted, looking into his sympathetic eyes and feeling as though she were about to jump over the falls.

"Do you want to talk about it?"

She shook her head. "No. I want to forget it. All of it. I just want to stay right here. Will you stay with me?"

"Hannah, you don't know what you're asking."

"I'm not trying to seduce you, Ram. I'm afraid I don't have the energy for that right now. But I don't want to go back to town, to Doc and his questions. And I can't go back to that awful place either."

"But there must be another solution. You can't sleep here," he said.

"Why not? You said you were partial to the stars. They'll be out soon, and we can see them clearly from here. We have this blanket, and the sound of the water close by. I slept here many a night when I didn't want to hear, to know, what was going on in the room outside my bedroom door. I'd sneak out my window and come here, where everything was beautiful and peaceful. I said I wanted peace. I didn't realize at the time that it was this place I was talking about. The only place I was ever able to find serenity. I want you to understand. And I want you to share it with me, Ram. For tonight."

A weaker man would have refused. A weaker man couldn't have stayed so close to this new, vulnerable Hannah and not taken advantage of the situation.

Unfortunately, Ram knew he was strong. He could deny himself what he most wanted at that moment for Hannah's sake. He didn't answer, just reached for her hand and drew her into the circle of his arms. He leaned back against his saddlebag and settled Hannah's head on his chest. They faced the sky as the first star twinkled to life.

It was full dark and a chill had settled over their niche when Hannah finally began to speak. Ram lay silent, fearful of breathing in case she remembered who she was talking to and ceased.

"She drank. A lot. At first I thought she drank because of what she did. With men, you know. But then, later, I realized she did what she did so she could drink. More and more. She drank away all the money my father gave her when he left. She sold off any furniture that was worth anything. Then she sold the house we owned in town and moved us into that place because it was abandoned and free. That was when I was about three, I suppose, although I can't say I really remember. Doc filled in some of the blanks for me, though he didn't like to dwell on it much himself."

Ram's arm had fallen asleep and he desperately needed to shift his body, but he remained perfectly still.

"I didn't really understand what it was she did until I was about ten. One of the boys at school had heard his father talking about my mother, and he told everyone she laid with men for money. I'd known about the men for years," she said simply, looking up into his face and then quickly away again. "It wasn't a very big house and she wasn't exactly discreet, you understand. But I didn't know that it was a sin. I thought all families lived much the same. I was incredibly naive for the daughter of the town whore."

"You were ten years old, Hannah. Everyone should be naive at that age," he told her. Himself included, he thought, remembering how he'd idolized his father in his youth and thought his mother was as perfect a saint as the Virgin Mary.

He'd thought at the time that he wanted to be a preacher. Now *that* was naive.

"I had never been invited to the parties and socials the other little girls went to, but I'd always thought it must be because something was wrong with me. Finally I understood. What my mother did nightly with men from all around Blue Springs was wicked and dirty, and I was wicked and dirty, too, because I was her daughter. I never wondered again why the children were mean and their parents ignored me when I passed them on the street. I knew," she whispered, the pain and humiliation nearly choking off her words. "I knew."

"Hannah, children can be cruel," Ram said, because he could think of nothing else to say to comfort her.

She laughed dryly. "You don't know the half of it," she told him, the resentment she'd felt still etched in each word. "You don't know anything."

"Then tell me," he invited her softly. "Make me understand. I'm not going to judge you, Hannah. I'm the last person you have to fear will cast stones."

She took a steadying breath. "I had just turned seventeen. I'd been out of school for some time, but no one in town would give me any kind of a job. So I continued to live out here, with her. She was beginning to get sick a lot by that time, and I couldn't just leave her. Not even when the Colliers offered me a decent home with them. She still brought in money, though not as regularly as before. Her looks had faded; liquor does take a toll. I would stash away money so we'd have food. Sometimes she'd find it, though, and drink it away. Sometimes we went days with nothing to eat but what I could find in the woods."

Ram felt a knot form in his throat. He didn't want to hear any more, but he knew Hannah needed to tell someone, and he wanted to be the one to help her through this. So he held her close and kept silent as she continued.

"I went into town one day with a few pennies I'd found in the salt tin. An old man by the name of Patty ran the general store, and he'd sell me the eggs that'd gotten cracked that day, or maybe a bit of cheese that had gotten a little moldy. He usually had something I could use to make a decent meal. That day he had a telegram. Said it'd

come addressed to me, but of course he couldn't get anyone to bring it out to our place."

Ram could hear the sorrow even that small slight had
cost her. His expression was grim as he reached for her
hand, entwining their fingers in a silent gesture of solace.

"Lordy, I thought I'd died and gone to heaven."

Her words held a ray of joy and he felt himself relax
slightly, knowing the tense moment had passed.

"I held that paper in my hand for the longest time,
feeling like a whole new world had opened up for me. I'd
never imagined that anyone outside Blue Springs knew I
existed, much less cared enough to send me a telegram.
I rushed out here and sat right in this very spot while I
opened it and read it."

Ram waited a full minute, anxious to hear the rest of
her story. When she didn't continue, he finally had to prod
her.

"Well? It was good news?"

"You haven't been listening." She grimaced and shook
her head. "There was no good news in my life at that
time."

Her eyes dulled, her voice softened. "The telegram was
from Francis."

"That candy . . . um, preacher from Fortune?"

Ram cringed at his slip, but when she spoke again he
could hear the difference in her voice and knew she was
smiling, if only a little.

"Yes. My father had been living in Fortune for some
time, and he'd gotten close to the Lord in the last few
years of his life. He'd always felt bad about leaving me with
my mother, but he still wanted no part of either of us while
he was alive. However, he'd instructed Francis to wire me
when he died. I was to inherit his house and a little money
he'd amassed through a mine he worked in California
years ago."

"That's how you came to own the cottage? But I thought . . ." Ram barely stopped himself before letting it slip that he'd checked up on Hannah. He hadn't found out about her father, though. Or the inheritance. Francis had hidden her secret well.

He hated the small spark of gratitude he felt for the milksop, but now he understood Hannah's unfailing devotion to the preacher a little better.

"It was perfect. I could take my mother away from Blue Springs, start over fresh. Maybe get her to see a doctor before it was too late."

But Ram knew it hadn't worked that way. He wondered what had gone wrong. He waited anxiously, but Hannah didn't go on for several interminable moments.

"Of course nothing ever turns out the way you plan. I left that night, but I left alone. And I truly thought nothing could ever bring me back. I can't wait for tomorrow," she said, her voice growing weak. "I'll finally be truly free."

The painful remembrance had left her drained, exhausted. She drifted off to sleep and Ram thought he'd go mad from unsatisfied curiosity. Something had happened to Hannah before she left Blue Springs.

Something worse than being an outcast and finding out her mother was a whore. Something that had driven Hannah into the arms of the preacher and over the edge of righteousness into fanaticism. But what?

His mind conjured images he hoped were only in his imagination. He couldn't stand to think of such things happening to Hannah. Would he ever find out the truth?

Only two people knew the answer: one wasn't talking and the other was to be buried in the morning.

Ram woke in time to see the sun come up the next morning, but Hannah was already gone. He jerked awake, searching the small cove, then spotted her down by the water's edge. She was tidying her hair, her arms stretched over her head. The morning sun outlined her profile and the rise and fall of her breasts. Ram swallowed hard and tried to will away the reaction his body often had upon waking.

He didn't want to make the morning's meeting any more awkward than necessary, and he doubted Hannah would understand that it was a common male occurrence and not a blatant attempt at seduction.

Or would she?

His night had been plagued with terrible pictures of what Hannah's past must have been like. He wondered how she'd escaped a life like her mother's. He wondered *if* she had.

Could it be possible she knew more about men and their ways than he'd believed?

She had seemed guileless, even innocent. But he accepted the fact that it would have been difficult, if not impossible, for that to be true.

Somehow, Ram wanted to let her know that none of that mattered to him. But, if he guessed right, Hannah would be feeling embarrassed and annoyed because she'd let her guard down with him. She'd see it as a sign of weakness, a skirmish lost to the other side. She wouldn't want his pity on top of that.

And they still had the funeral to get through. He couldn't make today any harder on her than it would already be.

He packed the blanket into her valise and gathered their things for the trek back into town. He wondered, belatedly, what Doc would think when they arrived together after being gone the entire night.

But as he watched Hannah turn her face toward the sun, the morning light kissing her cheeks and setting fire to her wild red curls, he couldn't summon an ounce of regret. He wouldn't trade last night with Hannah in his arms for anything.

"Ready," he said, coming up behind her. He saw her stiffen and suspected she was remembering all the things she'd whispered into the dark of night. He flashed her a bland smile, trying to ease the awkward moment.

"Yes," she said, pushing to her feet. He pretended to heft her bag, trying to keep his hand from reaching out to her. She wouldn't welcome his touch so easily in the light of day, he felt certain.

"I'll take that," she said, grasping her bag before he could protest. He watched her walk away, prim and precise, with the starch back in her sails and her back ramrod stiff, and he had to smile. Whatever had happened to Hannah Sullivan, it hadn't broken her spirit.

The funeral was a grim affair, Hannah and Ram the only two mourners in attendance.

Her mother had been refused burial in the little cemetery by the old church, so the undertaker had arranged for her to be laid to rest in the field of wildflowers that grew behind the abandoned mine.

The town's preacher had been one of the first to leave when the town started to deteriorate, and no one else would have considered saying words over the grave of a prostitute.

Even Doc Collier had been called away on an emergency.

Stan Bose Jr. stood at the head of the coffin, waiting for Hannah to pay her last respects so he could signal the men with shovels standing nearby. Ram waited as the coffin was lowered into the ground. He stood with his hat over his chest, wanting to offer Hannah comfort but uncertain of her reaction if he did.

As soon as the thud signaled the fact that the coffin had

reached the bottom of the hole, Hannah turned away. Ram blinked in surprise. With all her religion, Hannah hadn't so much as muttered a prayer.

Ram knew he couldn't just turn away without doing something. He tossed the undertaker a coin.

"Say something respectful, will you?"

The kid—for that was what he seemed like to Ram—shrugged and nodded. Ram turned away as he began to recite the Lord's Prayer.

Pushing his hat onto his head, Ram strode after Hannah's retreating form. Chasing her seemed to be becoming a habit, and one he wasn't too fond of.

"Hannah, wait."

"For what?" she asked, taking huge steps across the open field.

Ram clutched Hannah's arm, halting her retreat. "Where are you going in such a hurry?"

"Home."

"Home, as in Fortune?"

"It's the only home I have," she said sharply, as if daring him to bring up the shack outside of town. Soon enough, that would be nothing but another bad memory.

"What are you running from now?"

She snatched her arm away. "I'm not running. I did what I came here to do. Now it's time to leave."

"Just like that? Don't you want to see your friend Doc again? Maybe visit for a bit? Couldn't you have even said a few words over your mother's grave?"

Hannah winced but refused to let him see he'd hit a nerve. She lifted her valise higher. "There was nothing more to say. I said my prayers for my mother years ago. Either they were heard or they weren't; it's too late to worry about it now. Only one thing remains to be done, and then I plan to go back to Fortune and plague you and all the other whiskey-loving drunks and morally depraved saloon owners that would like to take over that town."

"Don't change the subject, Hannah. What are you planning? What one thing remains to be done?"

"None of your business," she told him, turning to walk away.

She wasn't getting off that easy. "Everything you do is my business. I thought I'd made that clear. So you might as well tell me, and then let's get on with whatever it is."

Hannah glared into his face, shadowed by the brim of his hat. She couldn't see his eyes, but she didn't need to. The kind, loving man she'd spent the last two days with was gone, replaced by the worthy opponent, who seemed much safer at the moment.

Secretly, she was glad he wasn't still treating her with kid gloves. She'd let her guard down last night, and she didn't ever intend to let that happen again.

With any luck, they'd go back to being bitter rivals and she'd soon forget the longing and desire she'd felt upon waking in his arms.

"Are you going to tell me where we're going?" he asked, coming up beside her.

"Not *we. Me.* I'm going alone."

"Not likely. I've followed you this far; I'll see you back to Fortune."

"Why? So you can announce to everyone the truth of my past and put down my fight for temperance once and for all?"

Ram grabbed her arm again, this time hard enough to make her drop her valise. He spun her around to face him, their noses nearly touching as she glared up at him and he stared down into her bright green eyes.

"Hannah, I was hired to keep you from harassing the saloon owners. I wasn't hired to dig up dirt about your mother. I plan to beat you and your group soundly. But I intend to do it in a fair manner.''

She held his gaze a moment longer, then looked away. Her spine softened, but she refused to let him see how truly relieved she was by his words.

''I still intend to see you put out of work when the saloons are forever closed in Fortune. That is my goal and the last two days have not swayed me from it in the least.''

She walked away, leaving Ram standing with his fists on his hips, shaking his head. ''I never thought it would,'' he called out to her. ''Damn stubborn woman.''

He followed her back through town to the trail that led to the shack. He kept his distance and remained quiet, knowing she had unfinished business at the place.

When they arrived, she stood for a long moment and just stared. Then she turned to him, still dry-eyed. She hadn't cried once during the whole ordeal, and he worried that she was holding in some serious emotions.

''Do you still have those matches?'' she asked.

Ram knew what she intended. He wasn't sure she knew what she was doing, however. ''You need something lit?'' he asked simply.

She cut him a wry look and held out her hand. Ram hesitated, then fished the matches out of his shirt pocket and handed over the box.

Setting her valise on the ground, Hannah disappeared into the house only to return a moment later. He could just smell the first hint of burning kerosene as she handed the matches back to him.

''We'll have to hurry if we want to catch the train. There's only one a day and I don't want to have to spend another night here.''

Ram saw the flames quickly consume the weathered boards and wads of newspaper. The tarpaper covering the roof curled into tight strips and disintegrated within seconds.

In no time the whole ugly shack was gone, nothing but the dirt of the floor remaining. He waited another minute, making certain none of the surrounding foliage caught a wayward spark. As the fire smoldered and went out, he turned and followed Hannah back into town.

Chapter Thirteen

The trip back to Fortune was long but uneventful. They took the train to Fort Smith, where Ram collected his horse and hitched it to a small rented buggy. Together they rode all night, mostly in silence, to reach town by daybreak.

Ram stopped the buggy outside Hannah's cottage, viewing it through different eyes now that he knew the story of how she'd come to own it. A father who hadn't been man enough to give her anything while he was alive had seen fit to leave her everything when he died.

Ram couldn't fathom the man's reasoning, but he supposed a posthumous gift was better than nothing.

"I'll see you inside," he said, setting the brake and tying off the reins.

"That's not necessary. I've seen myself home all my life. As you well know, now," she added, meeting his gaze.

Ram could see the question she refused to ask burning in her eyes. She didn't trust him, maybe with good reason.

She wondered if he would keep his word and protect the secrets of her past.

"Then it's time you were treated properly," he told her, stubbornly climbing to the ground and holding his hands up to help her down.

She pursed her lips and frowned, but he thought he saw a twinkle in her eye, a sign that she was secretly pleased, perhaps.

He carried her valise, noticing her feet were dragging the ground. She must be exhausted, he thought, both mentally and physically. The expected tears had never emerged, and he worried about that. It wasn't good to hold such raw, intense feelings inside. And she had to be hurting.

Ram knew the pain of loss. Even when you thought you didn't love the person any longer, grief was a drain on your heart and your soul.

It was obvious Hannah was suppressing her emotions. She'd been deeply affected by the loss of her mother, but she wouldn't allow herself to grieve. He suspected she was afraid of what would happen if she did.

He wanted to help but knew from his own experience that she wouldn't want that now. Maybe she never would— at least not from him.

She continued around to the back door, and he realized she must always use that entrance rather than the front. Another curious tidbit of information about her that he stored in his mental file.

Unlocking the door, she turned to face him, barring the opening.

"Thank you, Mr. Kellogg."

"Mr. Kellogg? Isn't that a bit formal under the circumstances?"

"There are no *circumstances*," she said, raising one eyebrow primly. "And now that we're back in Fortune, and back to our less-than-amicable association, I think it would be best if we kept our relationship strictly that of two leaders of opposing teams."

He stared at her uncompromising expression for a long moment, then touched his finger to his hat brim. "If that's the way you want it, Miss Sullivan."

"It is."

"Then I'll see you around."

"That you will," she told him, nodding as she disappeared into the small house.

Ram shook his head and made a noise, half laugh, half mocking sneer. *What a damnably irritating female,* he thought, making his way back to the buggy.

As he lifted his foot to climb onto the seat, a high, frantic scream cut through the still morning air and he stumbled back, startled.

He realized the cry had come from inside Hannah's house and bolted for the back door. She hadn't locked it behind her and he crashed through the kitchen, sliding to a halt when he saw her.

She was standing in the front room, unrecognizable beneath what appeared to be a river of blood. Her trembling hands were clutched to her cheeks and she continued to scream.

"Hannah," he cried, rushing forward and sliding in the puddle already forming around her feet. He went down on one knee, the seat of his trousers skidding through the sticky red pool.

Righting himself, he grasped her hands and held them out to her sides as he searched for what must surely be a horrendous wound.

And still she continued to scream.

"Hannah, where are you hurt? Tell me, sweetheart, what happened? Who did this?"

He surveyed her from head to foot and still couldn't

find any signs of injury. His eyes went to her face once more and he began the perusal again.

"Please, I can't see anything," he gasped, his heart racing in his throat until he could barely breathe. "Tell me where you're hurt."

"Not . . . nowhere," she choked out, terror still strangling every word. "Not mine . . ."

"What? What are you saying?"

"The blood. Not mine."

Ram leaned back, dazed and shaken. For a moment he couldn't understand what she was saying; then he surveyed the room and saw the bucket on the floor. A rope, still tied to the handle, had been strung across the top of the door frame and no doubt attached to the front door. Hannah must have gone to the door for some reason, opening it and sending the bucket of blood crashing down on her.

Ram sucked in a deep breath, anger and relief waging a fierce battle within him. He'd never been so scared, or so furious.

"Damn the sons of bitches to hell," he shouted, raising his face to the ceiling and making Hannah wince. He quickly gained control of his fury and clutched her shaking body to him, holding her tight, ignoring the bloody gore now soaking them both.

She tried to push away, but he held tight. All at once he heard a whimper and her body went limp in his arms. Great heaving sobs shook her and he slowly sank to the floor, cradling her in his lap and holding her as tight as he could without hurting her.

"Go ahead, honey," he told her, pushing the matted hair from her eyes, wiping her face with the sleeve of his shirt. "You go right ahead and cry. You hear me? Let it go, Hannah."

Ram had never heard such painful sounds coming from

another human being. It broke his heart to hear them coming from such a strong and vibrant woman as Hannah Sullivan. Knowing he could do nothing at that moment but hold her close and whisper soft, soothing noises, he hoped he was comforting her on some basic level.

He couldn't imagine how long they sat that way, her crying, him rocking her softly and murmuring. Soon he became aware of the stench of the old blood. She continued to tremble despite his hold, and he knew they couldn't continue to sit that way any longer.

"Hannah, honey, I'm going to let you go for a moment, but I'll be right back. Don't move. Count to ten and I'll be back." He saw her eyes widen with terror and he grasped her hand, forcing her to look at him. "Count, Hannah. One, two . . ."

"Th-three."

"Good girl. Keep counting," he said, backing out of the room. He broke for the door and raced to the wagon, snatched up his saddlebag and made it back to her side just as she reached ten.

"Good, good," he gasped, breathless. "Now stand up and let me help you out of those clothes."

"I—I can do it," she told him, trying to regain some semblance of control. Her hands shook and the stickiness of the blood made the task even more difficult, but he could see her determination.

"All right. You do that while I go draw a bath. Do you have a wrapper?"

She nodded. "Hook, back of the door, in my room."

Ram fetched the bathtub from the pantry and filled it with buckets of sun-warmed rainwater from the barrel on the back porch. It wasn't hot, but it would have to suffice. He didn't want to take time to heat water on the stove. Returning to the front room, he realized he hadn't fetched Hannah's robe.

No matter, it would probably be ruined if she tried to put it on before she'd bathed.

She stood in the middle of the floor, her skirt clutched in front of her like a drape. She wore only a thin, stained chemise.

"Come on, honey. It'll be all right."

He took her hand and dropped the skirt to the pile of soiled clothes on the floor. Sweeping her into his arms, he carried her into the kitchen and stood her beside the tub, steadying her when he felt her sway.

"Arms up," he ordered, hoping she wouldn't choose that moment to rebel against his control.

To his surprise, she lifted her arms docilely and let him remove the undergarment. Was this latest trick too much for her to bear after the emotional exhaustion of the last few days?

He again swept her into his arms and set her gently into the tub. Taking a tin ladle, he began pouring water over her.

He found a cake of soap and lathered her all over, beginning with her long, burnished hair and finishing with the tiny pink nails on her toes.

She sat, shaking and silent as he removed every trace of the horrible blood. She didn't say anything, and he worried that she was too quiet, too obliging. Was she in shock? Had the bucket hit her, injuring her in some way he hadn't realized? Would he ever see fire light her eyes and sparks of defiance aimed at him again?

As soon as she was clean, he went to her room and collected the wrapper, then brought it to the kitchen. He stood her up, toweled her dry as impassively as he could manage under the circumstances and pulled the robe over over her.

Stripping off his shirt so he wouldn't get her soiled, he lifted her up and carried her to the bedroom, where he set her on the bed. He covered her with the spread and brushed her tangled curls out of her face.

As he started for the door, she called out his name.

"Ram?"

"Yes? I'm right here."

"Don't leave me."

"No chance, Hannah, honey. I'll be right back."

He found several old rags in the back of the pantry and some strong lye soap and cleaned up all traces of the ghastly trick from Hannah's usually tidy house. Then he emptied the tub, refilled it and quickly cleaned himself, donning the change of clothes from his saddlebag.

He returned to the bedroom in less than fifteen minutes to find Hannah sleeping. She was curled up on her side, her hair spread across the pillow and her hand tucked under one cheek. He'd never seen anything so beautiful, he thought, going to her side.

Stretching out beside her, he curled his body against hers and held on to her. She'd chosen sleep to escape the terror she'd experienced.

Ram knew the only thing that would erase the memory from his mind was holding Hannah in his arms as she slept.

Just as he was about to drift off beside her, she jumped and cried out, and he knew immediately that she was reliving the horror of the incident. He held her tight and soothed her, and she turned in his arms to face him.

"You didn't leave?"

"I said I wouldn't."

"Who would do such a thing?"

"I swear to you I'll find out. And I'll make damn sure it never happens again."

"Thank you," she whispered, snuggling closer.

His body responded to her touch and he held back a

groan as her thigh accidentally rubbed against his swollen manhood.

"I won't let anything happen to you, Hannah. I swear it."

"I trust you, Ram. I know it's crazy. You work for the men who are doing this to me. But right now you're the only one I trust."

He couldn't resist her nearness any longer. She'd pressed tight against him, and before he could stop himself, his mouth had descended on hers.

Ram drank his fill of her lips, then gently touched his tongue to the seam of her mouth. She opened to him and he delved into the sweetness, knowing no wine had ever been so intoxicating.

His hand ached to touch every inch of her body, and he could feel her warmth even through the thick wrapper. It couldn't hide her curves, and he barely kept his hands from closing over the soft, full mounds of her bottom. He retraced the line of her spine to her waist and then flared his palms over her ribs, stopping just shy of the full undersides of her breasts.

He heard her sharp intake of breath and breathless sigh and took it for a sign of consent. His fingers gently covered her breasts, searching out the distended nipples that puckered beneath his light touch.

He'd never felt anything so good in his life and he wanted to go on touching her and kissing her until the stars fell from the sky and the world stopped turning. He wanted to live forever and die in her arms.

He wanted Hannah Sullivan, body and soul. Forever.

Chapter Fourteen

Hannah clutched Ram's head, dragging it down until his lips closed over hers once more. Her skin tingled and her muscles bunched. She could feel the tension between her legs growing, spreading out, sending ripples of longing through her belly. Wrapping her arms around his back, she tried to get closer, to feel his skin against every inch of her body.

Ram sensed her need and shifted his leg up between her thighs, nestling the hair-roughened skin against her most private place. Hannah gasped and cried out, shaking as the hunger consumed her.

Nothing had ever felt so good. She tightened her thighs until the pleasure was almost unbearable. When his hand slid over her stomach and settled in the soft curls covering her mound, she thought her mind and body would explode.

His mouth found the soft skin of her throat and she tipped her head back as he nuzzled her with kisses. Every

Take 4 FREE Books!

Zebra created its convenient Home Subscription Service so you'll be sure to get the hottest new romances delivered each month right to your doorstep — usually before they are available in book stores. Just to show you how convenient Zebra Home Subscription Service is, we would like to send you 4 Zebra Historical Romances as a FREE gift. You receive a gift worth up to $24.96 — absolutely FREE. There's no extra charge for shipping and handling. There's no obligation to buy anything - ever!

Save Even More with Free Home Delivery!

Accept your FREE gift and each month we'll deliver 4 brand new titles as soon as they are published. They'll be yours to examine FREE for 10 days. Then if you decide to keep the books, you'll pay the preferred subscriber's price of just $4.20 per title. That's $16.80 for all 4 books for a savings of up to 32% off the publisher's price! What's more...$16.80 is your total price...there is no additional charge for the convenience of home delivery. Remember, you are under no obligation to buy any of these books at any time! If you are not delighted with them, simply return them and owe nothing. But if you enjoy Zebra Historical Romances as much as we think you will, pay the special preferred subscriber rate of only $16.80 each month and save over $8.00 off the bookstore price!

We have 4 FREE BOOKS for you as your introduction to KENSINGTON CHOICE!

To get your FREE BOOKS, worth up to $24.96, mail the card below. or call TOLL-FREE 1-888-345-BOOK

Take 4 Zebra Historical Romances FREE!

MAIL TO: ZEBRA HOME SUBSCRIPTION SERVICE, INC.
120 BRIGHTON ROAD, P.O. BOX 5214,
CLIFTON, NEW JERSEY 07015-5214

YES! Please send me my 4 FREE ZEBRA HISTORICAL ROMANCES (without obligation to purchase other books). Unless you hear from me after I receive my 4 FREE BOOKS, you may send me 4 new novels - as soon as they are published - to preview each month FREE for 10 days. If I am not satisfied, I may return them and owe nothing. Otherwise, I will pay the money-saving preferred subscriber's price of just $4.20 each... a total of $16.80. That's a savings of over $8.00 each month and there is no additional charge for shipping and handling. I may return any shipment within 10 days and owe nothing, and I may cancel any time I wish. In any case the 4 FREE books will be mine to keep.

Name _____

Address _____ Apt No _____

City _____ State _____ Zip _____

Telephone ( ) _____ Signature _____

(If under 18, parent or guardian must sign)

Terms, offer, and price subject to change. Orders subject to acceptance.

KC0899

4 FREE
Zebra
Historical
Romances
are waiting
for you to
claim them!

*(worth up
to $24.96)*

*See details
inside....*

KENSINGTON CHOICE
Zebra Home Subscription Service, Inc.
120 Brighton Road
P.O.Box 5214
Clifton, NJ 07015-5214

sense was heightened suddenly—the scent of his warm, freshly bathed skin, the taste of his kiss still lingering on her lips, the feel of his hand gently caressing her.

The world disappeared and only this room remained, then the bed, then nothing but their bodies and the intense sensations he was creating. She couldn't think; she could only feel. And what she felt surpassed anything she'd ever imagined.

Suddenly she felt a rising momentum growing within her and, frightened, she grasped his hand and tried to still his strokes. Her actions only seemed to increase the intensity of his movements and he rocked against her harder, pressing his body against hers.

Hannah felt the throbbing hardness against her belly and her fear increased. Ram was blind to her sudden tenseness, his lust driving him beyond rational thought. She pushed against his chest, but he only groaned and rolled atop her, pressing her deeper into the mattress. She dug her heels into the bed, trying to remove his bulk, but the movement only offered him closer access to that part of her that burned with desire. He groaned again, calling her name.

"Hannah, my sweet, passionate Hannah. You're so good, so hot. Let go; just let it come."

What was he saying? What did he mean? She wasn't hot, passionate. She didn't want to be that way.

Again, she tried to still his hand, but he pressed his lips to hers and she felt herself slipping away. His finger slid inside her and she cried out as spasms rocked her and stars exploded before her eyes.

"Oh, God, Hannah," he cried, gripping her in tense arms. A shudder went through his body, and Hannah didn't know if her lack of breath came from what had just happened to her or from his tight hold.

Suddenly she panicked and her hands flailed out, catch-

ing him in the jaw and chest. He shook off the blows and
chuckled, rolling to the side and drawing her along with
him until they lay face-to-face on the bed.

"Settle down, sweetheart." He laughed, catching her
hands and kissing her tightened knuckles. "You're all
right."

"No, don't. What have you done? What have *I* done?"

"You've done what every woman dreams of doing. And
I was about to do what every man dreams of doing."

"No, I didn't. I mean, I don't. Dream of that, that is. I
never . . ."

"Of course you have. I know I have. Since the moment
I laid eyes on you I've dreamed of doing what I just did."

"You can't!" She backpedaled with her feet, scooting
across the bed and jumping off the mattress as if it was a
bed of hot coals. "We don't even like each other."

"I like you a whole lot right now," he said, still unaware
how truly upset she was by what had happened. He stared
at her for a moment, a wicked gleam in his whiskey-dark
eyes.

"No, you don't!" she snapped, straightening her robe
and pulling the sash into a tight knot. "We're enemies,
on opposite sides. How could this have happened?"

Ram leaned on his elbow and Hannah realized he was
naked to the waist. No wonder she'd been so aware of the
feel of his skin on her breasts, the seductive rub of his hair
against her nipples.

She swallowed hard and covered her eyes with a
trembling hand.

"It happened because we both wanted it to happen.
There's nothing wrong with that, Hannah. It's natural."

"It's not natural!" Her hands went to her flaming cheeks
and she fought to still a wave of shame and embarrassment
when she remembered her shocking display.

"Stop being such a prude, Hannah. It's not your style,"

he told her, tossing his legs over the side of the bed and pushing to his feet. She could see the outline of his erection against the placket of his trousers and she turned away.

"Ooohh." Again her hands went over her eyes and she heard him chuckle.

"Look at me, Hannah," he said, and she realized he'd come to stand in front of her. She shook her head, feeling foolish and childish but unable to face him.

He took her hands and pulled them down. He smiled at her. "I don't want to stop, Hannah. It was good, so good between us. And it can be even better. Let me show you." He brought her hand down and pressed it against his hardened manhood, and Hannah jerked away as though burned.

"Stop it! Can't you see I made a mistake? A horrible mistake. It should never have happened, and it'll never happen again."

"Oh, yes, it'll happen again," he said, his words sounding like a vow. "You can't stop something that strong, Hannah. You're a very passionate woman. Even more so than I thought. You can't deny that passion forever."

"I can. And I will, if I have to. I won't be that kind of woman. I'll never succumb to sin in that way again."

That snapped it. She'd hit upon the one thing Ram least wanted to hear in that moment.

"For crying out loud," he said, brushing his fingers through his hair and pressing the damp strands to his head. "Don't bring the Bible into this. Not now, not here. I won't go through that again. Besides, who do you think invented lovemaking in the first place?"

Hannah gasped. "You blasphemer," she whispered, shocked and appalled. "How dare you say something like that?"

"Because it's the truth. And, quite frankly, I'm tired of

having my normal male urges held up to His word and being found lacking in some way."

"I don't know what you're talking about. And I don't want to know. You should just go, now. This is wrong; this is all wrong."

"No, this is right," he told her, grabbing her hand and pulling her close. She leaned away, out of his reach, and he made a disgusted noise and slung her hand away. "God save me from pious women. They're a curse, and I swear I don't know why I let myself be taken in by another one."

"The Bible says 'Who can find a virtuous woman, for her price is far above rubies'," Hannah quoted senselessly, grasping at anything safe and familiar.

Ram closed the distance between them with one giant step and clasped her shoulders in a hard grip. He shook her once, hard, and glared into her eyes. "You can talk to me about drinking, you can talk to me about whoring, you can talk to me about how good my finger felt sliding into you as you jerked and twitched around my hand. But don't you ever quote the Bible to me while I'm standing here with a hard-on you brought on and encouraged, lady. He didn't make you cozy up to me and He isn't the reason you're backing out now."

"Let me go," Hannah cried, stumbling back when he released her. She fought back tears as humiliation swept over her. She'd never been treated so coarsely, or talked to so rudely. And the idea that Ram was even partially right—that she had led him on and even encouraged him—was more than she could bear. What had possessed her to behave so wantonly? To risk everything she'd worked for just to be in his arms? Shame engulfed her as she thought of Francis and her desire to be a good and faithful wife.

"What have I done? Francis will never forgive me. He'll never marry me now."

"Yeah, and you can thank your God for that," he snapped. "You had no business thinking you could tie yourself to a cold fish like that anyway. You're too much woman for a man like him, Hannah. He'd never be man enough to satisfy you."

"Shut up," she yelled, clasping her hands over her ears. "I don't want to hear anymore. You don't know anything about me, so stop pretending you do. Francis *is* the man I want. The only man I'll ever want."

"Don't lie, Hannah. Not to me. I was in that bed with you a minute ago. I felt you grow wet and shudder as I pleasured you."

"Stop!"

"You wanted me," he taunted, his voice low and hot. "You wanted me as much as I wanted you. And I could have had you at any time. You were ready," he said. "So ready. I've never seen a woman want it more."

She slapped him hard across the face and he glared at her. Then he started to laugh, rubbing the red welt forming on his cheek.

"There it is again. That fire, that passion," he drawled slowly, breathing each word into her face like an accusation. "You can't hide it, Hannah. You can't wish it away. And you'll never appease it with the rev."

"Get out," she ordered, trembling with rage and renewed humiliation.

"My pleasure. There's a woman at the saloon, a real woman, who wants what I can give her and isn't afraid of her normal feelings."

"A whore? You're talking about a whore? How could you! You bastard," she cried, rushing toward him and pummeling him with her fists. "Get out of here. I never want to see you again."

"You got it, lady. And believe me, the feeling is mutual."

Ram snatched up his belongings on his way out the door,

his anger and frustration driving him. He snapped the reins down hard on his horse's rump and left behind a cloud of dust as he raced the animal through the deserted street.

It was still early morning, and a few folks were just beginning to meander out to sweep their front steps and raise the shades on their windows. Some gave Ram curious looks as he raced past, but he ignored them, too overcome with rage to care what they thought.

His loins throbbed and he couldn't get to the saloon—and Sally—fast enough.

Why would any man in his right mind chase after a self-righteous prig like Hannah Sullivan when he had a willing and skilled seductress like Sally eager to share his bed?

"Because you're a damned fool," Ram cursed himself as he stabled the horse and snatched his saddlebag out of the buggy. "A damned fool who is destined to make the same mistake over and over until it finally kills you."

Hadn't he learned his lesson with Doreen? Why would he even waste his time with another woman like that, knowing only grief and pain lay in that direction?

Because he'd thought, hoped, Hannah was different. He'd wanted her to be different. Ram had seen something in her. Life, fire, whatever it was, it had made him hope again. Had made him think this time could be different.

"Like I said, a damned fool."

He made his way into the saloon through the back door, hoping he wouldn't encounter anyone on his way up to his room. But he saw Sally standing beside the long polished bar, drinking a cup of coffee.

The strong aroma of the brew drew him into the otherwise empty room.

"You look like hell, Ram," she said, going behind the bar and getting another mug. She turned it upright on the bar and filled it with coffee from the pot sitting next to her elbow. It was a porcelain container, with flowers painted on it and a gold trim around the rim, and it looked out of place in the masculine room. He figured it must be Sally's personal property, something she'd brought with her from her former life.

"Didn't mean to intrude," he said, sipping the coffee, which was excellent. He closed his eyes and let the flavor soothe his rattled nerves.

"Naw. I was just enjoying the peace of morning time," she said, nodding toward the rising sun visible through the bat-wing doors. "Don't get to see that sight too often in my business."

"I reckon that's true," he said, though he'd never really thought about it until that moment. Morning was a time he enjoyed himself, usually. When he was on a case, he'd be up before the sun, ready to ride. He seldom took time to look at the sky or watch the changing colors of a sunrise, but he'd always felt moved by the sight when he did.

It moved him now, and he felt his tenseness seep away. The black mood was nearly gone, replaced by remorse at some of the things he'd said to Hannah in anger. But she was wrong, dead wrong. And he'd been right to make her face the truth about her feelings.

He'd gone beyond that, he admitted to himself, now ashamed. She'd hurt him with her rejection and he'd wanted to hurt her in return.

Not a very honorable thing for a man to do to a woman he's just touched with such passion and abandon.

"Want to talk about it?"

"How's that?"

Sally smiled and refilled his mug. "You were a thousand miles away. I just wondered if you'd like to talk about whatever's got you troubled."

He stared at her for a moment, remembering his harsh promise to Hannah, then shook his head. "Naw. I reckon it'll work itself out in time," he said, sipping the coffee and staring at the flaming red ball the sun made coming over the tops of the buildings across the street.

"You went away. We were kind of thinking you might be gone for good."

"Just taking care of a little business."

She nodded and took a sip from her cup. "Another thing I always liked about mornings," she said, looking past him to the street as though absorbed in thought.

"What's that?"

"Good sex to start the day off right." Her eyes slid to meet his gaze and she raised an eyebrow as she took another drink.

"Yeah, that was always my favorite time of the day for a good roll in the sack," he agreed.

Ram knew only too well what she was asking. Hell, hadn't he as good as told Hannah that that was what he intended to do as soon as he arrived at the saloon?

But the thought held no appeal, though he touched Sally's hand where it lay on the bar. "It's been a long trip and I'm fairly exhausted," he said. "I'm afraid I'd be a sore disappointment to you right now."

She turned her hand over and clasped his fingers, tracing his knuckles with one long nail. "I'll take my chances," she told him, her tongue darting out to moisten her lips.

She wore no makeup, no kohl on her eyes or lip rouge. Her blond hair hung down her back, gathered at her nape with a soft blue ribbon. The tiny lines around her eyes and mouth only added to her appeal. She was very pretty this morning, and he could picture her smooth white skin as she lay on his bed upstairs. He almost felt aroused by the thought.

Almost.

But almost wasn't good enough. And Sally, though enticing and certainly welcoming, wasn't either.

Because she wasn't Hannah.

"I'm afraid I'm just not up for it this morning," he told her with a wink and a small grin. He liked Sally at that moment, felt close to her somehow. He didn't want to hurt her or spoil the moment.

He set down his cup and picked up his saddlebag.

"She's not for you, you know."

Ram stopped, the tension returning. He turned slowly to face her. "How's that?"

"The Sullivan broad. You're wasting your time. She ain't like us."

"Us?"

"Yeah, you know. She isn't cut from the same cloth, you might say. She doesn't know anything about pleasuring a man like you. Not the way I do. She's the flannel-nightie, lights-out-while-you-poke-her type. A prude."

Ram could tell Sally she was wrong about Hannah. No flannel nightie, no lights out. Enough fire to sear a man's skin off. But, of course, he wouldn't say any of those things. It didn't matter what Sally thought, or even what Hannah claimed to be the truth. He knew her better than she knew herself. And the pious, priggish act was a facade to cover her true nature—that of a loving, generous woman.

He didn't know the whole story about Hannah. But he would find out, and soon. What he'd learned about her mother went a long way toward explaining her aversion to drinking and saloons and women like Sally.

It even explained her need for Francis and his way of life.

He should have been more understanding, instead of pushing her. He'd told her she was passionate, which she'd assumed was synonymous with wicked.

Just like her mother, to her way of thinking.

She probably wouldn't let him near her now. And that

could be very dangerous. How could he protect her if she was avoiding him?

"You're wrong, Sally," he told the woman as he left the room. "About me and Hannah," he added as he made his way up the stairs alone.

Chapter Fifteen

"Well, look who's decided to join us once more."

Hannah spun in the direction of her front door, her heart racing absurdly in her chest. As she saw Mary Beth hesitate before entering, she felt disappointed, and she wondered who it was she'd really been looking for.

"Mary Beth," she said, rushing to the woman's side and pulling her into a happy embrace. She'd been so worried about her friend, and she was very glad to see her out and about once more.

"Hannah, how have you been?"

"Fine, Mary Beth. But that was supposed to be my question to you."

The other ladies crowded around and each gave Mary Beth a hug and a few words of welcome. She beamed at all the attention, and tears shone in her eyes.

"Hannah, Rupert told me you were suddenly called out of town last week. I do hope nothing is amiss."

Hannah felt every eye in the room turn on her and her heart missed a beat.

They'd all questioned her about her absence, most subtly. Only Agnes had been blatant in her curiosity, and even she hadn't pushed very hard when it became evident that Hannah didn't want to discuss the matter.

She fought back her nervousness and just smiled at them, quickly diverting the subject from herself. "Tell us how your family is doing, Mary Beth. We've been so concerned."

Everyone echoed Hannah's sentiment and soon the attention was once more on the new arrival. Mary Beth flushed and took Hannah's hands.

"I hope you won't take this the wrong way, Hannah. I know how you loathe the man. But we have truly found a savior in Mr. Kellogg."

A cry went up through the group, each woman loudly exclaiming her disbelief at Mary Beth's shocking statement.

"Listen, please," she said. "It's the truth. He challenged that day laborer to a game of draw poker, bet fifty dollars of his own money against our land and won it back. Then he just handed it over to Rupert and told him to go home to his family and stay out of the saloons. And," she breathed, obviously in awe of her benefactor, "Rupert has done just that. Now that we have those acres back, he's been able to give up working nights in town. I've never seen him so happy, or so content," she added, blushing.

"Oh, Mary Beth," Hannah said, trying to hide the mixed emotions coursing through her. "That's wonderful. Truly, I couldn't be happier."

Hannah felt happiness bubbling within her, threatening to spill over in the form of tears. Was it all for Mary Beth and her good fortune? Or was some small measure of it

for Ram, for what he'd done, and for the feelings she
hadn't been able to escape?

She hoped no one else noticed the strange sadness she'd
seen mirrored in her eyes for the past week. An odd lethargy seemed to have taken hold of her ever since Ram
walked out of her house, angry and bitter. And she couldn't
blame him.

Oh, she'd tried to. But, being Ram, he'd refused to let
her. He'd called her out for the way she'd behaved and
he'd been right. She was as responsible as he was for the
dreadful turn of events that had occurred that morning
in her bedroom. More so. Because she knew, deep down
in her heart, that she'd wished for that very thing to happen
since the moment she saw him on the train at Fort Smith.

That was why she'd allowed him to follow her to Blue
Springs, asked him to stay with her in the alcove that night.
Never in her life had she felt as safe and loved as she had
lying in Ram's arms, his heart beating in her ear, his body
surrounding hers in a protective embrace.

And that was why she'd absolutely avoided him for the
past seven days.

What had come over her that she'd allowed herself to fall
for a whiskey-loving, womanizing reprobate who relished
everything she most despised?

Her shame was boundless, her guilt endless. And still
the dreams woke her nightly, her body hot and trembling
with desire as she relived every touch.

Finally she'd thrown herself into her crusade. The only
way to rid herself of this tangled web of deceit and desire
was to rid herself of Ram Kellogg.

And that meant the saloons had to go.

"Hannah?"

Hannah drew herself back to the moment, and to Mary
Beth's happy homecoming to the group. She forced a
smile and took her friend's hand.

"I'm glad your gratitude doesn't prevent you from helping others who are still being adversely affected by the saloons in this town. We still need every hand to do the Lord's work."

She'd called on Him a lot more this past week as well, Hannah thought, hoping righteous thoughts would oust the sinful ones she continued to have. And she'd turned more and more to Francis.

After all, he was to be her husband. If she felt such yearnings for anyone, shouldn't it be him?

"Oh, no, Hannah. I would never desert your cause. I know better than anyone here how dreadful the effects of liquor can be."

Hannah bit her lip. She knew that wasn't entirely true. No doubt even Mary Beth's pitiful tale couldn't compare to her own. She was thankful that Ram had not found out the entire truth about her past, at least, and her last days with her drunken, despondent mother.

"Praise the Lord," she said, hugging Mary Beth once more. "Francis has been working on a speech for me to deliver after the Founder's Day race tomorrow. The whole town will be there. It's our chance to get the support we need to finally finish this thing."

"Do you really think we can get the men to sign a petition at a rally, with the whole town looking on?" Tabby asked, shaking her head and making her blond curls bounce and sway. She was a fetching sight, and Hannah knew Daniel had been sitting out on her front porch with her every chance he got.

"If you can't get Daniel to sign a petition, then that boy's got rocks in his head," Agnes said, slapping her hands on her knees and pushing herself to her feet. "And it's the same for the other men in this town. If they know which side their bread is buttered on, they'll sign. And be happy to do it, too."

"Agnes is right," Nan cut in, for once in agreement with the older, saucier woman. "It's time we had a say in how our town and even our country is run. Why, I'm twice as smart as that nitwit they elected mayor last election, and I'm not even allowed to vote."

"Forget voting," Margaret said, "I want to hold office. Just look at the mess those men have made with the whole Indian situation. A woman could have settled it in less time, and more equitably."

"If that ain't the God's own truth," Agnes conceded, nodding furiously. She whipped her bag open and showed Margaret the address for the organization for Indian rights, and they were soon absorbed in conversation.

Mary Beth glanced at Hannah and grinned, a dimple appearing in her smooth, pink cheek. Hannah knew Ram was responsible for putting the light back in her friend's eyes. She was grateful to him for that. Again she had to acknowledge that the man wasn't all bad. What he'd done for Mary Beth and Rupert went beyond generosity. It had been a truly magnanimous gesture.

Which only made it harder to resist the temptation he continued to present, no matter where Hannah was or what she was doing.

"Well, let's get busy, ladies," she called out, bringing order to the group. "We still have a lot of work to do to get ready for tomorrow."

"Francis, this is very important. It's the opportunity we've waited for. We can put an end to this dreadful situation once and for all if we only plan our strategy carefully to the last detail."

She'd located him beneath the huge oak in back of the parsonage, where he'd been chopping a few small logs for the barbecue the town had planned for the following day.

He'd removed the somber black coat he usually wore and his shirtsleeves were rolled to his forearm.

"You're pinning an awful lot of hope on one little rally, Hannah. I think you should just be patient. The Lord will see to our needs in his own good time."

Hannah couldn't help acting impatient. That was precisely how she felt. The sooner she was rid of Ram Kellogg, the better off she'd be. And the only way she could do that was to get rid of the saloons who employed him.

"There *is* a lot riding on this rally, Francis," she said, touching his shoulder and hoping to feel a measure of the excitement she still felt whenever she remembered her time with Ram.

Unfortunately, it was a bad mistake. When she touched that bony expanse, she couldn't help but compare it to Ram's broad, muscled shoulders. Her eye critically studied the narrow forearm exposed to view and she remembered Ram's tanned, sinewy arms wrapped around her. Francis's soft white hands looked almost feminine when she thought of Ram's big, calloused hands caressing her skin and making it tingle with awareness.

She withdrew her fingers and wrapped her arms together at her waist.

"We'll see the end of the saloons, Hannah, I assure you," he told her, patting her hand.

The movement was more platonic than romantic, and Hannah felt thwarted. She wanted to feel something—anything—that resembled the myriad of emotions just the thought of Ram Kellogg could bring on.

"I wasn't just talking about the crusade, Francis," she said, deciding to proceed more boldly. "What I meant was, our marriage. We've waited so long. I'm ready to be your wife. I don't want to wait any longer."

"I've been thinking about that very thing, Hannah," he told her.

Hannah blinked her surprise, staring at him for a long minute. Then she forced a smile and pressed her hand to her nervous stomach.

"You have?"

"Yes. And you were right: It's time I married and started a family. A preacher seems more stable, more settled, when he has a wife and children sitting in the congregation. We could even order an organ from Wells Fargo, and you could play it on Sundays."

"I don't play the organ, Francis." Her throat had gone suddenly dry and she fought to get out the simple words.

"Nonsense. Every minister's wife can play, either the piano or the organ. I've always been partial to the organ myself."

"I don't know how . . ."

"You'll take lessons," he said, waving away her arguments like worrisome gnats. "That way you can teach our children when they're older. The girls, anyway." He laughed, smoothing his thinning hair, which was wet from sweat. "Don't suppose the boys'll care much for that sort of thing."

"But, Francis, I'm not sure I *want* to learn. You're moving too fast." Hannah knew she was being illogical, discussing an organ when the real issue was his sudden decision to go forth with the wedding.

But, truthfully, now that he seemed eager to marry, she wasn't so certain she wanted to.

He caught her quick mood shift and looked down at her, plainly annoyed. "A moment ago you implied I was moving too slow."

"Well, perhaps I was mistaken. You were just being judicious, something you've told me many times I need to practice."

"That's so, Hannah, but not in this. It's time we wed. There's nothing standing in our way now."

"What are you talking about, Francis? What stood in our way before?"

"Well, darling, to be honest—your mother. She was a constant source of disgrace that could have appeared at any moment."

"My mother?" Hannah breathed, stunned. "She didn't even know where I lived. She was ill, and certainly no threat to us or our future together. Really, Francis, I don't understand where that line of reasoning came from."

"Your father confided in me, Hannah. Remember? I know what an affliction the woman was. Why, anyone who could run off a decent sort like your father . . ."

"Decent? The man may have found religion in the end, Francis, but let's not forget how he deserted his wife *and* daughter."

"A woman no man could be expected to contend with. She was a harlot."

Rage filled Hannah as this man degraded and demeaned her mother. Granted, she'd felt no love for the woman after that last fateful night. Indeed, she was surprised by her sudden need to defend the woman.

She'd think about her own change of heart later. Right now all she knew was that this man had no right to besmirch a dead woman.

Francis knew nothing about her mother or her troubles. He was just being judgmental, and that angered Hannah and made her want to defend the woman against his unfair conclusion.

After all, he hadn't been there when she'd cry to Hannah and beg her not to give her any more liquor, then slap her when she refused to fetch more. He didn't see her mother after some customer would beat her.

"I don't want to discuss this with you, Francis," she said. "You can't possibly understand."

Her heart felt heavy, and Hannah knew somehow she'd turned a corner in her life.

She realized she didn't hate her mother, as she'd thought she did for so long. Maybe she never had. At this moment all she felt was pity, and a great deal of sorrow for the way she lived and died.

It was an emotional revelation, and Hannah knew she would never again feel the same way about the woman who had been her mother.

"Wait. I'm sorry," Francis said, taking her shoulders and pulling her to him. "I always seem to say the wrong thing around you, Hannah. I'm afraid that's because you have me at a disadvantage."

"What do you mean?"

"You don't understand the ways of men, Hannah, and that's a virtue. But the truth is, I find myself tied in knots when I'm with you."

It was the closest thing to a profession of love Francis had ever murmured, and Hannah felt a small seed of hope blossom in her heart.

"Francis, do you mean it?"

"Of course, darling. After all this time, don't you know how I feel about you? How I've always felt about you? You're the one the Lord sent to be my helpmate, my Eve. To stand beside me and work with me for the good of the church. I knew it the moment I saw you."

Something about Francis's statement left Hannah cold. With a sinking heart she realized he'd still said nothing about love. Or desire.

She wanted to be in favor with the Lord and do his work. But she was also a woman. A woman who wanted to be loved for herself. Loved—and needed—the way Ram had made her feel.

"Francis, I'm not sure . . ."

"I'm sure enough for both of us," he said, drawing her

even closer. She felt his hands on her, but there was no
spark like she'd felt with Ram. He could have been anyone—or no one at all.

"Hannah, I think we should set a date and make the
formal announcement at Founder's Day tomorrow."

She felt a momentary panic as her mind raced. What
could she say? How did she feel about this new, determined
side of Francis? Hannah stood frozen as conflicting emotions assailed her.

"What do you say, Hannah? I think we've waited long
enough."

His lips came closer and she wanted to run, turn away,
anything to stop what she knew was about to happen. But
how could she? She'd wanted this for so long, waited what
seemed like an eternity. And now all she'd hoped for was
being offered to her.

So why did she feel as though everything was falling
apart?

His mouth covered hers and she squeezed her eyes shut.
She felt her whole body tense and was strangely aware of
the rough dryness of his lips. He continued to apply pressure, but he made no attempt to deepen the kiss, to wrap
her in an embrace.

Hannah stood there, conscious of everything around
her as the seconds drew on like minutes. Her spine was
rigid, her hands stiff at her sides. She felt wooden, and
soon her muscles protested the awkward position.

She cursed Ram for his skilled lovemaking and finally
admitted to herself that Francis had no hope of erasing
the fiery image seared on her brain—and on her lips.

Finally Francis pulled away, and Hannah feared his reaction to the miserable encounter. But his complacent smile
baffled her, and she frowned.

"I'm sorry, darling. I couldn't resist. Now that I've

decided we should go ahead with this thing, I find I'm rather impatient to get on with it.''

Hannah stared, stunned, for a long moment. What did he mean, *this thing*? He made it sound like a purchase of yard goods, or a choice of vegetable with dinner. Not a life decision, a step that would be the most important she'd ever taken.

She couldn't think of anything to say, so she forced a brittle smile and nodded.

''You run on back to the ladies, now. I'll stop by this evening and we can sit on your porch swing and discuss the matter further.''

Hannah didn't even flinch at his definitive tone. She felt numb, dazed. Everything felt off kilter somehow, and all she could think was that Ram Kellogg was to blame for this latest debacle.

The man truly was a menace, and for whatever reason he seemed to have set his sights on ruining her chances for a safe, respectable life.

Ram leaned against the side of the church house, his nonchalant pose in no way conveying the roiling turmoil of emotions flowing through him. A piece of hay was clenched in his teeth, forgotten when he'd caught sight of Hannah and her preacher.

At first he'd thought they were having a disagreement; Hannah's body language seemed to reflect irritation. But then he'd watched the man take her in his arms, and a fierce, instinctive jealousy swelled within him.

He didn't want to see but found he couldn't turn away as the man's lips closed over Hannah's. Ram remembered too well how those lips tasted, felt, moved beneath the pressure of a kiss.

He'd dreamed of Hannah in his arms for seven long

nights. Relived the moments of passion they'd shared during nearly every waking hour. For a solid week he'd done little else but rankle the nerves of his employers with questions concerning the threats against Hannah. Finding her tormentor had become his first priority.

And all the while she'd been furthering her pursuit of the respectable, acceptable reverend.

"Damn all fickle, feeble-headed women," he cursed, tossing aside the sprig of hay. He told himself the feeling in his gut—like he'd been kicked by a horse—was nothing more than anger at her perfidy. And disgust with himself for allowing her to get under his skin in the first place.

Hadn't he learned his lesson by now? When would he ever get it through his head that the only women worth messing with were the ones like Sally? No ties, no obligations. No useless emotions to knot a man's guts in a wad.

There was only one problem with that, he thought, turning away and heading back toward the Double Eagle. Somewhere in the last week he seemed to have lost his taste for that kind of woman.

Chapter Sixteen

The crisp morning air was charged with excitement. Children chased hoops through the street, squealing with pleasure and sometimes fright when they'd get too close to the horses in the road.

Hannah took a deep breath and let the warm sunshine bathe her face. It was a glorious day, with enough of a breeze to keep the heat under control. The sky was a beautiful shade of blue, the clouds little pillows of white.

And everywhere she looked her friends and neighbors appeared to be having a wonderful time.

Mary Beth and Rupert strolled through the square hand in hand like newlyweds, their children marching ahead like little ducklings. Ed Pearl had been put in charge of the huge barbecue pit the men had set up in the southwest corner, but it was Agnes, standing watch nearby, who was actually giving the orders. Hannah smiled as the men groaned and complained, then hopped to do her bidding.

Was there ever such a day? she wondered. Such a perfect,

ideal moment in time. Nothing could possibly spoil it, she thought.

And then she saw him.

He stood beneath the huge willow tree, his boots crossed at the ankle and hat tipped back on his head. He held a cup of what Hannah knew wasn't punch.

As he caught her eye, Ram held the glass up to her in a toast and downed the contents in one gulp.

Still morning, and the man was already on his way to being intoxicated. It was a disgrace, and if Hannah had her way, it would soon be a crime.

Dragging her gaze away, she ignored his presence, pretending she hadn't seen the insulting gesture. Trying to stop her mind from replaying that shameful, horrible, pleasurable scene in her bedroom over again. It served no purpose to try and forget it; Hannah knew she never would. But she would force herself to pretend it hadn't happened.

She refused to let Ram Kellogg's debauchery spoil her mood today.

She hadn't seen Francis all morning, and she was secretly thankful. After a long discussion on her porch swing the night before, she'd managed to put Francis off his announcement idea, insisting Founder's Day was not the proper time to herald their engagement.

But he'd hinted that he had a surprise for her today, and Hannah wasn't at all sure she'd find it a pleasant one.

She thought of her approaching speech, and that gave her a moment's pause. The occasional butterfly fluttered in her stomach. But she told herself it was all part of the work she'd vowed to do for the cause. If Carry Nation and Frances Willard could stand true to their beliefs in the face of all obstacles, so might Hannah Sullivan.

Her speech was all prepared, and she had to admit it sounded impassioned enough to stir even the most moderate soul to act on their behalf.

A horse race was scheduled for later in the morning, followed by the food and several planned festivities. Later in the afternoon would come the speeches.

Everybody had one, it seemed.

The mayor would expound on the virtues of the town, take credit for most of them and remind people of his bid in the upcoming election. Ed Pearl, as head of the school board, wanted to raise funds for a new roof on the school building. Agnes had decided to bring up the issue of Indian affairs and start a petition to send to Washington in favor of the Dawes Act, reformist legislation that provided for distribution of landholdings to Indians.

And, finally, Hannah would take her turn on the make-shift stage.

Again she felt the butterflies, this time stronger and more unsettling. For, unlike the mayor or Ed, or even Agnes, she would be looking down on the faces of her most obdurate opponents.

Her eye was once more drawn to the willow tree, where a small gathering of men had collected around Ram. They were all frequenters of the saloons, and each held a cup in his hand.

The only thing worse then facing your foes on the battle-field was facing them while they were well into their cups. Hannah could easily imagine a drunken brawl developing in the town square, with innocent women and children likely to be caught in the fray.

That would never do, she thought, suddenly realizing the dangerous possibilities and wondering why they hadn't occurred to her earlier. She had to take action to prevent such a thing from happening.

Unfortunately, there was only one person she could think of who might have a chance of putting down a revolt.

She squeezed her eyes shut and shook her head. How could she face him after that awful spectacle in her bedroom? How could she go to him for help when she'd slapped him and thrown him out of her house? She'd rather be stung by a thousand bees.

But Hannah knew she had no other choice. Taking a deep breath, she started toward Ram, resigned that he was her only hope.

He looked up as she came forward and his gaze locked on her face. Hannah felt the heat of his stare and her cheeks grew warm. One of the men noticed the direction of his gaze and turned to face her, muttering something as he nudged the man next to him.

As a group, they turned to watch her approach. The butterflies had turned into bats and then swooping hawks in the space of a single moment.

"Miss Sullivan."

Ram nodded and put his free hand to his hat brim in greeting. Several of the other men did likewise, but their welcome was laced with sly smirks and knowing jabs.

"Mr. Kellogg, I was wondering if I might speak with you," she said. He glanced around at the men, and Hannah heard several muffled laughs.

Ram shrugged. "I reckon if you talk I can't help but hear you."

She rubbed a spot over her eyebrow, trying to contain her temper and hide the flush of embarrassment she was sure colored her cheeks.

"In private," she murmured, her voice low.

"How's that?" He tipped his head as though he hadn't heard her, though she was certain he had and was only trying to provoke her.

She glared up at him and placed her hands firmly on her hips. "I said in private," she told him, speaking slowly and clearly.

A few low whistles and ribald chuckles came from the

back of the group, and Ram turned to grin at his entourage, enjoying her discomfiture.

She wanted to walk away, deciding this had been a bad idea. But she reminded herself that she was doing it for the good of the town. Fighting down her embarrassment, she stood firm.

"Yes, ma'am," he drawled, holding out his hand toward an empty bench under a nearby tree. "I aim to please."

This brought the group to life and the laughter grew louder, the comments bolder. Hannah seethed, knowing her face was crimson now. She hated to blush. She'd always thought the horrible red flash of color clashed with her hair.

It shouldn't matter. What did she care if she looked awful in front of Ram Kellogg? But deep down Hannah knew she did care. Against all reason, she'd begun to let his opinion matter to her.

She took a seat on the scrolled wrought-iron bench and adjusted her skirts to make room for Ram to sit next to her. But he surprised her yet again. He chose to remain standing, facing the bench and lifting one foot to rest on the seat.

Crossing his arms over his raised knee, he tipped his hat back and stared down at her.

"What can I do for you?"

The question seemed to have a double meaning and she shifted uncomfortably beneath his impervious gaze.

"I—I wanted to speak to you about the alcohol being served in the square today," she told him, trying to hold his gaze but finally giving up and glancing to the side.

"What about it?"

He wasn't going to make this easy for her, she realized. Obviously he was still upset by their less-than-amicable parting a week ago.

"I believe it might cause problems as the day wears on."

"Is that so?"

"Yes. You see, the festivities will continue into the evening, and you men have already started drinking. I don't want a bunch of rowdy, liquored up . . ."

"*You* don't want?"

Hannah was stopped midsentence, her mouth still open on her next words. "What?"

"Why is it that every time we're together we end up in a discussion about what you want?"

"I don't . . ."

"What about what I want?" he asked, leaning toward her. Hannah felt the breath rush out of her lungs and she quickly scanned the area to see if anyone was within earshot.

"What do you mean?" she whispered, feeling heat course through her body. A ripple of awareness started in her midsection and spread in an ever-widening pool until even her fingertips tingled.

"Maybe the men and I want to drink. Maybe we want to get stinking drunk and raise hell."

"You can't be serious! Why, that's outrageous. There are children here."

"And men who want to have a good time."

"Why must you drink to excess in order to have a good time? Join the race," she said, waving her hand toward the tethered horses that had been brought in to compete.

"I've already signed up for the race. And by the looks of the competition, I expect to win."

"Look, Ram," she said, her voice softening as she rose and took a step closer to him.

"What happened to Mr. Kellogg?"

Hannah met his gaze, and she could see the suppressed anger barely hidden in his narrowed eyes. She'd made an enemy of the man, at first intentionally and then unexpectedly. She hadn't thought it would matter to her.

It did.

"All I'm asking is that you keep the men under control so everyone can enjoy the day without any unpleasant incidents. As I'm sure you know, I'll be speaking this afternoon in favor of prohibition for Fortune. Perhaps you should just consider my request for a moment. You'll only be helping my cause a great deal if trouble breaks out due to the liquor being served here today."

"I'll consider myself forewarned," he said, touching his hat brim again.

As Hannah watched him walk away, something inside her longed to go after him and try to make things right. But she couldn't do that. And she disliked the anger and bitterness that now stood between them. Hated feeling like his enemy.

But the fact remained, they *were* enemies. And nothing, it seemed, would ever change that.

The riders mounted their horses, the line stretching clear across the main street through town. It was an awesome sight, most of the horses reacting to the excitement, prancing and sidestepping majestically.

Hannah's gaze had immediately sought, and found, Ram on a huge bay stallion.

"Isn't it exciting?" Mary Beth breathed beside her.

Hannah glanced sideways and smiled at her friend. Yes, it was exciting. There was something incredibly captivating about a man astride a horse. Especially a man with as commanding a presence as Ram. The horse moved with the slightest nudge of his thighs.

Heat raced through Hannah as she recalled the way those same thighs had held her and commanded her. A swell of desire rose in her throat until she could barely breathe.

"You know the winner gets a twenty-dollar gold piece."

She frowned at Mary Beth. "A gold piece donated by Martin Pollock, the saloonkeeper. Why, you know he only did it to gain support for the saloons."

"I don't care why he's doing it. What I wouldn't give to get back some of what we've lost to him and his establishment."

Hannah continued to frown, thinking how the offer of a twenty-dollar gold piece could corrupt even the most faithful at heart. Just look how it had affected Mary Beth, and who knew better than she did how dangerous the saloons could be to their men?

"Besides," the woman said, trying to draw Hannah out of her dour mood, "the winner also wins a kiss from the lady of his choice." She winked at Hannah and squeezed her elbow. "Who knows, you might be the lucky lady."

Drawing her gaze from Ram's imposing figure, Hannah stared with widened eyes. Had Mary Beth noticed her watching Ram? Were the feelings she'd tried to keep hidden so obvious? Lord, what would people think?

"What are you saying, Mary Beth? Why would you think anyone would try to win a kiss from me?"

"Hannah, don't be silly. Of course if he wins he'll kiss you."

She must have noticed Hannah's horrified reaction. She placed her hand gently on Hannah's arm and smiled.

"Don't look so scandalized. Even if he is a minister, he's still a man. And everyone knows you two are practically engaged."

As the words sank through the confusion whirling around in Hannah's head, she shot a frantic glance toward the riders. Indeed, there was Francis.

She gasped. "What is he *doing* out there? He can't seriously be considering racing. Why, Francis isn't an experienced horseman. He could be killed."

She took a step toward the street, but Mary Beth refused to relinquish her hold. "Hannah, where are you going? You can't just walk out there. The race is about to begin."

"But I can't let him do this, Mary Beth."

"He's his own man, Hannah. You can't stop him. Besides, he said it would only be fitting for the wages of sin to pay for the new hymn books he's been longing for."

"This is awful," Hannah moaned. Her gaze darted between Ram and Francis, and the differences between the two men had never been more obvious. Francis was thin and pale from spending most of his time indoors, studying and writing. Ram was muscular and tanned and at least four inches taller.

Hannah felt ashamed to be comparing them in such a way. But what really upset her most was that Ram was the one who made her heart race, while all she felt for Francis was concern that he'd be injured.

Of course, Francis was the better man in every way except the physical. He was a man of God, devoted to his congregation and this town's best interest.

Ram was a womanizing whiskey-lover with few redeeming qualities.

Except that he had come to her defense more than once, her traitorous heart reminded her. And he'd kissed her like no man ever had or, she feared, ever would. He hadn't judged her for her mother's sins or questioned her about her own.

Truth be told, he'd been a lot more fair to her than she'd been to him. And she couldn't forget how kind and generous he'd been to Mary Beth.

A shot startled Hannah out of her musings and she pressed a hand to her racing heart as the riders bolted forward on their eager beasts.

There were about twenty riders in all. The course led north out of town, circled around behind the small block of residences on the west end, past the side street where Hannah's house stood and ended with a reentry onto Main Street from the south.

At times the riders would be out of sight, but only for brief periods.

As they approached the first turn at the north end of town, the group in the lead thinned out. Four riders rounded the corner together: Ram, Rupert Gray, a day laborer Hannah didn't recognize and Francis. That surprised Hannah, to say the least. She hadn't realized that Francis even knew how to ride.

After the second turn, at the end of Main Street, the riders disappeared from view. The crowd of spectators hurried to the small knoll behind the bank, where they could better see the route the men would take.

Mary Beth clutched Hannah's hand and dragged her up the incline.

"There they are," she cried, dancing on tiptoes to see over the taller heads in front of her. She pushed a little farther through the throng and finally gained a place in the front of the pack.

"You can just see them coming out of the trees. Rupert's still toward the front," she said.

Hannah didn't want to look. She couldn't bear to see the men racing along at such breakneck speeds, their mounts coming within inches of colliding with each other. Her heart was in her throat and seemed to have stopped beating completely. She held her breath.

"Look! Hannah, Rupert's taking the lead." Mary Beth grabbed Hannah's arm and shook her, her enthusiasm too immense to be contained.

Forcing herself to watch, Hannah saw that Ram and Francis were side by side, just ahead of the other riders. Rupert was indeed coming up fast on the outside, though.

What Francis lacked in experience, his horse was more

than making up for. The gelded roan, owned by Ed Pearl,
was having no trouble carrying the light weight since he
was obviously used to a much heavier rider.

They rounded the last curve and started back for the
opposite end of Main Street. Once more the crowd rushed
to vie for the most advantageous viewing spot to see the
riders as they neared the last stretch. Mary Beth had
released Hannah's arm, and as she hurried away, Hannah
kept her gaze on the riders for one more instant.

A fateful moment, as it turned out, for Francis's unre-
fined skills on the crowded turn brought his horse too
close to Rupert's, who had just managed to draw even with
him. The horses' hooves collided. Hannah clasped a hand
over her pounding heart.

Ram was in the lead by a nose, but he'd glanced back
to gauge Rupert's approach. As Hannah watched in horror,
Rupert's horse went down, stirring up a great cloud of
dust as it landed atop its helpless rider.

Chapter Seventeen

As Hannah stood, too stunned to move, she saw Ram rein his horse in a circle so tight it seemed he picked it up and set it down in the same spot. The horse reared and cried out at the sudden pressure on his mouth from the metal bit. Hannah couldn't believe that Ram was going back.

But what shocked her even more was, Francis wasn't!

Could he not have realized what he'd done? That didn't seem likely. But, as she stood, frozen in disbelief, she saw him take the lead and continue on.

A frightened cry from behind her propelled Hannah forward, and the thought was immediately wiped from her mind. She hurried down the hill toward the commotion, Mary Beth and half the town on her heels.

As Hannah reached the chaotic scene, Ram was trying to force Rupert's stunned, struggling horse to stand. She could see the figure lying still on the ground and her heart dropped to her feet. A sheen of icy sweat broke along her brow and she just caught Mary Beth before the woman plunged forward into the commotion.

"Stop! You can't go in there. Not until Ram gets the horse out of the way. He could trample you," she said, struck by the terrifying notion that the animal might very well do just that to Ram.

She held her breath and clutched Mary Beth in trembling arms as the woman sobbed.

The horse finally righted itself, and one of the other men went forward to take the reins. The mount was limping as it was led away from its prone rider.

Ram knelt down beside Rupert, and Hannah released her hold on Mary Beth. The woman hurried to her husband's side as Hannah stood back, the crowd closing around her, and watched.

After what seemed like an eternity, but was in reality no more than a few minutes, Hannah saw two of the men help Rupert sit up.

He cried out in pain, and Hannah felt tears of relief well in her eyes. At least he was alive.

"Bring a wagon," one of the men called out. "And someone fetch Doc."

"Right here," Albert Snell said, pushing his way through the throng.

Hannah remembered that she'd seen him at the beginning of the race, watching along with the rest of the town, and wondered what had taken him so long to get to the scene.

Then she saw that he carried his black satchel and she realized he'd gone straight to his office to retrieve it as soon as he'd seen what had happened.

He was a young man—not more than thirty—and it had taken several months and several minor miracles to convince the skeptics in town that he was a fine doctor.

Hannah knew he was, and she breathed a relieved sigh

when he kneeled down next to Rupert. She knew her friend's husband was in the best possible hands.

She heard the wagon rolling forward, and the crowd parted to let it through, then closed together again. The day had taken a surprisingly bad turn and the excitement brought on by the race dissolved into anxious chatter and a lot of nervous handwringing.

While several of the riders had stopped to help, or just to watch the commotion, Francis and most of the others had gone on to finish the race.

Finally the men loaded Rupert into the back of the wagon, and Hannah winced as he cried out again. Then the doctor scrambled up beside him and the wagon took off for the little clinic in the center of town.

Ram bent to pick up Rupert's hat and whack it soundly against his thigh. Dust danced off in every direction, and as the crowd followed the wagon back toward town, Hannah discovered that she and Ram had been left alone.

He paused, watching as the last person disappeared behind the small knoll, leaving them alone and unobserved.

Finally his eyes met hers, and she thought she saw a flash of something warm and tender. Then he looked down at the hat in his hand and started to walk past her. Her hand shot out to stop him, and she didn't know who was the most surprised by the action.

"How is he?" she asked, liking the feel of his muscular forearm beneath her palm. "Really, I mean."

"Got the wind knocked out of him, that's for sure. I didn't think he was breathing when we first reached him. But he came around. Leg's pretty messed up."

"Broken?"

"Yeah. He won't be dancing any time soon."

He glanced down at her hand and she hesitated for a moment, then forced herself to relinquish her hold. She missed the feel of his warm skin chasing the chill of fear from her. She wished he would take her in his arms and hold her until the trembling stopped, but she knew she couldn't expect that with all that had happened between them. And, she admitted to herself, she was wrong to want it so.

Hadn't she just been trying to convince herself he would never be the man for her?

"Ram, wait," she called, unable to let him walk away. He turned to face her, and an awkward moment followed. What could she say? Why had she called out to him instead of letting him go, as she should have?

"Mary Beth told me what you did for Rupert, getting back the acres he lost. That was a wonderful thing to do," she told him, realizing she should have said something sooner about his generosity. "Now, with this accident, your gift will be even more valuable."

"It'll be more of a burden, you mean. The man won't be working in the fields anytime soon, Hannah. The extra acres will just mean more unharvested crops left to rot in the fields."

"Oh, no," she hurried to tell him, taking a step closer, since he hadn't rebuffed her efforts at conversation thus far. "Everyone'll help out; they always do in a situation like this. The crops will be brought in, and the extra will get Mary Beth's family through the winter until Rupert is back on his feet again."

Ram looked at her for a long minute, then nodded. "I see. Well, that's just swell."

He took another step, and Hannah knew she had to stop him. She may not agree with his views on liquor, but she couldn't let him walk away with bitter feelings still between them.

"Ram, I also wanted to thank you for rushing to his aid the way you did. It could have been dangerous, and you didn't even stop to think before you turned to help. Something like that says a lot about a man."

He shrugged. "Instinct, nothing more. Don't go putting any more stock in it than that."

"But you were in the lead. You would have won. Aren't you even a little upset that you didn't win the twenty-dollar gold piece?"

His eyes came up to stare into hers and she felt her face grow hot under his perusal. He took a step toward her.

"I didn't enter the race for the twenty bucks," he told her.

Hannah licked her dry lips and met his bold gaze. "You didn't?"

He shook his head.

"Then why did you?"

He glanced to the side and rubbed his hand across his jaw. Hannah could hear the soft scrape of his knuckles on the short growth of beard that had developed during the day.

Once more he pinned her with a stare, and this time she definitely saw a hint of something in his eyes. Longing, anticipation, disappointment. She couldn't tell, but she found that she desperately wanted to know.

"What would you say if I told you the only reason I entered the race was to win the kiss?"

"The kiss?" she breathed.

"The winner got a kiss from the lady of his choice."

"Yes, I remember now."

Her heart raced, her palms tingled and she could feel that heaviness in the pit of her stomach that she'd come to associate with Ram's nearness. She knew she should turn around, follow the others into town. But, at that moment, this was the only place she wanted to be.

He arched a brow, obviously waiting for her to say something, and Hannah scrambled to remember what they'd been talking about.

"I'd say the lady must be something pretty special," she finally managed.

"I thought so," he told her, and the look in his eyes softened. She was certain now it must be longing.

"But you don't think so now?" Her voice was low and raspy and she swallowed to wet her parched throat.

"I'm not sure. Could be." His voice sounded oddly rough, with an uncertain quality she'd never heard before. "Of course, a really special lady wouldn't let a man miss out on his kiss on account of him stopping to help someone. She'd offer him the kiss anyway."

"Well, why don't you ask the lady? She just might," she challenged him boldly, hiding the nervous tremble his words caused in her.

"I don't know. If I ask, she might say no. And I'm in no mood to be turned down. Maybe I'll just take the kiss."

He stepped closer, and Hannah felt hypnotized by the amber glow of his eyes boring into hers. His look held an undeniable question, one she wasn't sure she had the answer to.

Her heart fluttered wildly against the walls of her chest and her body felt heavy and warm. Especially that secret place he'd brought to life once before.

Shame threatened to engulf her, but she had no more time to think or rebuke herself as he reached for her and she found her arms going eagerly around his neck.

He clutched her to his chest with enough force to lift her off her feet, and Hannah could only hold on and drown in the feel of being in Ram's arms once again. Her mouth opened immediately and he pressed deeper, his tongue darting into the dark heat of her mouth.

Hannah had accused him of drinking, and he hadn't denied it. But she tasted no liquor on his lips as they came together. Only maleness, and a hint of peppermint. She adored peppermint, and right now she couldn't get enough of it.

He'd dropped Rupert's hat, and she could feel both his hands clasped around her waist. Her toes were now touching the ground, but she felt as though she was still up in the air.

His mouth worked hungrily over hers, his lips hard and searching. This was no gentle, comforting kiss. He demanded a response from her, and Hannah could not refuse him. She reached out daringly with her tongue and met him thrust for thrust.

As he continued to hold her, she could feel the hardness of his arousal pressed against her. His hand came up to cup her head, his fingers raking through the wild strands. He pulled the ribbon from her hair and grasped a handful, wrapping it around his wrist.

With a gentle tug, he turned her head first one way and then the other to plunder every inch of her mouth. She couldn't breathe and didn't care if she ever drew breath again, as long as he kept kissing her.

Finally, when she thought she would faint from sheer pleasure, he released her. Her feet settled firmly on the ground, she let her arms drift slowly down his shoulders to his chest, where they settled.

His eyes were dark as wood smoke when he gazed at her, his lips full and slightly damp. She felt another jolt rocket through her stomach.

"Worth more than a twenty-dollar gold piece any day," he said, clasping her hands.

"I adore peppermint," she whispered, still dazed by the moment.

He chuckled low in his throat, and she thought he'd bring her hands to his lips and kiss them, then kiss her again until she indeed collapsed from exhilaration.

Instead, he lowered them to her sides and bent to pick up the discarded hat. At her frown, he only grinned.

"I believe you're late for your rally," he said.

Hannah gasped and whirled toward the direction of town. She'd completely forgotten about her speech in all the excitement, and she belatedly realized they'd been standing there for some time.

"You did that on purpose," she accused him.

"Kissed you? You bet, I did. And if you don't get moving, I'm likely to do it again, your rally be damned."

She huffed and gathered up her skirts, racing for the town square before anyone thought to come looking for her.

Ram watched her hurry away, his heart stuck in his trousers for the moment. He was damned uncomfortable, and knowing he'd done the right thing in sending Hannah away didn't ease his suffering any.

He shouldn't have kissed her, but he'd been unable to stop himself. How could he remain angry at her when her mere glance set him on fire? Her concern for his safety, her praise for his having won back the twenty acres, stoked his ardor. Which he'd kept barely banked since their last encounter.

But the lady didn't want him, he reminded himself sternly. Not the man he was, warts and all. And he wouldn't even try to change for a woman. That thinking only led to disaster, as he well knew.

So, where did that leave them? Her, uptight and repressed. Him, rock-hard and frustrated.

He groaned and adjusted the placket on his trousers, knowing they couldn't go on like this much longer. And that meant there was only one solution: If he didn't plan to change himself, he would have to change her way of thinking.

He grinned as he remembered her breathy comment after they kissed.

The lady liked peppermint, did she? Well, he might just have to introduce her to the newest thing in liqueur—a German treat one of the men had brought to the square earlier. Schnapps.

"I told you, Hannah, I didn't see him go down. Hand me that pitcher."

She tossed out the warm lemonade and set the tin container in the box Francis carried, already full of the dishes and utensils they'd cleared from the tables in the square. Only a bit more remained to be done, and Hannah was bone tired.

"But you caused him to fall, Francis. I saw it with my own eyes. And then you just continued on."

"So you've said. But you were all the way up on the knoll, and no doubt excited by the race. How can you be sure what you saw? Or what actually happened? I was right there, and I can't say I know for sure what caused Rupert's horse to stumble. It could have been a rabbit hole. Besides, no one else seems to have seen what you claim."

"They were all turned around the other way, as I've already told you. Everyone was heading back toward town. Besides, that isn't the point I'm trying to make. Whether you realized what had happened at the time or not, you didn't win fair. Mr. Kellogg would have surely beaten you if he hadn't stopped to help Rupert."

"Why are you still going on about this, Hannah? The race was declared final." He clutched the ends of a table-cloth, and together they folded it into a neat square. "I won, and the church is finally going to get those hymn books from St. Louis.''

As she watched, his eyes lit up and he nodded. "They're the best money can buy, with real red leather covers and gold script on the front. We'd never be able to afford anything half that fine on what this town pledges.''

"I think you should give the money to Rupert and Mary Beth," she told him outright, tired of beating around the issue he seemed determined to avoid.

She'd been astonished to arrive in town and see him accepting the prize from a dour-looking Martin Pollack. She was even more astounded that he didn't seem to consider himself to blame for the incident.

She'd gone on to give her speech, but she'd had trouble working up the righteous indignation she usually felt for her cause. She'd feared at first that it might have been Ram's kiss that had distorted her perspective, but she quickly dismissed that notion.

Everything else had seemed anticlimactic after Rupert's accident, that's all. Most folks had been subdued by the brush with tragedy. Very few had remained to hear the entire series of talks, even fewer to sign her petition for full prohibition in Fortune.

"Now, why would I do something as foolish as that?" Francis asked, pausing as they emptied another table and several men came to haul it back to the schoolhouse. As soon as the men left, he continued. "You know as well as I do that the man would probably just gamble it away, as he nearly did his farm.''

Hannah clapped her hands on her hips, her jaw dropping in astonishment. "Why, Francis, how could you say something so unkind?''

"Because it's the truth, and you know it. I know the woman is your friend, and I feel sorry for her. But the fact remains, she and the children probably wouldn't benefit from the money anyway. That useless husband of hers would see to that," he said in disgust.

She opened her mouth to lament his uncaring attitude, but he held up his hand in front of her. "And don't say I didn't try to help him, because I did. I counseled them countless times."

"For crying out loud, the man has a badly broken leg. Besides, he's sworn off the saloons, the drinking and gambling. And Mary Beth says she thinks he really is sincere this time."

"That leg will just be another excuse for him to avoid honest work. As for him swearing off the saloons, he's made that promise before, many times. He always goes back to his old habits. Take my word for it, that money would be right back in Pollack's pocket before the week was over."

"You can't be sure. Maybe Rupert really has learned his lesson."

"And maybe it's just an act to placate everyone so we'll dole out charity as we always have in the past. No, that money should go for a good cause. The church needs those hymn books."

"But we could do with less expensive ones."

"Why should we shortchange the Lord for a man like Rupert Gray? I promised everyone we'd get those St. Louis hymn books, and I mean to see we get them."

"So, you're just giving up on a fellow human being? You're selling him out, only your price is a twenty-dollar gold piece, rather than thirty pieces of silver. I wish the rest of the people in this town had witnessed what I saw today, Francis. Then they'd realize, as I have, what kind of man you truly are."

Francis stopped and glared at her, and Hannah could see that he was truly angry. She'd never seen Francis express any negative emotion in public. In fact, she'd never

seen him express any emotion in public, except to occasionally get carried away by his sermon in the pulpit.

"How dare you say something like that to me. After all
I've done for you. Who do you think you are?"

Blinking her surprise at the harsh attack, Hannah took
a step back and straightened her spine.

"Your fiancée, remember? If you'd had your way, we
would have made the announcement today, right here.
You said you wanted me to be your helpmate. I'm trying
to help you see that it's our Christian duty to assist this
family. We can still get new hymn books, just less expensive
ones."

"As if I need advice on what my Christian duty is from
the likes of you. What would you know about being a
Christian, except what I've taught you?"

The words stung like a whip, the rebuke cutting painfully
into her newfound self-esteem. Taking a deep breath, Hannah tried to force back her trembling rage. But her words
shook with anger.

"I know the way you're behaving at this moment certainly is not appropriate for a minister."

"Again, you know nothing of propriety but what you've
learned from me. Really, Hannah, you should show more
gratitude."

"And you should show more humility. I've studied the
Bible. Everything I've learned in the last two years hasn't
come from you, Francis. I know this, because if it had, I
wouldn't be so certain now that what you're doing is wrong.
And I wouldn't have the nerve to say what I'm about to
say. You are a mean-spirited man, Francis, and no amount
of praying and sermonizing can hide that any longer. Nor
will I excuse you for the hurtful, cruel insults you hurl at
me. I've wondered for a long time why you chose me as
your future wife. Now I'm afraid I've finally figured it out.
You don't want a helpmate; you want a whipping post.

Someone inferior to make you feel superior. Well, that someone won't be me, Francis. Not any longer.''

She tossed the tablecloth she held in his face and stormed away.

Chapter Eighteen

Dark had settled by the time Hannah reached her street. For some reason the gaslights at the corner had not been lit. She shuddered, disliking the shadowy stillness, then felt her anger blossom again.

Of course there would be no light. Dewey Denton, the man who lit the lamps each evening, had been one of the men drinking with Ram in the square that afternoon. No doubt he was passed out somewhere, pickled to perfection.

That man was a curse on this town, she thought, clutching her shawl tighter as she passed beneath an overhanging tree limb. And, worse still, on her.

Hannah knew more than Francis's enmity was responsible for their final breakup. Ram was responsible.

She'd thought about Francis's kiss a great deal since yesterday, but not because it had touched her in any way. Just the opposite. She'd felt nothing when he held her, kissed her, told her he finally wanted to announce their engagement. He was the man she'd thought she loved for nearly two years. But tonight, in the square, she'd finally admitted the truth to herself. What she'd mistaken for love had really been a need to *be* loved.

Francis had helped her. When she'd first arrived in Fortune, he'd been kind and sympathetic. He'd taken her under his wing and enjoyed teaching her about religion. She'd never had any connection to a church, so she'd been fascinated and eager to learn. He'd shaped her and molded her into the perfect little follower.

And, because respectability was more important to her than anything else, she'd grabbed at the chance to align herself with a man of God. After all, who could be more respectable than a minister's wife?

She'd had doubts from time to time, but she'd always dismissed them quickly from her mind. But she'd finally realized Francis had a cruel streak that seemed to peak only around her.

For two years she'd convinced herself that it was her fault that she brought him to exasperation. After all, he was hiding her past, covering for her slips. It stood to reason he would occasionally lose patience with her less-than-perfect characteristics.

"No more," she muttered, happy to see her gate outlined before her. She closed it behind her and moved toward the back door.

She would not pardon his behavior any longer. For one thing, it was too hard to bear unfeeling barbs after suffering them her whole life. Secondly, there was no longer any reason she should dismiss his derision.

The moment Francis kissed her behind the parsonage she'd realized what a mistake they'd made. His kisses didn't move her. She didn't long for them to go on forever.

Not the way she had with Ram.

"And I don't even like the man," she thought out loud,

opening her door and stepping into the darkened interior of her kitchen.

What an irony—that the one man she couldn't tolerate should be the only one who could make her come alive and remember she was a woman without feeling shame at the fact.

"Oh, Ram," she whispered, pushing the door closed.

A dark shadow shifted from behind the door, and Hannah gasped, startled. At first she thought her mind had conjured him; then a heavy, damp hand closed over her mouth and she knew whoever was in her house, it wasn't Ram.

"Not this time, little sister." His hot breath whipped past her ear and she felt something cold press against her neck.

She smelled sour whiskey, and immediately she was back in the tarpaper shack, a little girl again, being punished for some supposed indiscretion.

Her stomach turned to liquid, her mouth cotton. She tried to hold on to her control, but fear swirled around her tighter, cutting off her breath. She thought surely she would faint soon and be spared whatever was about to happen next.

Her fingers clutched and clawed at the rough hands holding her. She felt a jab in her lower back as her attacker brought his knee up to still her struggles. The blow took the last of her breath and she went limp.

"Not so full of piss and vinegar now, are you? Nothing but another dumb snatch, thinking you can best a man." His hand closed over her breast and he pinched her nipple hard. Hannah started to struggle again in earnest.

"Yeah, I know what you need, missy. If'n you had a real man between your legs, you wouldn't have no time for all that harping and cawing and troublemaking."

Hannah gripped his hand with renewed vigor and pulled

it far enough from her lips to issue a high wail. He bopped her on the side of the head with whatever he held. She staggered but didn't go down.

"I bet you ain't even worth pokin'," he said, lifting her up, one heavy arm wrapped around her just under her breasts. His hold cut off her air. She had to scream now, or be lost to whatever fate this man had in mind for her.

Whipping her head first one way and then the other sharply, she caught him off guard, loosening the hand covering her face. She opened her mouth and, as he clutched for her again, sank her teeth into the flesh between his thumb and forefinger.

He released her with a howl and Hannah turned for the door, screaming as long and as loud as her diminished air supply would permit.

Ram stopped, one foot on the front porch, the shriek freezing the blood in his veins. Raising the package he carried over his head like a club, he lifted his boot and kicked the door open, bursting into the darkened room. For a moment he couldn't see a blessed thing; then his eyes adjusted and he could make out shapes.

"Hannah!"

Stumbling over a table and then what must have been a low stool, he tripped toward the kitchen, trying to remember the lay of the place from the last time he'd been inside.

"Dammit," he muttered, cracking his shin on another table and sending something crashing to the floor. "Hannah!"

"Here, Ram," he heard her call out, her voice shaking and weak. "I'm in here."

He rushed toward the kitchen and collided with Hannah, trying to reach him in the dark.

"Shit," he muttered, rubbing the spot over one eye where they'd knocked heads.

"Hurry, Ram, he went out the back. Get him," she cried, her fear quickly dissipating beneath what sounded like pure rage. She shoved him toward the back door, and he thrust the package into her hands and shot out after the intruder.

Ram raced to the street, but he couldn't see anything in the dark. He paused, listening for running footsteps, straining futilely to see through the shadows. Nothing.

He retraced his steps, wishing he could see well enough to search the yard for a clue as to whom the man might be and where he'd gone. Of course, there were several ways he could have gone, and Ram wouldn't be searching for clues until the light of day.

Concerned for Hannah's safety, he hurried to return to her.

He found her in a bright kitchen, sitting at her small round table. She'd lit several lamps throughout the house, and the illumination momentarily blinded him.

"I'm sorry, Hannah. He got away."

Ram saw her nod slowly, holding her mouth rigid. He'd expected to find her in a crumpled heap, crying hysterically. He realized that she was downright mad. Too mad to give in to the terror that she must be feeling at that moment.

His own blood continued to race through his veins, and his heart still pounded furiously with fright and the exhilaration of the chase, however brief and unsuccessful. The rush he'd always experienced when he was closing in on a suspect was nothing compared to this.

"Hannah, what happened? Do you know who it was?"

She shook her head, and he thought she must be too frightened to even speak. Then she raised her head, and he could see the fierce light in her eyes as she met his gaze.

"If I knew who it was, I'd be out there right now, swearing out a complaint with the sheriff. I'm not a complete fool, you know. Besides, you're the detective. Why haven't you found out who's doing this?"

Ram rubbed his hand over his mouth to cover the sappy grin he couldn't keep from sliding over his face. This was no time to find humor in Hannah's fortitude. Indeed, there was nothing funny about the situation at all. But sheer relief made a smile break across his face, and he couldn't hold it back.

Hannah looked up and saw the expression before he could hide it.

"Are you laughing about this?" she cried, pushing out of her chair and bowing up like a cornered rattler.

Ram held out his hands and shook his head. "No, I swear it. I'm not laughing." But to his horror a chuckle chose that precise moment to slip out. "I was just so damned scared, and then I found you in here, mad as a wet setting hen and ordering me to sic him like a trained dog."

"This isn't funny, Ram," she told him, her eyes going wide as he fought to contain his laughter. "Someone broke into my house and frightened the living daylights out of me."

"I'm sorry," he said, trying to keep a serious face. "Come here." He held out his arms and she slapped them away.

"No. I can't believe you find this funny."

"Oh, Hannah," he said, sobering instantly and catching her shoulders in his shaking hands. "I don't, trust me. It's just the relief, that's all. I'm just so glad that you weren't hurt." His last words trailed off, and he grasped her to his chest in a fierce hug that threatened to force the breath out of her. "God, I don't think I've ever been so scared, Hannah."

He cupped her face in his hands and lifted her chin. "Do you understand what I'm saying?"

"No, Ram, don't," she said, trying to turn her face away from the intensity of his gaze. He refused to let her look away, holding her eyes with a heated stare.

"I have to, Hannah. You don't understand what I'm feeling, but I have to."

"I do understand," she whispered. "And I feel the same. That's why you must stop. Now."

"Impossible."

His mouth came down over hers and he kissed her with all the emotion coursing through him at that moment. Parting her lips, his tongue thrust inside her mouth, darting and dancing in rhythm with hers. He gripped her bottom and drew her body into the curve of his, not bothering to hide the fact that he was already aroused. The blood that had pounded from his racing heart seemed to have settled in his nether regions.

At first Hannah tried to protest, but she couldn't manage more than a whimper. Finally she gave in to the driving need and struggled to get closer, then realized they were pressed so tight, she could feel the buttons on his trousers cutting into her lower belly through the fabric of her dress.

His hot mouth raked over her ear and down the curve of her throat, and she felt a shiver start at her spine and shoot out to encompass her whole body. Her knees shook and gave way beneath her, and Ram caught her up in his arms.

"It's all right, Hannah honey," he soothed her, his lips teasing her earlobe. "I've got you."

"Don't let go, Ram," she pleaded, wondering what had happened to her anger, her fear. They'd dissipated like smoke in a hurricane beneath Ram's desire.

"Never, Hannah honey. Never," he vowed, carrying her
through the house to the room down the hall. He shoved
the door open with his foot and then kicked it shut behind
him, turning the key in the lock.

She still held the paper-covered package he'd handed
her, and he removed it from her hand and tossed it onto
the chair by the window.

Dropping her on the bed, he followed her down, refusing to let so much as an inch of space separate them. His
lips found her neck, and she made a soft noise in her
throat that fueled his need.

"If anything had happened to you . . ."

"Don't say it," she begged, placing her fingers lightly
over his lips. He drew the tip of one finger into his mouth
and gently sucked it. Hannah moaned and shifted beneath
him, her knees instinctively falling open so his hips could
settle between her thighs.

The hard mass pressed against her intimately, and she
felt the shock zip straight up her spine to the top of her
head. Her scalp tingled and her toes drew up.

"I need to explain, Hannah. I swear I wasn't laughing
at you."

"Shut up, Ram. Just shut up and kiss me again."

He did. Over and over, until Hannah couldn't breathe,
couldn't think, couldn't have protested if she'd wanted to.

She didn't. The time for thinking was gone. There was
no room for anything but feeling now. And she'd never
felt so good.

Ram knelt before her, pushing her skirt to the top of
her thighs. He lifted her feet and eased each one out of
the soft slippers she wore. His eyes held her gaze as his
hand slid over the outside of her leg to the top of her
stockings. Rolling the first one down, he followed it with
his lips, leaving hot little trails of kisses on her bare skin.

Hannah fell back against the pillows with a groan, and

Ram smiled at the tiny pebbles of gooseflesh his mouth left in its wake.

After he'd bared both legs, he took her hand and pulled her up, lifting her legs over his and scooting their bodies closer together. He wrapped one arm around her and meticulously began to unfasten the prim row of buttons that marched up her back.

When the last button surrendered, he eased the bodice of her dress down to her waist. The satin ribbon on her chemise had come untied and one shoulder fell, revealing a plump white breast.

Hannah tried to cover herself, but Ram took her hand and guided it to the back of his neck. He bent to kiss the soft flesh he'd revealed and she clung to him, both arms linked behind his head.

He gripped her buttocks and lifted her into his lap, wrapping her thighs around his hips and drawing her breast more firmly into his mouth.

She wiggled, unnerved to be straddling him so intimately, and her little movements nearly sent him over the edge.

"Hannah, honey, don't move or you're going to embarrass me something fierce," he begged, one hand holding her bottom firmly in place.

She shifted experimentally, feeling a surge of power and control when he gasped and grabbed her legs, throwing his head back with a low growl.

"You are heartless, Hannah," he accused, his knuckles white with the effort to hold back his reaction.

"No," she whispered, taking his hand as he'd taken hers. She lifted it to her breast and placed it gently over the stiff peak of her nipple. "Feel that?"

His eyes widened and he gently squeezed the soft mound.

"My heart, Ram," she said, laughter in her voice. "My

heart is racing like mad, threatening to burst from my chest. For want of something I don't even fully understand."

"You've never . . ."

"No, Ram."

Ram had wondered, but he'd told himself he had no right to ask. Whatever had happened in Hannah's past had not been in her control.

But now that he knew, he felt a wild rush of protectiveness surge through him. Was he the right man to introduce Hannah to this exciting new experience? Did he really want that responsibility?

Hell, yes, he did. And, what's more, he'd kill any man who tried to take his place.

"I want you, Hannah. I want to show you how it's supposed to be between a man and a woman."

"That's what I want, too, Ram. Please," she begged, "show me. Now."

He quickly removed her dress and underclothes, then removed his own as she watched boldly. For the first time in his life Ram actually felt shy.

He paused, awed that this woman could make him feel something no other ever had. Not the baudy whores he'd spent time with. Not even his wife.

God, he thought, *especially not Doreen.*

He thrust those repulsive memories from his mind. He refused to let any of that touch what he'd found here with Hannah.

Their relationship was too new to put a name to, but Ram had a gut feeling this wouldn't be a one-night affair. Not if he had anything to say about the matter.

Naked and hard, he returned to Hannah. She tried not to look, but her gaze dropped and her eyes widened. Instantly, she turned her head away.

"Look at me, Hannah. It's all right." He turned her

chin toward him and placed a kiss on her lips. He felt her relax. "I like it when you look at me. And I sure plan on looking my fill at you," he teased, raising her arms over her head and stretching out alongside her.

He let his hand drift down her side, across her belly and up her back, following it with his eyes. She shivered, and he closed his eyes and sucked in a deep, calming breath.

Then Hannah pushed on his shoulder and rolled him over, taking the position he'd held a moment before. Ram chuckled in surprise as she touched him the way he'd touched her.

She didn't understand what she was doing to him, but she was doing a damn good job. And he was loving every minute of her naïveté.

Raising his body over hers, he kissed her hard, plundering her mouth and waiting until she was responding fully to his kiss before he thrust himself inside her. She stiffened for a moment, but Ram began to move, and in an instant she was rocking in rhythm with him.

He couldn't stop kissing her, couldn't get close enough. Grasping her knee, he drew her leg up and wrapped it around his waist. She instinctively raised the other one and linked them behind his back.

Ram felt her muscles tightening around him and knew she was close to fulfillment. Gritting his teeth, he held back until he felt the first spasms rock her. She dug her nails into his back and cried out his name and he was lost. Together they spiraled to a climax.

He held her as their breathing returned to normal, afraid of what she might be feeling, thinking in the aftermath of their passion.

That had always been the test with Doreen. A test he'd never passed.

He wanted to hold her quietly, fall asleep inside her and wake up and do it all again. But after several minutes passed and she hadn't moved, his doubts grew. He couldn't put it off any longer. If she was repulsed, horrified by what they'd done, he had to know.

"Hannah, honey," he whispered, smoothing her hair from her cheek and placing a kiss on the side of her mouth, her chin, her closed eyes. "Are you all right? Say something, please."

She opened sparkling green eyes and stared at him. Then a smile split her face and she squeezed her pelvic muscles around his shaft.

"Can we do it again?"

Chapter Nineteen

"I mean it, Ram. I never dreamed it would be like that."

Hannah scooted up on the pillow so they were eye to eye, lips to lips.

"At first I was terrified. Then I thought something inside me was going to burst. And when it did," she exclaimed, clasping her crossed hands over her chest, not even conscious she was fully exposed to his view, "I swear I saw stars explode right in front of my eyes."

Ram laughed, and his member twitched to life. Her words were a balm his soul had needed for some time. He wanted to tell her what it meant to him to hear the wonder and joy in her voice and know their coupling was the cause.

Instead, he decided to show her. He eased over her once more and moved his hips.

"Ah, good answer," she whispered.

Hannah woke in the night and was frightened for a moment. She couldn't move, and a heaviness lay across her chest. Raising her hand, she felt above her ribs and found a hard-muscled forearm, sprinkled with soft hair.

Ram.

The night's events came rushing back as she also noted, belatedly, her lack of clothes and sore thighs.

How shamefully she'd behaved, practically begging Ram to make love with her. Not once, but twice. Her cheeks grew hot and she longed to slip away before he woke.

But where could she go? This was her house, her bed. Besides, his arm was very heavy, his hand softly clutching her breast. If she tried to move, he would surely wake.

For a long moment she felt confined and confused. Trapped. But then she listened to the sound of his soft snore and a lightness touched her heart. He tried to be so bad, she thought. And she couldn't deny he was a rogue.

He drank. A lot. Despite his knowledge of the Bible, she'd bet he'd never set foot inside a church. And he associated with loose women.

The last thought made her tense. Surely he didn't consider *her* that kind of woman?

Why not? she thought. Hadn't she acted immoral? Brazen even? How could she have done such things with any man, let alone one like Ram Kellogg?

She stared down at his features, barely illuminated by the thin beam of moonlight peeking between the folds of her window curtains. She could see his full lips, firm jaw, dark shadow of beard, and again her heart gave a little leap.

In that moment Hannah had to face the truth. She might be a lot of things, but she'd never lied, not even to herself.

She loved Ram.

She'd loved him since the moment he'd finagled a seat next to her on the train outside Fort Smith. Her love grew when he staunchly defended her against the mean-spirited old Widow Crumb. And again when he'd needlessly stood up to Doc Collier. But Hannah's fate had truly been sealed when Ram held her in his arms by her special place and refrained from commenting on the horrible shack she'd lived in, and the life her mother had chosen to live.

Even when she'd set fire to the place in a final, desperate effort to put an end to that part of her life, he hadn't uttered a word of rebuke. Instead, he'd left it to burn and brought her home.

And finally, last night, he'd saved her once again.

A shiver ran along her spine as she remembered the man in her kitchen, his evil voice and rough hands. She didn't know what he would have done if Ram hadn't burst in. She prayed she'd never have to find out.

She couldn't ignore the facts any longer. Her tormentor had taken his terror tactics another step further tonight. He'd actually waited to ambush her, and physically attacked her instead of merely trying to scare her, as he had in the past.

She briefly considered going away but knew she'd never be able to do that. This was her home, the only one she'd ever had, and she wasn't about to be chased away from it by somebody with a grudge against her. No matter how terrified she might be to stay alone.

Another frightened tremor shook her. Ram's arm tightened around her, drawing her body closer within the circle of his comforting embrace. One hard, heavy leg slid over her thigh and rested there.

Instantly the trembling ceased. Hannah realized that drunk or sober, she trusted Ram more than she'd ever trusted anyone in her life. She knew, deep down, that he was a good man. Or could be, if he let himself.

She also realized that he, too, had demons that haunted him. She'd seen the signs. A sudden sadness would come into his eyes at an odd moment, or he'd say something to indicate he'd been hurt.

He refused to elaborate, though, always hiding the pain behind a wicked grin or baudy comment. But, Hannah suspected, a man who drank with as much vigor as Ram was drinking to forget something—or someone.

And she still hadn't figured out the mystery of Ram's Bible learning. Someone, somewhere, had schooled him well in religion. Certainly better than she'd been able to teach herself in two years of striving to absorb every detail.

That first day in the alley she'd discovered quickly that she couldn't best him with scripture. She doubted if even Francis could.

But where did a man who drank and caroused like Ram, who was probably a frequent guest of every saloon west of the Mississippi and knew every whore by name, learn so much about the Lord? And why did he detest that knowledge?

"Ha'penny for your thoughts."

Ram's sleep-roughened voice rolled over Hannah, raising gooseflesh on her arms. Her skin tingled and her stomach tightened reflexively.

"A waste of money," she teased, but she heard a distinct thread of uncertainty in his tone. What did he have to be anxious about? She was the one who'd behaved so wantonly. The one whose reputation could be destroyed if a mere hint of such an indiscretion got out.

He would no doubt be heralded as a hero if the men he worked for learned of his conquest over the prim prohibitionist. She felt a moment's panic; then she relaxed again, letting the feel of his hand softly caressing her breast soothe her. This was Ram. She knew he'd never do anything to hurt her.

"I never thanked you properly for coming to my rescue last night," she said, speaking into the darkness and thankful for it at that moment.

Ram let his fingertip swirl a pattern around the sensitive

tip of her nipple, and Hannah was shocked to discover she wanted him again despite her misgivings.

"Yes, you did," he breathed into her ear, raising her passion to a boiling point. "And a finer thank you I've never received."

She couldn't help the tiny giggle of pleasure that escaped her. He was teasing her, like a lover, and she found she enjoyed this banter between them much more than the angry exchanges they'd had in the past.

"I could fix you something to eat. If you're hungry, that is."

"I'm hungry all right," he said, nuzzling her neck below her ear.

Hannah wriggled away a bit and he tried to draw her back.

"What is it, Hannah?"

Again the note of alarm was in his voice. Almost as though he expected her to push him away and dissolve into tears over what they'd done. His hands stilled in readiness for her reaction, whatever it might be.

She should push him away, she supposed. She couldn't. Instead she rolled to her side, facing him, and let her own hands explore the contours of his chest, his shoulders, his sides.

"I was curious, that's all. I wake to find a strange man in my bed. I'd like to know a little more about him."

He smoothed her hair over her shoulder and gently tucked it behind her ear. "What do you want to know?"

Where to begin? Hannah wondered frantically when she realized Ram was allowing her inquiries instead of rebuking them as she'd feared. There was so much she wanted to know, and this might be her only chance to find out.

"Where did you learn so much about the Bible?" she blurted, drawing on the first thought that came to mind.

"My father."

She waited for him to continue, but he fell silent, his hands stroking her skin to life.

"Go on," she prompted, nudging his chest and admiring the strength of the hard-muscled wall of flesh.

"He had a traveling revival when I was growing up. I'm sure you've seen the type."

She leaned on one elbow and stared down at his shadowed face in shock. "He was a minister?"

She felt him shrug. "Of sorts."

"Why, I'm speechless. I never would have guessed. Where is he now?"

Again the wordless shrug, followed by a long moment of silence. "I don't know. Dead, I suppose, though I reckon it's just as likely he's still alive. Unless he started to believe his own chicanery about faith healing."

"Ram, how can you be so disrespectful? To your father, and to the Lord? Of course faith heals. Everyone who's ever read the Bible knows that."

"Do they? I've read it cover to cover more times than I can count. I've yet to see a miracle."

"Ram, you've just said your father was a minister. How can you be so cynical about religion?"

"He had a tent and about twenty chairs. He dragged my mother and me from town to town from before I was born, preaching and *healing* and passing a collection plate. And folks would come and pray and sing and turn over money they couldn't afford, hoping for a miracle. But he was only a man, not a prophet. He was a showman. My mother told me one time before he started doing the revivals he ran a traveling show with a midget and a man who could eat fire. My father fought bare-fisted any takers in the crowd."

He stopped talking, and Hannah felt his body tense beside hers. "Ram? What is it?"

"Your mother."

She'd reached for his cheek, but her hand stilled in midair. "What?" Why was he bringing that up now? she wondered, a sinking in her stomach.

"She might have sold herself for money, but at least she was honest about what she did. My father was a fake, Hannah. All my life I thought he was a saint, the right hand of God. I looked up to him, admired him. I believed he could heal. But it was all a lie. And when *I* needed a miracle, all he could do was cry and say how sorry he was."

Hannah wanted to ask Ram why he had needed a miracle. She wanted to give him what his father hadn't been able to. But it was too late for that, she could tell by the way his tone had changed from disappointment to bitterness.

His father had let him down terribly at a time when it had apparently mattered a great deal to Ram that he succeed. She wanted to know what had happened between them, but she sensed that Ram wasn't ready to reveal everything just yet. She decided she could wait.

"He was just a man, Ram. I'm sure he would have done what you asked if it had been within his power."

"That's the point, don't you see? He had no power. Not the kind he made everyone think he had. He made me believe he had. It was all a big fallacy. God, miracles, faith."

"Oh, no, Ram. You're wrong. And you're not being fair. Just because your father ran a traveling show doesn't mean he didn't truly find religion and dedicate his life to the Lord's work. I'm sure it hurt you at the time, but his not being able to make a miracle didn't mean he didn't have faith. The Lord answers all prayers, Ram. It's just that sometimes the answer is no."

"Hannah, honey, are you real?"

"Don't I feel real, Ram?"

He squeezed her so tight, he threatened to cut off her breath, but Hannah refused to utter a protest. There was a deep need in his embrace, and she desperately wanted to fill whatever void he had in his life.

He was a whiskey-loving rogue, but there was a gentle soul somewhere beneath all the roughness. And a pain that prevented him from seeing the good in others.

Hannah wanted to be there when he opened his heart again. More than that, she wanted to be the one he opened it to.

He released her and rolled to the side of the bed. Hannah felt bereft without him, but she couldn't bring herself to ask him not to go.

She couldn't just let him walk away.

"Are you angry?"

"No," he said, leaning in to plant a deep, hungry kiss on her mouth. "Just thirsty."

"Oh," she breathed, relieved. Scrambling from the bed, she searched the shadows for her wrapper but could only find Ram's shirt. Feeling decidedly wicked, she slipped it on and breathed the scent of his skin that clung to the fabric. He'd fumbled for the lamp, and the sudden brightness brought her back to the moment.

"I have lemonade or buttermilk," she offered, noting that he'd donned his trousers before lighting the lamp. She appreciated his concern for her modesty, but she was a little disappointed that she wouldn't get another chance to see all of him in the light.

Ram eyed the offer with obvious disdain. "Thanks anyway, but I brought my own."

He glanced around, and then his gaze settled on the paper bag he'd given to Hannah to hold when he'd first arrived. "You might want to get a couple of glasses, though," he told her, retrieving the package.

"What is that, Ram? Not liquor?" But she could already see it was.

She was stunned that he would bring alcohol into her

house, knowing how she felt about it. And more than a little hurt that he still felt the need for it after what they'd shared together.

"Well, it ain't buttermilk," he said, removing a bottle and twisting off the top. He held it out toward her. "You prefer to drink from the bottle?" he asked, noticing that she hadn't moved to get the glasses.

"You can't mean to drink that here? In front of me?"

"Why, that would be rude, Hannah. What do you take me for?"

Hannah released a breath and started to smile, thinking he'd been fooling with her.

"I planned to drink it with you." He held out the bottle to her. "Ladies first."

"Ram Kellogg, you put that away right now. I refuse to allow you to drink liquor in my home."

"I brought it for you, Hannah. You said you adored peppermint, remember? It's a gift; you can't refuse."

"I certainly can! And I intend to. How dare you?"

"Just try it, Hannah. Taking one little sip isn't going to turn you into a drunk or make you like your mother. It's just a little refreshment."

"That I have fought long and hard to get banned from this town."

"Only because you don't know what you're talking about. How can you be so dead set against something you've never tried? For all you know, you might enjoy it."

"I won't!"

"How can you be so sure? You might not have thought you'd enjoy sex so much either, but I dare say you've got a different attitude toward that now."

Hannah gasped and pressed her hand to the base of her throat. "Is that all I was to you, Ram? Just another tumble like the many you've shared with women like Sally at the Double Eagle?"

Ram paused with the bottle of schnapps to his lips. He could see the pain in Hannah's eyes, and though he might like to pretend it didn't affect him, he knew it did.

"Hannah, honey," he said softly, regretting the little game he'd been playing with her. He made a show of setting the bottle on the bedside table. "You could never be just another tumble to any man. Especially not to me. I was just teasing you. Forgive me?"

He held out his arms and she went into them, leaning her head against his bare chest and feeling his hands smooth over the tail of his shirt to cup her buttocks.

"You're not going to drink that liquor, then?"

"I'm not going to drink that liquor in front of you, in your house."

"Why did you bring it here in the first place?" She tipped her head back and narrowed her eyes, staring up at him. "What were you planning to do, get me drunk and seduce me?"

"Well, now, I might have done just that, if the thought had occurred to me and the occasion had presented itself."

"But you didn't."

"No, I didn't. You were sensible and saw the benefit in allowing me in here all on your own."

"Sensible?" She shook her head. "I don't know that I'd call anything about tonight sensible."

"Pleasurable, then?"

"Yes, indeed, pleasurable," she admitted, placing a kiss on the round masculine coin of his nipple.

"Delightful?"

"Uh huh," she whispered, nodding as she let her tongue make tiny swirls around the small nub.

"Worth doing over, just to be sure?" He gripped her bottom, and she could feel the hardness behind the straining placket on his trousers.

"Definitely worth doing again," she agreed, wrapping

her arms around his neck as he swept her off her feet and carried her toward the bed. "Just to be sure," she said, before his lips came down on hers and ended all conversation between them for some time.

Chapter Twenty

Ram stood in the open bat-wing doors of the Double Eagle and fought a grin. Here they came, Hannah's ladies, with their painted signs raised in protest. He should be heading them off, but he found he couldn't wait to see her again.

He'd finally had to sneak out of her house as the first rays of dawn crept over the town, and he'd hated leaving her. It had been one of the hardest things he'd ever done. Only saving her reputation, and knowing the importance of respectability to Hannah, had forced him away.

But now she was back, her red hair pinned primly beneath a hideous gray bonnet that hid none of her beauty, though he was sure that was its sole purpose.

"Evening, ladies," he greeted the group as they marched up to the walkway outside the bustling saloon. He thought he saw a pink flush creep over Hannah's smooth, pale cheeks, but she ducked her head quickly, hiding it from his view.

When she glanced back up at him, there was no trace of the soft, willing woman he'd made love to time and time again last night. In her place was the saucy, determined little prohibitionist.

Oddly enough, Ram found he now liked that side of Hannah as well. She had spunk, spirit and a strong conviction in her beliefs.

He still couldn't help but wonder what had happened before Hannah left Blue Springs for good that had left such an indelible mark on her personality. Soon, if their relationship continued to progress as he hoped it would, he'd have to find some way of getting her to talk about that last night she'd spent in the tarpaper shack.

Of course, if he began to probe her past, there was a good chance she would do likewise, and his former life was something Ram refused to delve into. He kept the guilt and bitterness at bay by refusing to talk about, or even think about, that time in his life.

"Good evening, Mr. Kellogg," Hannah replied, trying to keep from blushing as Ram's hot gaze raked her face like a caress. Every detail of their night together burned into her memory, and each time she closed her eyes she could see it replayed.

If she concentrated hard enough, she could still feel the imprint of his hands on her breasts, her stomach, her thighs. She could even smell his scent on her skin.

For hours after he left her bed she waited for the guilt and remorse to attack her. It hadn't happened. She couldn't feel bad about something that had been so good, so right. If, later, she came to realize it had been a terrible mistake, she would face the consequences at that time.

Right now, all she felt were the remnants of the wonder and glory he'd shown her.

"We'd like to come inside for a moment and speak to

your clientele about the petition we're circulating to enact prohibition in Fortune.''

Ram grinned and tucked one thumb into the gunbelt he always wore around the rowdy saloons. So far he hadn't had need of the weapon, but in his line of work he'd feel naked in public without it.

Ironically, he'd chosen to leave the sidearm behind last night when he'd gone to Hannah's house. He wouldn't make that mistake again, he thought, remembering the paralyzing fear he'd felt when she'd screamed and he'd rushed in to find she'd been attacked. He now knew, beyond a doubt, that whoever had been threatening her was not just playing pranks anymore.

The man had taken his threats to a new level, and that worried Ram. He would like to tell Hannah to go somewhere safe until he found the culprit, but he knew she would never do that. Hannah loved her house, and the more the man invaded her home and threatened her, the more stubborn and courageous she grew.

He didn't have one damn clue to go on. Except to search the hands of every man in town, looking for some sign of Hannah's teeth.

But neither was he ready to give up. Not until he had the bastard by the short hairs.

He tried not to think about Hannah's safety because it distracted him from his other job—the one he'd stayed in Fortune to do.

"That is never gonna happen, Miss Sullivan," he told her, forcing his mind back to the business at hand. If he continued to remember their actions of the last twenty-four hours, he'd fold and give her whatever she wanted.

"If you're so certain these men want and need what these sin emporiums are offering, Mr. Kellogg, then why not let us have our say? If you're right, the customers will send us on our way soon enough."

"Ah, but not before giving you a little pinch and tickle," he said, reminding her of their first encounter and the disaster that had been for her group. "And frankly, I'm not sure I'd be so quick to come to your rescue this time. As I recall, you weren't exactly appreciative."

He was certain he caught a glimpse of crimson flash across her cheeks. He fought another grin.

"Nevertheless, we are entitled to speak out for our cause. It is in the very Constitution the great founders of this country set forth as one of the incontrovertible rights."

"Oooh, that's a mighty big word for such a little thing like yourself."

Hannah heard Tabby snicker and saw Agnes poke her in the side. Nan looked embarrassed by the whole situation, while Margaret just stared at her feet.

The other women wouldn't be much help this time. Half had fallen in love with Ram at the Founder's Day race, and the other half were more than a little intimidated by him.

"Insult me all you want, Mr. Kellogg. I will not back down. No matter what sort of tactics you use to divert me from my purpose."

Ram caught the double meaning in her words and rubbed his jaw to hide a sappy smirk. So, the little minx wanted to play word games with him, did she? He looked forward to another round with her. Their banter was almost as much fun as their lovemaking.

And he enjoyed all the things she did with that luscious mouth of hers.

"Mosey on home, Hannah," he told her, silently hoping she wouldn't obey him. If he couldn't touch her, he wanted to at least fill his eyes with the sight of her. It was a view he couldn't get enough of.

"Not a chance, Kellogg," she baited, fighting a grin of her own.

"Are you two gonna stand here all night making google eyes, or are we gonna roust the joint?"

Agnes's sharp retort startled Hannah, and she turned to look at the older woman. Agnes had propped her hands on her hips, her protest sign hanging by her side. The other women peered curiously at Hannah, and then at Ram.

"We—well, I think we should . . ."

Hannah fumbled over the words, not certain what to say. Had she been so obvious about her feelings for Ram? Could Agnes have guessed the truth about their relationship? Oh, that would be dreadful, Hannah thought, truly afraid for the first time since Ram had burst into her house the night before. She'd worked so hard to win the respect of the people of Fortune. She looked to Ram for help, not sure what she thought he could do under the circumstances.

"Mrs. Pearl is right. You can just stop making doe eyes at me. It won't help you get into this saloon or any of the others," he said, giving Hannah a look of bored indifference. "You might as well cut the act and go on home."

Hannah breathed a silent sigh and forced herself not to reveal the gratitude she felt toward him. He'd seen her fear, and just like that he'd read her thoughts. And, as always, he'd rushed to her rescue.

"You can stop us from going inside," she said, forcing herself to sound stern and imperious, "but this is a public sidewalk. You can't stop us from waiting outside and speaking to the men about the petition as they come out. Unless you intend to douse us with beer again."

Ram eyed her for a long moment, as though considering her suggestion, then shook his head. "I'm too thirsty to waste good booze tonight. I reckon you can't hurt nothing standing out here on the sidewalk. Just don't block the doors, don't pray out loud and for the love of Pete don't sing." He pointed a finger at Hannah. "Especially you."

Tabby giggled, and Hannah caught Agnes's grin out of the corner of her eye. Nan flushed and avoided Hannah's gaze, as did Margaret.

"What does that mean?" she asked. She tried to meet the eyes of each woman, but they refused to look her in the face. Finally she turned back to Ram. "Why can't I sing?"

"I don't know the answer to that," he told her, looking puzzled. "All I know is, you sure as hell couldn't carry a tune in a steamer trunk."

"Why, I never . . ." she stammered.

"Nope, and it's likely you never will," he told her seriously. "But don't fret. I'm sure you have *other* talents," he added suggestively, offering her a rakish wink as he returned to the saloon.

Hannah returned to her house later that evening, walking hesitantly up to her back door.

Would she ever feel safe entering her own house again? She hated the terror that met her each time she stepped onto her porch. Her house had been such a source of pride and comfort before. The intruder, whoever he was, had stolen that from her.

"Nice night for a protest."

She froze as the disembodied voice came out of the darkness. Then her stomach settled back into place and a flutter of excitement replaced the momentary fear.

"What are you doing here, Ram?"

"Came to see that you got in safe, without any surprise guests tonight."

"I was just thinking the same thing myself. Thank you

for coming. I hate to admit it, to let a bully like that get the upper hand, but I was a bit afraid of going in alone.''

"Let me," he said, stepping out of the shadows. He approached the door and turned the knob. It didn't move.

"I locked it," she said, pulling a chain from beneath the collar of her dress. A brass key dangled from the heavy silver strand.

"Good girl," he said, reaching for the key and wrapping his hand around hers. He squeezed her fingers slightly and offered her a smile rich with suggestion.

"I'll just have a look around and make sure everything is as it should be."

Hannah followed close behind as Ram went into the house. They filed through each room, lighting lamps and checking every nook and corner. He even peered under the bed and dining table, and behind the drapes in her room.

"Really, Ram, I think it's pretty obvious there's no one here but us."

As he drew the living room curtains back into place, she stopped behind him. He whirled, pulling her into his arms and kissing her breathless.

"Good," he said, when he finally stopped to take a breath. "Because I've been waiting all day to do that and I don't think I could have waited another second."

Hannah gasped for air, even as she realized she didn't ever want him to stop. She, too, had thought of little else but being in his arms again. She'd wondered how she could see him, be close to him without stirring up any more suspicion. Ram must have been thinking the same thing.

"So it wasn't chivalry at all," she teased, pushing against his chest in mock protest. "You wanted to get in so you could seduce me again."

"You can believe it, Hannah, honey," he said, cupping

her buttocks and drawing her into the curves of his body. "How am I doing?"

"Um, not bad," she whispered, feeling the hardness of his body. Her own body grew hot and pliant and she couldn't wait to be with him again in that way.

Lord, she'd never dreamed she could be so wanton. But here, with Ram, she couldn't pretend indifference.

"We shouldn't do this," she said, feeling she should offer some protest, no matter how feeble it sounded.

"Why?"

"Surely it's wrong."

"Does it feel wrong, Hannah? Do you dislike being in my arms?"

"No. I swear I should, but I don't."

"How about my kisses? Do they make you uncomfortable?"

"Yes," she told him. "Decidedly uncomfortable. In a most appealing way," she added.

Ram smiled and cupped her cheek with his hand. "Let me love you, Hannah. I swear I've thought of nothing else since I left you this morning."

"Nor have I," she said, laying her head on his shoulder.

Ram swept her up into his arms and carried her the now familiar route down the hall to her room, closing the door behind them.

Ram let his fingers slowly drift through the hair at Hannah's temple as she rested her head on his bare chest. Their bodies were still moist from their lovemaking, and he could feel her skin fused to his beneath the light quilt. Her body was exposed from the waist up and her soft white breast rested warmly against his side just under his arm, which was draped around her.

"Hannah, I know you probably don't want to discuss

that time in your life. I understand by burning the shack you were putting an end to your past. But I admit to being curious about every aspect of your life.''

"It's gone now," she whispered drowsily. "I just want to forget."

Her nails made slow circles across his stomach, the sensation driving him to distraction. He stilled her movements by entertwining their fingers and bringing her hand to his lips. He kissed each knuckle slowly.

"I know, honey. But I know you were a virgin. I'm a little surprised you were able to escape that kind of life untouched."

"Just because I'd never lain with a man before you doesn't mean I escaped untouched. I assure you, living with my mother I got touched plenty."

Ram could hear the bitterness in her voice, the trace of fear she couldn't completely hide. Anger suffused him that she'd had to endure anything so unpleasant. He never wanted Hannah to suffer, not even in the smallest degree.

And she never would again, if he had anything to say about the matter.

Maybe he should let the questions rest. She didn't seem to be eager to share that part of herself with him. Neither was he eager to get into a discussion of his haunting past. He held her quietly for a few minutes; then she took a deep breath.

"I'd been pawed by more than one of my mother's customers from the time I was about fourteen. That was why I made good use of the window in my room. It allowed me to get out of the house when I heard someone arrive. Especially if they both were drinking. Mama tried to keep me away from the men when she was halfway lucid, but after she'd pass out, I couldn't count on any help from her. So I learned to take care of myself. And that meant staying out of sight and out of reach."

"Smart girl."

"Not smart enough, apparently."

Ram heard the bitterness, and something more in her voice. Whatever had happened that night, Hannah still harbored the hostility deep inside. He wanted to purge her of the resentment that he knew ate at her otherwise gentle soul.

"Tell me. I want you to share that part of yourself with me."

She looked up, into his eyes. Probably searching for some sign of insincerity. What she saw must have assured her. She started to talk again.

"I went home that last night, more excited than I can ever remember being in my whole miserable life. I had the telegram from Francis, which meant a house and some money. I thought Mama would finally be able to put that way of life behind her and we could start over. I was still under the misconception that she drank because of what she had to do with those men."

"That would seem likely. It couldn't have been a very pleasant life."

"No, it wasn't. Sometimes they'd beat her up after. Sometimes they'd steal what little food or money we had. Or leave without paying; that always made Mama furious. But somehow she always managed to get enough money for another bottle.

"That night I didn't know she had a man with her. When I came through the door she looked really glad to see me. I tried to tell her about the telegram, the house and all. She hushed me, and then she told me she needed me to do something for her. I said all right. I always did things for Mama. Going into town, whatever she needed."

Ram heard the tension strain her voice, felt the slight stiffening of her muscles. He stroked her hair until he felt her relax again.

"She led me to the door of my room and kinda gave me a little push. I went in, but I didn't know what she wanted. Then I saw him. It was hideous. He was naked, lying on my bed, on the pretty quilt Doc's wife had given me that year as a Christmas present. He was fat, and all I could see was all that flesh, white and wrinkled. I stepped back, in shock I guess, and Mama was behind me. She gave me another push."

Bile rose in the back of Ram's throat. Hannah's body was shaking and he could feel her pain, hear it in each shaky word she spoke. He wanted to tell her not to go on. He didn't want to know. But he'd started this and he would see it through for Hannah's sake. She needed to get it out once and for all. He was sure she'd never told anyone about the horrible incident, not even Francis.

"She leaned close to my ear and I could smell the sour liquor on her breath. Her teeth had begun to rot and there was always a putrid odor. She didn't take time with herself; sometimes she wouldn't even change clothes for days. I looked at her then, really looked at her. I wondered how anyone could want to be near her like that. But I still didn't understand what she was trying to do.

"She said, 'We need the money. You're young and pretty. You'll make a potful with your looks.' And finally I understood. God, I felt so stupid. I just stood there with my mouth open, my eyes wide in horror and disgust. I couldn't believe she was offering me to that odious man just so she could buy another bottle."

A shudder went through Hannah, and Ram tightened his arm around her shoulders, drawing her closer to the warmth of his body and trying to protect her from the painful memories.

"I yelled something at her. I don't remember what. I tried to walk away, but she grabbed my arm. She said she *needed* a bottle, I had to get her one. She looked so mean, so angry. She said all those years she'd taken care of me by doing *that* with men. Now she was getting too old, and it was up to me to take care of her.

"I think I laughed in her face, then. I'd been taking care of her for years. She might have provided what money we occasionally had, but I was the one who took care of everything else. She slapped me, hard. But I just walked away. I knew she was already drunk. I wouldn't have given her another drink even if I had the money. Not then; not ever again."

She stopped talking, and Ram was secretly glad. He didn't know how much more he could have listened to. It tore out his guts to think of Hannah that close to becoming what her mother had been. No wonder she hated liquor. It was easier to blame the bottle for what her mother had done than to believe a woman could actually try to prostitute her own daughter.

Her story also explained her obsessive need for respectability. She wanted the one thing she'd never had growing up.

"I left right then, with nothing but the clothes on my back and the telegram from Francis in my pocket. I walked to the road and hitched a ride with a family leaving town. They took me as far as Fortune, then continued on their way. I went to Francis, explained who I was. His wife had passed on the year before and he gave me some of her clothes, the key to my father's house and the money he'd left for me. Then he gave me his wife's Bible and told me he'd see me at services the next morning. I went, gladly. Even eagerly. That Sunday, and every one since."

And that explained a lot about the pious woman she'd become, Ram thought. Liquor, or her mother's need for it, had nearly destroyed her life. Of course she'd try to get as far away from it as possible. And how better to do that than by marrying a staid, sober fellow like that dandy preacher.

But Ram knew Hannah would never have been happy with Francis Healy. She had such fire in her, such life. He didn't know what had happened between the two of them, but she hadn't mentioned the man recently. And Ram sure as hell didn't want to be the one to remind her of her engagement.

He had to know, though. Now that they'd become lovers, now that he knew he felt something for her he'd never experienced with any woman, he needed to know if she still planned to go through with the farcical marriage.

And what if she did? How would he feel, knowing she would be lying in Francis's arms this way some day? Jealousy almost choked off the words he knew he had to speak.

"Hannah, I can see how you'd be grateful to that man for what he did. But that isn't love. If you plan to marry someone, you need more than gratitude."

She sighed, and he could feel her breath skirt across his skin. "Yes, I know. I didn't realize it before, but you're right."

"Does that mean you're not planning to marry him, then?" he asked, aware that he was suddenly holding his breath as he awaited her answer.

"No, Ram. I couldn't marry Francis now, even if I still wanted to. Not after being with you like this. I don't think he'd be so understanding about my not being a virgin."

Ram knew he should feel guilt at her words, but he didn't. He wouldn't go back and change what had happened between them, even if he could.

He felt a knot in his chest and tried to breathe normally, but his next question, and more importantly, her answer, meant a great deal to him. He didn't want to examine too closely why that should be true, though. Or why he felt nervous and tongue-tied now. The words jumbled around in his head, and he tried to sort them out logically, in a way that wouldn't seem threatening or too forceful to Hannah. Just in case she didn't feel the way he did.

"What do you plan to do now, Hannah? What did you hope would come from our being together this way?"

She peered up at him again and must have seen the worry in his eyes. Her lips thinned and she pushed to her elbow. Had she misread his concern?

"Don't worry, Ram. I'm not trying to hook you into marriage by letting you into my bed."

"Hannah, I never thought . . ."

"About marrying me? No, I expect not. After all, what could we possibly have in common? Outside of this room, we are still bitter rivals. And if gratitude is not enough to base a marriage on, certainly sexual compatibility would be even less reason."

"Hannah, that's not what I meant. You misunderstood."

"No, I didn't, Ram. And I hope you didn't either. This is all we have. All we'll ever have. Because I might be fool enough to fall into bed with a whiskey-loving rogue, but I'd never be fool enough to fall in love with one."

Chapter Twenty-one

"You should go," Hannah said.

Rising from the bed, she turned her back to him and wrapped her naked body in her worn chenille robe. She took her time fastening the belt so she wouldn't have to look at Ram.

What would he see in her eyes? Hurt, anger? Or the love she'd so vehemently denied? Even she couldn't be sure at that moment. She'd told herself she wasn't in love with Ram Kellogg. She liked him, certainly. He'd come to her rescue more than once, like a knight of old. But she couldn't be fool enough to love a man who reveled in everything she most detested in the world.

Could she?

"Hannah, wait. Let me explain what I was trying to say."

She turned to look at him, lying in her bed. His hair was tousled from their lovemaking, his bare chest a strong, solid wall of comfort waiting for her to rest her head upon.

His eyes pleaded with her not to spoil what had been so beautiful between them.

She couldn't help herself. Her heart softened and she managed a small smile.

"Ram, don't say anything right now. We both need time to adjust to what's happened between us. We need to consider what we're doing here for a moment. I can't live the kind of life you do, nor will I ever want that. You've been a good friend to me, despite our differences, but you can never be what I need in a man."

"Dammit, Hannah, stop talking like we live in separate worlds."

"But that's the point, Ram, we do." As much as it hurt her to think of her life without him in it now, she knew that time would come. He would go on to the next town, the next case. And she would continue her work to close the saloons here and possibly across the country. She had to. Now, more than ever, she needed to hold firm to her convictions regarding liquor.

Because when Ram left, as he surely would, they would be all she had to keep her going.

"We're both here now, Hannah," he told her softly, his eyes caressing her, offering her the comfort she wouldn't take in his arms. "When two people have been this close, they can't be that far apart."

"We are worlds apart in every other way, Ram. I will never tolerate drinking in any man. And I can't see you attending church with me on Sunday mornings."

A cold hardness swept his features, and Hannah knew she'd struck a nerve. She didn't know very much about Ram's past. He'd been very careful not to allow her too close to that part of his life. Now she wondered why. What could he have in his background that could be worse than what she'd told him about herself?

She went to the side of the bed and knelt on the edge, taking his hand.

"Would you, Ram?" she asked, holding his gaze with anxious eyes.

"What?"

"Would you go with me to church?"

"No."

She wasn't surprised. It was the answer she had expected.

"Tell me why," she pleaded. "You know every horrible detail of my past. I know next to nothing about yours."

"There's nothing to tell," he said, pulling away from her.

She was stung by his withdrawal. She hadn't expected him to pour out his soul as she'd done; it wouldn't be his way. But she'd hoped he would feel close enough to her to open his heart a little.

"I told you everything about myself, Ram. Now it's your turn. Share something of yourself with me."

He reached out and touched the curls hanging near her face, coiling them around his finger.

"I thought that's what I just did. If you want more, come back to bed."

"Don't be glib with me, Ram," she said, pushing his hand away before she gave in and crawled in next to him.

"What do you want to know?"

His sudden acquiescence caught her off guard and she couldn't think for a minute. The moment was slipping away, and she knew she had to keep him talking or lose the chance to find out what she most needed to know.

"Why do you drink so much?"

He looked disappointed, but he propped the pillows behind his head and sat up. "Because I like it."

"The taste?" She found that difficult to believe. True, she'd never tasted liquor, but she couldn't imagine it was all that flavorful, considering how it smelled.

"Sure. You should have given the peppermint schnapps a try. I think you'd have found it tasty."

She quirked one eyebrow at him and decided this argument would get her nowhere. She tried another tactic.

"Do you still have family?"

He shrugged. "Maybe. I don't know."

"You don't see them?"

"No, not since . . ."

He stopped, and she felt a surge of excitement. Finally they were getting somewhere.

"Not since what?"

"Not since my wife died."

Hannah sat back, stunned. She felt the edge of the bed and nearly toppled off onto the floor before righting herself. Ram didn't move; he just continued to sit on the bed, his face devoid of emotion.

"You were married," she breathed.

"It was a long time ago."

"You never said a word."

"It didn't come up."

"Well, it's come up now. I want to know."

"There's nothing to know. We married very young, and she died very young."

"That can't be all there is to the story, Ram," she pleaded, scooting closer on the bed. "What happened? How did she die?"

"In childbirth," he said flatly, with no hint of the emotions he must surely be feeling.

Hannah gasped, leaping from the bed as though it were made of hot coals. "You have a child?"

"Had. For about three hours. He died with his mother."

"Oh, Ram, I'm so sorry."

He looked up at her, his features were hard, unyielding. Hannah knew it must be excruciating to talk about such an enormous loss, but he showed no outward sign of the pain he must be feeling.

How long had he kept his feelings tamped down? she wondered. How much longer could he continue without going mad? Was that the reason he drank, to dull the pain? Did he wander from town to town, trying to escape his memories?

She didn't dare ask him. He'd deny it, in any case. Ram was the kind of man who would never offer excuses for his bad behavior.

"Don't look at me that way," he said, propping his hands behind his head.

"What way?"

"With pity. Don't pity me."

"It's not pity, Ram. It's compassion. I would feel that for anyone who'd suffered such a loss." She came back to the bed and sat beside him. "That's a terrible tragedy for you to have endured."

"Well, I'm still here. I survived. How bad could it have been?"

Hannah recoiled from his harsh words, stunned by his callousness.

Then she remembered what she'd just told herself. Ram would never make excuses for his actions, even if he was justified, and he refused to allow her to make excuses for him.

She softened and stretched out on the bed beside him. She cuddled close to his side, and for a long minute he didn't respond, didn't reach for her. Then, finally, he lowered his arms and circled them around her.

He'd suffered a terrible heartache. That explained a lot.

Hannah could see in her mind how it must have been. How he'd come to this point in his life. If he drank to lessen the pain he must still feel at the loss of his wife and child, then he must have loved his wife very much. And

Hannah could only imagine how awful it would be to lose a son.

Her mind whirled with thoughts as she placed the pieces of the puzzle where she thought they must fit.

She knew his father had been a minister. No matter what Ram said, the man must have been dedicated to travel the country preaching the gospel.

It stood to reason that Ram must have turned to God when his wife and child were in danger. And turned away from God when they died, despite his prayers.

It was like one of the tragedies by that English playwright, Shakespeare. She'd never actually read any of his work, but there had been a troupe of actors who traveled through Blue Springs once, doing vignettes from his stories. Hannah hadn't had money for a ticket, but she'd snuck up to the back of the tent and listened to the full, rich voices of the actors inside.

Her heart felt even heavier now than it had that day.

She never should have forced him to think about that awful time in his life. She'd imagined him as always being the brash, carefree man he'd seemed when he'd arrived in town and decided to stay.

She hadn't thought he might be running from something as devastating as this.

Suddenly their petty differences didn't seem so important. She thought she understood him, and it made her care for him even more.

Although it might be a mistake, she wanted to comfort him as he'd so often done for her. She stood, dropped her robe and climbed back into bed beside him. Her lips burned a trail of kisses over his shoulder, his chest, his belly. Then lower.

Ram sucked in a deep breath. He didn't know how his rotten past had brought him to such a glorious moment, but he wasn't one to question such a gift.

* * *

Ram returned to the saloon late, just as Martin was closing up for the night. He took one look at Ram's face and opened a new bottle of whiskey.

"Whatever it is, it can't be that bad," he said, sliding a full glass across the polished bar.

Ram caught the drink just before it reached the edge and crashed to the floor. He downed a huge gulp and waited for the liquor to hit his stomach. When he felt the first rays of warmth seep out to his frazzled nerves, he took another sip.

"Only thing puts a man in that shape is a woman," Pollack said, picking up a rag and polishing the glasses stacked on the bar. "Thing is, I cain't figure who she'd be." He raised an eyebrow, but Ram didn't take the bait.

"You don't have to tell me if you don't want to." He paused, and Ram gave him an irritated glance. Martin just laughed. "All right, I'll shut up. But I'm here if you need to talk."

He went back to the glasses, cleaning each one and then placing it on the pyramid he was making by stacking them behind the bar.

Ram waited until he'd finished his first drink and Martin had refilled his glass.

"Found out anything about what we talked about?"

Martin frowned and scratched his head. "What's that? Oh, you mean about that Sullivan broad claiming she'd been threatened?" He shrugged. "I asked around. Most everyone agrees with me. She probably made up the tale to turn folks against us. You know, by making us out to be bullies and criminals and all."

Ram shook his head. "I told you, I saw the broken window." And the animal blood, and the actual culprit, though he got away. But Ram couldn't admit to any of that without admitting he'd been in Hannah's house. And he couldn't do that without Hannah losing what she'd fought so hard to gain—the respect of her neighbors.

Pollack snorted. "She could have done that herself. Makin' it look like she'd been vandalized to get sympathy."

Ram glared at him, disgusted. "How could she get sympathy? She hasn't told anyone else about it that I know of."

"So how come she confided in you, then, huh? You think that was just an accident? She didn't tell none of her goody-two-shoes friends, but she told you. Don't that seem a bit peculiar?"

"I was there; I saw the broken window. She had to explain how it had happened."

"Yeah, yeah," the man said, bored with the same story he'd heard before. "And you just happened to be there 'cause you was going to talk to her about all the trouble she'd been stirrin' up."

"Civil conversation works with intelligent people," Ram snapped, hoping the man got the full meaning of his words.

Apparently he didn't. "You ain't dealing with intelligent people here," he said, leaning in close. "You're dealing with a female. And everyone knows there ain't nothin' smart or reasonable about them."

Ram knew he should be angry with the man's ignorance, but he wasn't. Martin Pollack was a salty old bachelor who'd worked in or owned a saloon most of his life. The man probably couldn't remember his own mother. And he'd never had any use for a wife. The only women he saw a purpose for were ones like Sally.

Ram thought women like that certainly served a purpose. Lord knows, he'd let them satisfy his own needs many times over the years.

But he thought of his own mother, and Hannah. Women

like that needed to be protected. And he *would* protect Hannah, if it was the last thing he ever did.

He finished his drink and Martin raised the bottle to pour him another.

Ram surprised himself by putting his hand over the glass. "No, thanks. I've had enough," he said.

Suddenly he didn't have the taste for getting drunk like he normally would when a case wasn't progressing the way he thought it should.

"Your call," the man said, putting the stopper in the bottle and replacing it beneath the bar. "Anything else, just let me know."

"Yeah, there is one thing you can do for me."

"What's that?"

"Spread the word. From now on, I'm working for free. Anyone comes up with the name of the person threatening Hannah Sullivan, he gets my pay."

"You don't mean all of it!" the man exclaimed, dropping his cloth on the floor. He bent to retrieve it and continued rubbing the glass he held.

Ram chuckled at the man's shock. "Yeah, I mean all of it. Everything you and the others have paid me."

"But you ain't even finished the job. She's still dogging us like a hound on the scent of a rabbit."

"Well, she isn't doing it inside the saloons anymore. You paid me to keep her out—she's out. Doesn't mean she doesn't have the right to say her piece in the street. You just get the word out. I'll handle Hannah Sullivan and her band," he said. Grabbing the other side of the rag, he pulled Pollack closer over the top of the bar. "And I'll damn sure handle whoever has been threatening her."

Ram left the bar and made his way up the stairs to his room. He was tired; exhausted, actually. Reliving the pain of his past had taken a lot out of him, much more than he'd let on to Hannah.

He smiled, thinking about her. Hannah had taken a lot out of him, too. The woman was amazing. For someone who knew so little about men, she damn sure knew how to please this one. They were good together, as though their bodies had been made for each other.

He opened the door to his room, his hand going to the gun on his hip. He drew it soundlessly and reached for the knob on the gaslight next to the door. Turning up the light, he glanced around.

Taking a deep breath, he replaced the gun. "What are you doing here?" he asked Sally, as she stared wide-eyed at the hand that had held the gun on her.

"I came to see if you might want some company. Business was slow tonight," she added with a nonchalant shrug, leaning back on the bed in a seductive pose.

Though she tried to hide it, Ram could see he'd frightened her when he'd drawn down on her. But he told himself that it was no more than she deserved for sneaking into his room. "I could have killed you," he told her, irritated that he might have done just that.

Again she shrugged. "I didn't realize your senses were that good. You knew I was here the minute you opened the door."

"It's a little trick I learned to keep myself alive when I was tracking killers. I usually shoot first and wait until later to sort out the whys and wherefores."

"Glad you didn't?" She sat up on the bed, and he could see she wore a see-through robe of some flimsy red fabric with puffs of fur at the neck and wrists. She looked like a hideous animal some predator had left behind after an attack.

"Yeah. Now get out."

She laughed and went to the table in the corner where

she helped herself to the bottle of whiskey he kept there. She poured a glass and took a sip, then offered it to him.

He shook his head, and she set it aside.

"Come on, Ram. We're both here and lonely. No reason we can't keep each other company for a while."

"I'm tired. It's been a long day," he explained, trying not to hurt the woman's feelings. "All I want to do is crawl into bed."

"Oooohhh," she purred, sidling up to him, "that's all I want, too, darling."

Ram grinned and set her away. He didn't want her cloying perfume on his clothing, where he'd be smelling it all night. All the way home he'd imagined he could still smell Hannah's lilac soap on his skin. He wanted to hold on to that image a little longer.

"Not tonight, Sally."

"Come on, Ram. Who have you been seeing?"

He eyed her cautiously. Could she still suspect he had his eye on Hannah? Had she already guessed what had happened between them? How could she? He'd vehemently denied her earlier insinuations, hopefully putting any thoughts along that line to rest in her mind.

"You won't play with me, you must be playing with someone else. Who is she? One of the other girls?"

He felt his muscles relax and forced a sly smile. "A gentleman never kisses and tells," he said, touching her nose and then giving her bottom a pat as he gently pushed her toward the door.

She stopped before leaving and turned to look back. Her smile was gone, and a serious look had replaced the seductive twinkle in her eye.

"Careful she doesn't hurt you," she warned.

Ram scoffed. "A big fellow like me? Not likely."

She walked over to him and placed her hand on his

chest. "Here, I mean. Careful she doesn't steal your heart. I've seen bigger men than you broken by a woman."

She placed a kiss on his cheek, let her fingers drift along his jaw and then turned and left the room.

Ram touched his chest where her hand had been. The same spot where Hannah liked to rest her head. It felt full. He could feel the steady beat and see the gentle thumping that moved his shirt slightly in and out.

Hannah hadn't stolen his heart. Not yet. But she'd certainly made it come alive again.

Chapter Twenty-two

"Hannah, wait," Francis said, taking her arm as she stood to leave the church following Sunday services. He said good-bye to the last of the parishioners as they filed toward the back door and then took Hannah's arm, leading her toward the altar.

"Francis, I said I'd stay and help with the supper on the grounds today, and I will. But I don't want to talk about us anymore. There's nothing left to say."

"Hannah, you're being ridiculous. We had a little tiff. All couples have them. It's no reason to act rash, or make impulsive decisions you'll regret later."

Hannah looked at Francis and wondered why she'd thought for so long that he was perfect. He wasn't perfect; he was just a man. Sometimes thoughtless, sometimes kind. Not a saint or a savior.

No better or worse than most of the men she'd known in her life.

"Francis, you have to let this go. I've told you I won't

marry you. I'm not going to change my mind. I'll still help out, just like always. Although you seem to have more than enough help today," she said, motioning toward the small group still milling at the back of the church.

Unable to work in the fields, Rupert had made good use of his time by studying his Bible fervently. And he seemed to have gotten the spirit within him. Maybe because of the accident, maybe in spite of it.

He talk continuously to anyone who would listen about the wonderful things he'd discovered. As though he was the first person ever to find comfort and salvation in religion.

Mary Beth glowed with pride as she stood by her husband's side. Even the children seemed better behaved somehow, dressed in their white shirts and gray knickers, each scrubbed clean and combed to perfection.

Looking at the group, you'd think Rupert was the minister, gathering his flock for one last bit of parting wisdom before they went their separate ways.

Hannah smiled at her fanciful thoughts but couldn't help feeling delighted for the family. Their happiness had been hard won and was well deserved.

"You should make him your assistant pastor, Francis. Or at the very least your song leader. He has an excellent voice, you know."

"Who? Gray? You must be joking."

Hannah turned to look at Francis and saw the derisive glance he cast at Rupert.

"I'm not joking. He could be a big help to you. And Mary Beth knows how to play the piano. In fact, she has one her mother brought all the way from Virginia."

"Hannah, the man is a drunk and a gambler. He's lucky I let him *in* church."

Hannah's heart hardened a little more toward Francis, and she knew she'd live alone the rest of her life before she would ever again settle for less than her heart's desire.

But what was her heart's desire? Ram?

It couldn't be. He drank, hung out in saloons, probably spent time with the women there.

She stopped her careening thoughts and reeled them back in. She hadn't asked Ram for any promises, and she wouldn't. What he did or didn't do when they were apart was really none of her concern.

"Was, Francis," she said. "Rupert *was* a drunk and a gambler. That man," she added, pointing toward the group, "has been redeemed."

"Nonsense. He'll be back in the saloon inside a month. Mark my words."

Hannah turned her full attention on Francis and shook her head sadly. "You have a hard heart for someone who is supposed to be generous of nature and forgiving of others. And you'll never change, Francis. On second thought, you should ask Mary Beth to help with the supper this evening. I feel a headache coming on."

She left him standing by the front row of pews. On her way out, she stopped and offered Rupert a hug.

"I'm very happy to see you taking an interest in church, Rupert," she told him sincerely.

"It's time I started thanking the Lord for all the blessings he's given me, don't you think?" he said, drawing Mary Beth close to his side, despite the unwieldy crutch, and tousling the blond hair of one of the younger boys.

"I do, indeed," Hannah said, offering Mary Beth's hand a small squeeze of affection as she left.

Hannah hadn't missed a Sunday supper on the grounds in two years. But today she felt restless, edgy. And it wasn't all because of the encounter with Francis. It was due in part to the fact that she hadn't seen Ram in nearly a week.

Oh, he'd spoken to her in passing on the street, and she'd continued her nightly excursions to the saloons with the other ladies, but he hadn't come to her house since that last wonderful night they'd spent together.

She knew he was only trying to protect her. Once again, he'd known her fears without her even voicing them. She loved that about him, among other things. And she had to admit she missed him terribly.

As she took another step, she stopped, amazed at her thoughts. *Loved?* Had she really used that word? About Ram Kellogg? Could it be true?

Lord, could she have let herself fall in love with a man so completely wrong for her?

And was it really love?

How could she know for sure? She'd never been in love before, not even close.

But she thought about him all the time, even dreamed about him when she slept. The things they'd done should have horrified her, especially after living with her mother and her way of life for so long. But Hannah thrilled at every moment spent in Ram's arms and couldn't wait for the next time they'd be together that way.

She wanted to fall asleep in his arms and wake beside him every day for the rest of her life. She wanted to give him a child to replace the one he'd lost.

Feeling a moment of panic, she realized she might be expecting at that very moment. She'd had no signs, but it was certainly a possibility, considering all the times and ways they'd made love together.

She felt her cheeks burn as she hurried toward the shelter of her house. Her thoughts were too new, too disturbing for her to take them all in. She needed time alone to consider what they meant.

How could she have been so foolish! Making love with Ram was one thing. Falling in love with him, possibly starting a family and staying together the rest of their lives— that was another thing altogether.

She drew the key from around her neck and started to unlock the back door. But the knob twisted easily in her hand and she felt a wave of apprehension.

How could she have forgotten to lock the door after the terrible scare she'd had? After being so careful for the past week?

But nothing had happened in seven days and Hannah had begun to think, hope, her tormentor had given up when he'd realized she wouldn't be frightened away. Not to mention being thwarted by Ram, not once, but twice.

Going into the kitchen, she felt a nervous tingle spiral out from the center of her stomach and tickle its way to her fingertips and toes. She checked the space behind the door carefully and breathed a raspy sigh when she saw that it was empty.

Nothing seemed to have been moved, nothing was out of place. She stepped softly through the front room, checking every corner as Ram had done that last time.

Hannah was inching toward the hall and the back part of the house when she heard a noise. Someone was at the kitchen door. Had she locked it behind her?

She couldn't remember, and she cursed her stupidity as she quickly looked around for a weapon. Nothing was handy. Pressing herself close to the wall, she slipped slowly toward the kitchen.

The sun was just past the midway point in the sky and beginning to throw shadows. Behind the lace curtains hanging over the window she saw the silhouette of someone approaching her porch.

Hannah ducked and reached for the nearest drawer. Opening it, she felt inside until her hand closed around the handle of a heavy metal meat mallet.

It would have to do; she only had two knives and they were both lying next to the sink, under the window. She crawled on her hands and knees toward the table in the center of the room and crouched beneath it.

She held her breath as the doorknob rattled and turned. The hinges gave a low, eerie squeak as the door was slowly pushed open. Hannah gripped the meat mallet with sweaty palms and closed her eyes, praying whoever it was would turn around and go back out before she was discovered.

The scrape of heavy boots on the floor near her made her jump and she pressed a hand over her mouth to keep from crying out. When she opened them, a pair of denim-clad legs stood before her.

Taking a deep breath, Hannah swung the mallet and caught the man in the right shin. He bellowed loudly and went down on one knee as she scrambled toward the back door. Just as she got her feet beneath her, she heard the man curse. Her hand froze on the doorknob and she winced. Turning back, she faced her worst fears.

"Ram, what are you doing?" she cried, dropping the mallet and rushing to his side.

He was sprawled on the floor, sweat covering his face and his leg drawn up beneath him.

"Trying to think of all the reasons I shouldn't throttle you right now," he breathed, clutching his leg and moaning as he gingerly touched the front of his shin.

"I mean, what are you doing sneaking around my house, scaring the daylights out of me?" she snapped.

"You weren't supposed to be home," he accused angrily, as though she was the one in the wrong. "You're supposed to be at that damn church supper until late."

"I had a headache. I came home early. That doesn't explain what you're doing here."

"I was passing by and decided to check on the place while you were gone. When I found the back door was unlocked, I thought something might be wrong, so I came in to have a look around."

"Ram, I'm so sorry," she said belatedly, kneeling beside him. Placing his arm around her shoulders, she clutched his waist. "Come on, let me help you up. You don't think I broke anything, do you?"

"Smashed it to pieces, more like it," he said, hobbling to the sofa in the front room. Hannah settled him on the cushions and tried to remove his boot. He bellowed like a wounded bull and she propped her hands on her hips.

"I've got to have a look at it. Stop being such a baby."

"A baby! You damn near knock my leg off and then you have the nerve to call me names? Come here, you little imp, I'll show you a baby," he threatened, clutching her around the waist and dragging her down on top of him.

She tried to be careful of his leg, but he held it up out of the way, making a pocket between his thighs for her to lay.

"Now then, what were you saying."

"Take your trousers off," she whispered, her lips close to his. He could lean up a fraction of an inch and claim her mouth in a mind-drugging kiss.

"You're an eager little thing, aren't you?"

"So I can see your leg, silly," she told him, slapping playfully at his chest. He caught her lips and kissed her until he felt her settle her weight atop his body. For a long minute he reveled in the feel of her after so many long, torturous days of forcing himself to stay away.

Hannah pulled out of the heated embrace, reminding herself of his injury and the time of day. It was still light outside, and someone could have seen him coming to her house. One of her friends might decide to stop by on her way home from the supper to check on her.

She rolled off him and stood, straightening her dress.

"You take off your boots and trousers; I'll get the linament and some bandages in case we need them."

He made a grab for her hand, but she skittered away

out of reach. If he kissed her again, she would be begging him to make love to her and never mind the consequences.

She couldn't do that. She couldn't risk someone finding them that way. And she wouldn't risk another chance of becoming pregnant until she'd had time to think through the numbing realizations that had assailed her earlier.

By the time she returned to the front room Ram had removed his boots and trousers and sat on the sofa with one of her petit-point pillows over his lap.

She smothered a grin and knelt in front of him.

"That looks really painful," she said, eyeing the raised lump on his bone and the red, swollen skin around it.

"Thank you, Nurse Sullivan," he mocked dryly, wincing when she pressed around the area, inspecting it closely.

"It doesn't appear to be broken, and the skin isn't torn. You might have a pretty nasty bruise for a few days, though." Opening the jar of foul-smelling linament, she scooped a glob into her hand. She rubbed it into his injury, trying to be gentle.

"Yow!" He scowled and pulled away from her. She gave him a scornful look, reaching for his leg once more.

"Serves you right for sneaking into my house and scaring me half to death. I still haven't forgiven you for that."

"Yes, you have," he said, not seeming to notice her ministrations now. She suspected he'd been playing up the pain for her benefit, teasing her a little.

"What makes you think so?"

"You know I only did it because I was worried about you. Because I care," he said, and her heart did a little flip and then seemed to skip a beat.

Hannah struggled to keep her eyes on his leg, but she was noticing other things now. Like the way his muscled calf felt in her hand, and the sexy little sprinkling of hair across his long, lean foot.

She hadn't noticed his feet before, and she wondered

how she could have missed such a perfect, masculine part of him.

After she finished with the linament she recapped the jar, taking the towel she'd brought and cleaning her hands. The swelling was going down a bit, and she suspected it wouldn't be that bad after all.

"I'll be right back," she told him, carrying the things back to the pantry, where she'd gotten them. In truth, she was trying to put some distance between them before she forgot her resolve and asked him to stay.

That way would lie disaster, she knew. Too many things might go wrong. Things they wouldn't be able to right afterwards. She needed time, and a clear head.

She couldn't think rationally with him sitting half naked on her sofa.

That thought made her grow warm with desire as she remembered what lay hidden beneath her petit-point pillow. Pleasure. Sinful pleasure.

Feelings she'd never felt before, but desperately wanted to feel again. Now.

Who was she trying to lie to? She wanted to go in there and take Ram by the hand and lead him down the hall to her room. She wanted him to stay with her, tonight and forever.

Tossing aside the soiled towel, she lifted her chin and walked purposefully into the front room.

Where Ram stood, fully dressed once more.

Her heart sank and she knew immense disappointment, but she tried to tell herself it was for the best. Again, it was as though he'd read her thoughts.

"If you're sure you're going to be all right, I guess I should get back to work."

She arched an eyebrow and tipped her head questioningly.

"You said you had a headache?"

"Oh," she said, suddenly remembering why she'd left the church supper and realizing the dull pain had miraculously subsided.

"It seems to be gone," she told him.

"Good. That's good," he said, prolonging the moment. He leaned over and kissed her on the cheek. "Lock the door behind me," he reminded her.

"You can count on it," she said, walking behind him through the kitchen. He limped, and she had to smother a small giggle. Oh, he should be truly sorry he ever got involved with her. She had certainly turned out to be the menace he'd predicted at their first meeting.

"Good night, Hannah."

She offered him a contrite smile. "Good night, Ram. And thank you."

He nodded and stepped out, closing the door behind him. Hannah turned the key in the lock and drew the curtains aside, watching him walk away in the fading light of the late afternoon sun.

As she stood staring out the window, the orange fireball dipped below the horizon and the shadows inched across the yard, creeping toward her house and devouring the last dying rays of light.

She stayed that way for several minutes, trying to sort through the mass of emotions overwhelming her. He'd said he cared for her. What did that mean?

Love? Desire? They were very different feelings. With different outcomes.

And what did she feel for him? When she'd seen him lying on her kitchen floor, her heart had ached because of the pain she'd caused him. Likewise, his concern for her touched her deeply, and she liked the notion that someone worried about her. She couldn't ever remember feeling needed, wanted.

Cared for.

Wasn't that enough for now? Did she really need to examine their very new, very fragile bond more closely? Time would certainly sort out the details, for both of them. For once in her life, Hannah just wanted to enjoy the feeling of being in love.

Yes, she admitted, knowing it was futile to lie to herself any longer. She loved Ram Kellogg. God help her, she had given her heart to the very man she'd sworn to fight with her last breath.

She smiled. Admitting that fact hadn't brought the world crashing down around her. In fact, it made her feel lighter somehow. She wouldn't tell him, not yet. There was still too much standing between them—seemingly insurmountable differences that they might never be able to work through.

But if they could, if she somehow got him to see that she was right about the saloons and the liquor, their possibilities were bright. They might just have a chance at a real future together.

Would he give up liquor for her? She didn't know. A few days ago, a week, she wouldn't have thought so. But hope was a funny thing. Love, stranger still. It made you believe in the impossible.

Finally, she turned away from the window. It had grown dark in the house, and she considered lighting the lamp and fixing herself a bite of something to eat. After all, she'd missed supper.

But she wasn't hungry. At least not for food. Maybe she'd just slip into her nightgown and read a bit. She had a book of English sonnets that had belonged to Francis's wife. She'd borrowed it some time ago but had been too busy to read it before now.

It sounded like the perfect end to a very trying, eventful day.

She made her way through the house without a lamp,

familiar with every turn and obstacle. This was her home and she loved it for the freedom it had given her.

The bitter resentment she'd once felt for the man who'd left it to her had long since faded to a dull sense of loss at having not had the chance to know him or share part of her life with him.

She'd missed out on having a father. For a while she'd blamed her mother for that as well. Now Hannah felt a certain peace with her past. Maybe because her mother was dead, and pity took the place of bitterness. Maybe because her heart was full of love for Ram and she had no room for any negative emotions. Maybe she'd finally grown up.

Whatever the reason, she was thankful.

As she went into her room, she felt the hairs on the back of her neck tingle in alarm. It suddenly occurred to her that she'd never checked the back of the house after coming home to find the door unlocked. Ram had distracted her.

Something in the stillness alerted her, and she whirled, certain now that she'd felt or heard something out of place.

A black shadow lurched toward her. A heavy object struck her forehead. She felt a deep, searing pain, and then nothing at all.

Chapter Twenty-three

Ram made his way through the dark streets, approaching the Double Eagle from the back alley to avoid the cluster of men who usually converged on the front sidewalk to smoke and spit tobacco over the rail.

He wasn't in the mood for fun and games tonight. Not that kind, anyway.

Hannah was on his mind, and he couldn't shake the feeling that something had been troubling her earlier.

More than the crack she'd given him on the shin, he thought, though she'd been upset by that. He fought a grin, then wondered what he found so damned funny about the situation when his leg was killing him.

A pile of crates were stacked by the back door, and Ram sidestepped them as he went in the saloon, headed for the back stairs. His foot hit something. The impact sent an empty bottle skidding across the floor and another needle of pain knifing through his leg.

He heard the crash and cursed silently. Who would have left an empty bottle by the back door? he wondered. Damn careless fool.

No doubt it was that odd little man who delivered whiskey to Martin and the others. Snooks, or something like that. They hadn't been formally introduced.

Ram remembered the man only because he'd made such a stink about Hannah and her group busting up his load of whiskey while he'd been filling his plump belly at the café.

Ram thought back to that day.

It seemed like a lifetime ago. He'd been surprised by Hannah's beauty, and momentarily distracted. She'd gotten the best of him, dousing him with whiskey. He'd wanted to kiss the satisfied smirk from her lips, so he had.

Only his plan had backfired. Instead of putting her in her place, he'd found himself at a loss.

If the sheriff hadn't shown up when he did, Ram might have embarrassed himself further. Thankfully, he'd been spared that, though he'd had to deal with the angry whiskey-seller.

Something tugged at his brain and he paused on his way to the back stairs. What had stopped him? A thought, almost there, and then gone. A memory?

No, just a feeling. The kind he got when a particularly difficult case finally started coming together after a long struggle. Worry continued to gnaw at his gut as he turned back toward the barroom.

Despite his own misgivings, Martin had put out the word that Ram was looking for information about whoever had been threatening Hannah. Perhaps Ram should just stop in for a minute and see if the man had turned anything up.

Not that he expected it anymore. The bounty he'd offered was high, and it had been a week since he'd upped the stakes. If anyone had knowledge of the culprit, they'd certainly have come forward by now. Ram assumed it was just a case of nobody knowing anything.

But what had made him think about that now? Was it just nerves because he'd left Hannah alone?

He saw Martin at the bar, leaning on one elbow as he talked to a customer. Ram held up two fingers to indicate the amount of whiskey he wanted in his glass and went over to get it.

"You favoring your leg?" Pollack asked, sliding the glass to Ram at the end of the bar.

"Huh? No."

Martin frowned and scratched his beard. "You sure about that?"

"I guess I'd know if I was," Ram said, motioning for a refill.

"Don't get yourself all riled up. I was just curious."

"Well, keep your curiosity to yourself. Or, better yet, make good use of it—by finding out about that problem we discussed."

Martin shook his head. "Ain't heard a damn thing. Asked ever'one I know. I swear, that broad made it all up, mark my words."

Ram shook his head and sipped his drink. Damn, but he enjoyed a good whiskey in the evening. Did that make him a drunk?

Hannah would say yes.

He absently reached down and rubbed the goose egg on his shin. She was a feisty lady, his Hannah. If he hadn't been in such pain, he'd have made a point of telling her how proud he was that she'd clobbered him that way. At least he knew she could defend herself.

But would she be as effective against someone set on

doing her real harm? He tried to tell himself she would, but the tension in his neck never seemed to let up anymore. And Ram knew it wouldn't until he'd found the man threatening her and put a stop to the malicious acts once and for all.

And then what? his mind asked.

Soon his job here would be finished. Either he would win, or Hannah and her group would. There didn't seem to be any way they could both emerge victorious.

How would that affect the growing closeness they'd shared? If Hannah was unsuccessful in her fight for prohibition, would she give up her ideas on liquor and saloons and accept him the way he was?

It didn't seem likely.

At the same time Ram knew he couldn't change what he was to suit her, or any woman. Not and keep what little self-respect he had. If he altered his way of life to make her happy, he might one day wake up and find he resented her.

He couldn't bear that.

What was the answer? Was there some middle ground where he and Hannah could meet and resolve these seemingly overwhelming differences between them? And if they could, where would they go then?

Was he ready to offer Hannah the kind of commitment she deserved? Would she accept him if he did? She'd made it clear she didn't expect anything from him.

There again, she'd proved she was like no other woman he'd ever known.

Certainly she was nothing like Doreen.

Ram started to push aside the bad memories, as he'd grown accustomed to doing over the years. But something stopped him. Maybe it was time to take them out and dust them off, and then get rid of them once and for all.

If only it was as simple to discard old remembrances as it was to toss out empty whiskey bottles. Just shatter them against a wall so they could never return.

Ram knew the time had come to at least face them. He found he wasn't as quick to shy away from the memories now as he had been. He didn't feel the familiar heaviness in his gut, or the usual stab of pain in his chest.

Hannah was responsible for that as well, he supposed.

For a long time he'd believed that marriage and family would never be for him. His union with Doreen had been a disaster from the "I do's." But maybe that hadn't been all his fault.

Doreen had problems when they first met, emotional difficulties. He'd thought his love alone would help her over them, make her happy. Of course, it hadn't worked that way at all.

In fact, it was his love for her that had eventually driven them farther apart, until she hated the very sight of him. His love. His desire, really.

At least he knew he and Hannah were compatible in that area. More than compatible, insatiable. He'd never felt the way he felt with Hannah before. Never cared for someone else's well-being the way he was concerned about hers now.

And never so frustrated that he didn't seem to be getting anywhere.

"Another?"

He glanced up at Pollack and nodded. "Yeah."

The whiskey was smooth tonight, he had to give the man that. Best he'd had in a long time. Maybe he'd tell Martin to leave the bottle and drink himself into oblivion. Maybe there he'd find the answers that seemed to elude him.

"Best whiskey around these parts," Pollack said, setting the bottle down.

Ram saw that his other customer had left, leaving the talkative barkeep with only Ram's ear to bend.

Not that it mattered. He was too keyed up to relax in his room or even take his usual stroll around town to check on the other saloons.

"It does seem particularly good tonight. I guess I'm just in a drinking mood."

"Naw, it's special all right. Snooks has been working on a new blend. That man takes his whiskey making serious, and he says he's gonna take this one to ole Jack Daniel himself and hit it big."

"That right?" Ram just nodded at the little man's fancy dreams.

"Yep. Says that's why he won't be making his usual run next week."

"How's that?"

"Next week. He come today and said he wouldn't be back for at least a month. Left those extra cases around back. By the way, I was wondering if you wouldn't mind . . ."

"When was he here last?" Ram asked, straightening. He felt the alarm go off in his brain and suddenly all his muscles were tensed like coiled springs. Could he have been that blind? Had the answer been right in front of his face, literally, he thought, looking down into his glass.

He'd questioned every saloonkeeper in Fortune about the threats against Hannah. He'd put the fear into most of them and felt sure they weren't behind the acts.

But why had it never occurred to him that of all the men in the business of selling liquor, none would be more hurt by the saloons closing than that squatty little man, Snooks.

The last attack on Hannah had been this past weekend. The first one he'd encountered with the rock, also on a weekend.

And the search for someone with a bite mark on their hand had turned up nothing. Was that because Snooks had remained out of town a full week, more than enough time for a wound like that to heal?

Snooks didn't look dangerous, had appeared perfectly harmless. But Ram knew by now that looks could be deceiving. And being a fool could get you killed.

Or someone else.

"Where is he now?"

"Who?"

"Snooks, dammit. That whiskey-seller. Where is he?"

"How should I know? He left out of here early this morning." Martin frowned at Ram. "Was you wanting something special?"

"Yeah," Ram said, pushing his glass away. "Answers."

Ram turned and rushed from the saloon, certain he was on the right track. Finally.

As Ram left the last saloon an hour later, some of his enthusiasm had dimmed. He walked along the sidewalk until he came to the rocker outside the postmaster's office. Slumping into the wicker seat, he dropped his hands between his knees and leaned forward.

Snooks had made all his usual deliveries, all right, then left for home sometime before noon.

Ram had been with Hannah later than that and she'd been fine. There'd been no sign of any new threats.

Each saloon owner told Ram the same story Martin had. They all showed him their extra cases of whiskey, meant to suffice until the man returned in a month.

No one reported the whiskey-seller acting strange or upset in any way. No one knew much about the man, but everyone agreed he was just a quiet, harmless old guy who lived alone somewhere and got a lot of joy out of making whiskey.

Maybe he was on the wrong track, after all, Ram thought, disgusted. The little fellow had been riled at Hannah for busting up his booze . . . but then, Martin said he took his whiskey serious.

That didn't make him vicious or capable of perpetrating those terrible acts against Hannah.

Yet Ram couldn't shake the itchy feeling at the base of his neck. It was too much of a coincidence. And Ram hated coincidences.

He needed to see Hannah, to assure himself that she was all right. But he knew he was asking for trouble going to her house this time of night.

It was late; she'd probably be asleep. He'd have to wake her. She'd come to the door tousled, in her nightgown. Maybe the same thin white one he'd dressed her in after bathing her in the sun-warmed rainwater. He felt the familiar tightening in his groin.

It would be better for both of them if he waited and spoke with Hannah tomorrow. There was no hurry, after all. Snooks was gone and wouldn't return for a month.

If nothing happened within that time, Ram would have his answers. And he'd be waiting for the little man when he returned.

But Ram's resolve weakened when he thought of Hannah lying in her bed, her face peaceful in repose. He'd tried to keep away because he understood Hannah's need for a pristine reputation. But he didn't know how much longer he could wait to be with her again.

He wouldn't be able to hold out forever. He wanted her as he'd never wanted any woman. But, more than that, he missed her. Especially the little things.

Her smile. Her laugh. The way she looked up at him

through her lashes like a shy maiden and then loved him
better than any seasoned whore.

She cared for her friends, her town. And she'd defend
them like a banty rooster guarding a henhouse.

If only she weren't such a prude about his taste for
whiskey.

Ram smiled. Even that was pure Hannah. It was a part
of her, a big part. A piece of the puzzle that he now
understood, after seeing where she'd come from and learning how she'd lived. Her fear of alcohol and its effects
were as much a part of Hannah as her green eyes and
glorious red hair.

He couldn't love part of her without loving all of her.

And he did love her, he thought. He hadn't expected
to. Certainly hadn't planned to.

But, he finally admitted with a little flare of hope, he
did.

He was certain she loved him, too, despite his drinking.
Hannah was a good soul, true in her beliefs in God and
the church. She wouldn't have made love with him the
way she had if she didn't love him, truly, somewhere deep
down inside. Maybe she wasn't even aware of it herself yet.
Maybe she was and it frightened her.

She wouldn't want to live with another drunk.

That was a sobering thought. One that didn't sit well
with Ram. It meant he would surely have to change if he
intended to further their relationship. Or she would.

He could always try the peppermint schnapps again, he
thought lightly. But he knew it wouldn't be that simple.
Nothing worth having ever was.

And Hannah Sullivan was certainly worth having. Now
and forever.

To hell with the hour and his good intentions, he thought,
jumping to his feet. He needed to see her. He ached to
hold her. Damn the gossips and the rumors. He loved her,

and he was going to tell her so. Together they would work out the rest of it.

"Mr. Kellogg?"

Ram turned to see a young man strolling toward him.

"Howdy. Daniel, isn't it?"

"Yes, sir," the boy said, puffing out his chest with pride that Ram knew his name. Ram had seen the sort before. A small-town kid who saw Ram's way of life as exciting, thrilling.

"What can I do for you?" he asked, feeling anxious to be on his way but not wanting to cut the boy off short.

"Mr. Pollack said I should come and find you. I was out of town, over to Lone Grove, visiting my ma's folks for near about three weeks. Just got back day 'fore yesterday."

Now Ram was really getting impatient. He didn't want to seem rude, but this just wasn't a good time for the kid to ask for shooting lessons or stories of Ram's escapades. He'd decided to tell Hannah how he felt and he wanted to do it now, before he changed his mind.

"Look, Daniel, maybe you could see me at the saloon some other time. Say in the morning, maybe. I'm kind of busy right now."

"Sure," the boy said, stuffing his hands into his back pockets and kicking dirt with the toe of one boot. "Sure, I can do that."

"Fine. Good," Ram said, turning away.

"Thing is, though, that's an awful lot of money. I'd hate to lose out on it, if you should talk to someone else before then."

Ram stopped, slowly turning back to face the kid. Twice tonight he'd almost screwed up. Dammit, if he didn't get his head out of his trousers he was going to get him and Hannah both killed.

"You've got information?" he asked eagerly, stepping right up in front of Daniel in two long strides.

The boy took a step back, intimidated by Ram's sudden vehemence.

"Ma-maybe," he said finally.

"No maybe about it, boy. Either you do or you don't." Ram didn't try to hide his eagerness. He didn't care how much it cost; if the kid knew something, he'd pay and pay well to know it, too.

"Might be nothing," Daniel said, looking sheepish now that Ram's full attention had focused on him.

"Let me decide that. Even if it doesn't pan out, I'll still see that you get something for your trouble."

"That's right nice of you. 'Course, Tabby said you was awful fair-minded. That ain't all she said, either," he added, somewhat peevishly.

"I was looking for information about whoever was threatening Hannah Sullivan," Ram prodded, frustrated with the boy but trying not to show any displeasure. The kid was a little mousy; he didn't want to scare him off.

"Yeah, I know. And I don't really know anything about Miss Hannah," he said. "That's why I said it might be nothing after all."

"But you thought it might?"

"Yes, sir."

"All right then, why don't you just tell me about it and let me decide for myself?"

"Well, I was out for a walk one night. It's been near about three weeks back, I reckon. Since as I done told you I been out of town."

Ram nodded and forced himself not to grab the gangly kid and shake the story out of him.

"Miss Sullivan was out of town, don't know where to."

Ram did, but he kept quiet.

"Reason I know she wasn't home, I'd been to sit with Tabby on her porch and she remarked how they were supposed to have a march that night but Hannah had disappeared real sudden-like. So Tabby didn't have to march and we got to sit out on her porch swing.''

"Go on," Ram prompted.

"I'm walking home from Tabby's and it's already way past dark. I took the short cut, across that little patch of field next to Miss Hannah's, and I seen this man coming from around the corner of her house. Now I'm thinking how funny, a man coming from Miss Hannah's like that. But then I remembered what Tabby said, about Miss Hannah not being home. I called out to him, something like, 'Hey, you.' He looks up, real nervous like, and then starts to run. I didn't see no reason to chase him; everything looked all right, far as I could tell. I went on home."

"Do you know who it was?"

"Don't know his name. He looked kind of familiar, though. Like someone I'd seen around a time or two before."

"What did he look like?"

The kid scratched his head and shrugged. "It was dark. Couldn't see his face."

"Tall, short? Fat, skinny? Anything at all you remember?"

"Short, shorter than me. And bigger 'round. Yeah, I guess you'd say fat, or stocky, anyway."

"Clothes? Hat? Anything else that might help?"

"Walked funny. Like he was balancing on the outsides of his feet. Not bow-legged, exactly, but not regular."

Snooks.

Dammit, Ram should have known. He *had* been blind, and a fool to boot. He remembered the odd way the man had of walking. Ram had never found any tracks in Hannah's backyard after the attack, but if he had he'd just about bet they'd have shown the outer edge of a man's boot dug in deeper than the rest of the sole.

"You did great, kid," he said, slapping Daniel on the shoulder. "And I'll see you get the reward money. Now, do one more thing for me?"

"Sure, if I can."

"Get Martin from the Double Eagle, and the sheriff. Tell them the man I've been after is the whiskey-seller, Snooks. And tell them to meet me at Hannah's house right away. Now that I know for sure he's the one, I'm not waiting a month to get my hands on the bastard."

"Sure thing, Mr. Kellogg," the kid said, hustling away toward the saloon as Ram started down the street toward Hannah's house.

Finally she'd be able to relax. Soon the threat against her would be removed. She could rest easy in her house once more.

He knew how much Hannah's little house meant to her. And how upset she'd been that all of the attacks had occurred there, stealing some of the pleasure from her.

But that was about to end. Wherever Snooks went, Ram would find him. He'd find him and make him pay for the way he'd tortured Hannah.

The house came into view, and Ram noticed that it was dark. No light shone in the windows.

He'd been right; she was in bed. He paused for a moment, wondering if he should wake her to give her the news. Then he hurried on.

Of course he should wake her. She'd be fit to be tied if he didn't. She told him she hadn't gotten a moment's decent sleep since the first note arrived.

Tonight Hannah would sleep like a baby. Ram would make sure of it.

He eased around the back, remembering the way she'd clubbed him earlier with the meat mallet. If he went bursting in, there was no telling what she'd do. The only solution was the most obvious: He'd just have to knock loud enough to wake her and wait for her to answer.

The door was a black void as Ram stepped onto the porch. Something about that struck him as odd. As he drew nearer, he realized what it was.

Hannah's door wasn't black, or even dark. It was white. And even at night it should stand out.

Unless it was open.

He leaped over the last two steps and through the open doorway, his heart pounding in his throat. A hot wave of panic washed over him and his knees felt liquid. He saw the overturned table and scattered chairs, and a sick wave of nausea gripped him.

"Hannah!" he cried, racing through the house, crashing over furniture like a wild bull. "Hannah, honey, where are you?"

He made his way down the hall to the open bedroom door. She'd taken to locking it at night when she went to bed. It wasn't locked now. It wasn't even closed.

He slipped through the opening and eased along the wall to the table that sat next to the bed. Hannah kept a candle and a small silver box of matches there.

He felt for the box, withdrew a match and lit the candle. Raising the hammered brass holder, he could see the whole room. Could see it was empty.

A large dark puddle stained the floor in front of the door.

Ram sucked a deep breath through clenched teeth and bent to examine the wet stain.

Blood. Quite a lot of it.

Ram's face tightened, his jaw clamped shut. Around the pool of blood were smears, like someone had slipped in the wetness. Ram lowered the light.

Snooks had stepped in the puddle. His boot prints made

half moons on the polished floor, the outer edges more
defined than the rest of the sole.

Snooks was his man, no doubt about it. And now he had
Hannah.

Chapter Twenty-four

Ram held up the light. His hand shook.

In his whole career he had never been on a case where he'd felt true fear. Not once had he ever been frightened for his own safety, even when he'd had guns trained on him and cold-blooded killers tracking him.

But the sight of Hannah's blood spilled on her polished wood floor made him sick to his stomach. And somehow he knew it *was* Hannah's blood. He desperately wanted to think otherwise but knew that was foolish. If it wasn't Hannah's blood, where was she?

Again he felt the need to puke but refused to waste the time it would take.

Drops of blood led him back to the kitchen, where he could now see another smaller puddle under the toppled table. If Hannah had been knocked unconscious, then she'd come to in the kitchen and fought her attacker. That explained the overturned furniture, the smears on the floor that looked like a desperate hand reaching for a weapon.

Ram closed his eyes, but the image of Hannah fighting for her life, trying to grasp something she could use to fight off her attacker, burned into his brain. He remembered her slamming the meat mallet into his shin earlier.

Maybe his coming upon her like that had lessened her resolve. Had it made her wary of hitting first, without waiting to see who she was striking out at? Had she hesitated a split second too long this time because of their earlier encounter?

Ram swallowed hard. He was being ridiculous. He couldn't know what had happened. Because, dammit, he hadn't been here. If he'd stayed with her, no one would have gotten close enough to lay a finger on her.

But he'd let the fear of gossip and innuendo drive him away, leaving her alone, helpless.

"Kellogg, what the hell went on here?"

Ram stood and faced the sheriff, who looked as though he'd been roused from his bed.

"He got her," he said, his voice not quite steady. "I didn't figure it out in time and the bastard got to her."

"Who?"

"I'll be," Martin Pollack muttered, shuffling his way past the sheriff and scratching his head as he surveyed the room, now bright as the lanterns they carried blended with Ram's candle. "I'da swore that little gal was spinning a yarn."

"Well, it's plain she wasn't," the sheriff said. "Daniel said you knew who it was that'd been threatening her."

"Snooks," Ram said, his voice now hard and cold as ice.

"Say what?" Martin cried.

"You sure about that, Kellogg?" the sheriff asked, rubbing his jaw.

"Of course I'm sure. If I hadn't been blinded by—other

things, I'd have figured it out sooner. God, I've been stupid. Blind and stupid. And now Hannah's life is in danger because of it."

The sheriff pushed past Ram and made his own tour of the house. When he returned to the kitchen, his face was grim.

"That's an awful lot of blood in there, Ram. It could be she's . . ."

"No," Ram snapped, spinning so hard that the hot wax from the candle ran over the base of the holder onto his hand. But he couldn't feel the pain or the heat. All he could feel was a fierce emptiness in his chest every time he thought of Hannah's fate.

Why had the bastard taken her with him? If he'd reached the point of wanting her dead, why not kill her here and leave her body behind?

"She was still bleeding when they left the house," Pollack said, coming in from the porch. "There's blood across the porch and some more outside on the walk."

"I'm going after them," Ram said, setting the candle down and grabbing two more lanterns from Hannah's cupboard.

"Now just hold on there a minute," the sheriff said. "We'll get some more men and go along. It's not going to be easy to track them in the dark, and he's already got a pretty good head start."

"You wait for the men," Ram snapped. "I've already waited too long." He hoped that wasn't true, that it wasn't too late.

Martin grabbed his arm. "Sheriff's right. You might be some fancy ex-Pinkerton detective, but we've all got a stake in this, too. Hell, none of us wanted any harm to come to Hannah. We just wanted her to stop harrassing us. Nobody said nothing about murder, but if Snooks has taken that notion upon himself, we all share the blame."

Ram glared at him, then swallowed hard and nodded. "We're wasting time here," he said. "If you're going, let's move."

"See how many men you can round up from the saloons that are sober enough to ride," the sheriff told Martin. "I'd better let Francis know what's happened."

Ram started to tell the man there was no need, that Hannah was no longer engaged to the preacher. That she loved *him*, would marry *him*.

But was that true?

Hannah said she wouldn't marry him. He'd thought he would have time to change her mind, to convince her that they could make a go of it together, despite their differences.

With a sick feeling in his gut, he knew he might never have the chance now.

"I'm going to follow this trail," he said, careful to avoid mentioning it was a trail of Hannah's blood he followed. He had to think unemotionally, keep his distance from the feelings assaulting him, or he wouldn't be able to do his job. And he had to do that, better than he'd ever done it in the past. Hannah's life depended on him.

"Get the men together, fill them in on what's happened, try to find anyone who knows where this man might live or anything else about him that'll help us know what he's planning. Then find me. I'll be wherever the trail leads."

The two men rushed to do their part, leaving Ram alone. He looked back inside Hannah's house one last time. He would bring her home safe. He had to. There was no other option for him; he knew now. He loved her, and he wanted the chance to tell her so.

He held one lantern high, the other low, and closed his mind to all emotion. He was on the trail of a possible killer. He'd done this many times. He wouldn't think about who the victim was. He would think about one thing and one thing only: finding the man responsible and bringing him in. The only difference this time was that he wouldn't be doing it for money. He'd be doing it for Hannah, and for himself.

The blood trail continued for better than a block. Ram's gut tightened every time the light illuminated another drop. So much blood. Could she lose so much and still be . . .

He cut off the thought. *Close your mind,* he told himself. *Close your heart. Don't think, just go on instinct.*

The trail finally ended in a narrow alley around the corner from Hannah's house. He could see the obvious signs of wagon wheels leading out of the back street.

So, they were traveling in a wagon. With Ram riding horseback, that would make his chances of catching them even greater.

Ram fought the urge to rush out of town in a cloud of dust. As anxious as he was, this was not the time for haste. He needed to hurry, but by the same token he would have to take his time and be careful, methodical. Speed was important, but so was accuracy. He wouldn't do Hannah any good rushing off half cocked, only to find he'd followed the wrong tracks.

He left the trail long enough to go to the livery for his mount. As he came out, leading the animal, he was met by the sheriff, Pollack and at least a dozen other men including the kid, Daniel.

"It's like I told you," Martin said, motioning to the eager group. "They all feel the same as me. No one intended for Hannah to get hurt."

Ram noticed someone was missing from the group, though. "Where's the preacher?" he asked.

Sheriff Dobson snorted. "That candy-ass said he was going to stay here and hold a vigil with the women. He's going to pray Hannah home safely," he mocked derisively.

"Damn coward is what he is," Martin said. "I knowed it all the time. He wasn't fooling me with that holier-than-thou act. Sum-bitch don't deserve a woman like Hannah Sullivan."

Ram frowned at the saloon owner. "You don't even like Hannah."

"Oh, hell, I never said that. That gal has spunk, and a hell of a lot of nerve. I might not of liked it, but you cain't help but admire her for it."

The other men in the crowd nodded and agreed, and Ram felt proud, as proud as he'd ever been in his life. Hannah would be surprised and, he was sure, honored to know she'd won the respect of the people in this town. And she hadn't done it by being righteous. That sure as hell hadn't gotten the preacher any supporters.

No, she'd done it by being Hannah. Stubborn, strong, dedicated Hannah.

"Well, let's quit wasting time then," Ram said, feeling somewhat better. They would find Hannah before Snooks had a chance to harm her further. They'd find her and bring her home. To Fortune, where she belonged.

"Your ma know where you're going?" he asked the kid as they climbed atop their horses a minute later.

The boy made a rude noise and muttered a curse. "I ain't no baby," he said, patting the gun strapped to his thin thigh.

"Daniel's the best tracker I've ever seen in my life," the sheriff told Ram. "Better than any bloodhound. Wouldn't want to face a task like this one without him. Why, he's been tracking since the first time he sniffed dirt crawling on his knees as a babe. And he knows the area around these parts better than most."

"That so?" Ram asked. Daniel nodded, and puffed out his bony chest. "Well, go to it, kid," he said, waving his hand. "We don't have any more time to waste." He didn't like letting a boy lead him, not in this, when Hannah's life was at stake. But he knew the argument was sound.

Many times he'd hired trackers or locals to help him with a case, since they nearly always had the detailed information on their particular area. It saved time and lives. And that mattered more than Ram's pride.

"Yes, sir," Daniel crowed, wheeling his horse toward the edge of town. The other men followed with a couple of whoops and cries, Ram in the lead.

Daylight crept over the horizon slowly, as though it sensed Ram's growing anxiety and feared his black mood.

They should have caught up to the wagon by now, he thought, gripping the leather reins until his knuckles turned white and his horse snorted in protest. He eased off, giving the animal some slack.

"What do you think?" he called out to Daniel for the hundredth time. The kid looked up from the ground, rings of purple around his bloodshot eyes, and shook his head.

"I don't know. He had a pretty good head start, but we should've took him easy by now. From the depth of his tracks I'd say he's running them horses pretty good, but they got to be tiring."

"So why haven't we caught up to them?"

The boy shrugged and climbed back on his horse. "Don't know."

Ram heard horses and turned in the saddle to see the sheriff riding in from the east with his posse. They'd split up some five miles back when they lost the wagon's tracks on a crop of rocks. Martin and the saloon owners had gone one way, the sheriff and half the remaining men another. Ram, the kid and the rest had continued on straight.

Now, they were all together again, but still they'd had no sight of Hannah or the whiskey-seller.

Ram's nerves were strung tight. He was exhausted, sore from riding all night and frustrated with the whole ineffectual search.

"There's a hill overlooks a canyon about two miles farther," Sheriff Dobson said. "I say we ride to the rim where we can get the bird's-eye view. They can't be that much farther ahead of us."

"Let's do it," Ram said, forgetting his vow to go slow and proceed cautiously. To hell with caution, he wanted to find Hannah now. He couldn't take the dread, the uncertainty any longer.

He spurred his horse, draining the last remaining ounce of energy from the tired animal and made for the rise he could just make out on the horizon.

As they neared the hill he slowed, and the others caught up to him one by one. They came to a stop on the highest point overlooking a lush green valley with a narrow stream running through it.

It was a beautiful place, Ram thought. Peaceful somehow. Under different circumstances he could see himself enjoying such a place. It would be a good choice for a farm, if a man had a mind to settle down and live out his life quietlike.

The thought was more than a little tempting, especially if it included Hannah and a passel of kids with green eyes and curly red hair.

"There he is," Daniel cried, knocking Ram out of his daydream with the force of an exploding cannon.

Ram tensed, peering down into the canyon.

"Where? I can't see a damn thing," he snapped, searching the seemingly empty area and convinced the kid was imagining things in his excitement.

"Daniel's also got eyes like a hawk," the sheriff said, reading Ram's look.

"There, by the stream," Daniel said, pointing. "He's just gone under that second copse of trees."

Keeping under cover, Ram thought. He must have been visable for only a split second, and yet the kid had spotted him. Damn, but that boy was wasting his time and talents in a hole like Fortune. The Pinkerton Agency would pay handsomely for his gifts.

"Did you see Hannah? Was she with him?"

"I don't know," Daniel said. "Couldn't tell. He was gone before I got a good look."

And maybe it wasn't Snooks at all, Ram thought. But maybe it was.

"Let's go," he said, telling himself that idle thoughts were for later. After they'd found Hannah, made sure she was all right and returned her safely home. He wouldn't even consider any other possibility, he told himself, driving his horse down the steep incline closest to where Daniel had seen the wagon.

Several of the less experienced riders circled the rim to where the slope appeared less treacherous, but Ram, Sheriff Dobson, Martin Pollack, Daniel and the rest proceeded straight down.

As they reached the bottom, Ram hauled back on the reins, scanning the scene for any sight of the wagon. Pure adrenaline pumped through his veins and nervous sweat poured off his skin. Pushing back his hat, he swiped the drops from his forehead and shaded his eyes so he could see beyond the flaming ball of the sun in his eyes.

"I see him, over there," he shouted, kicking his horse into a full run toward the water's edge. The sound of his voice echoed off the walls of the canyon, and as he drew closer he saw Snooks turn, as though in slow motion. Their eyes met for a moment, and then the man stood behind the reins and whipped his horses into a frenzied run.

Ram had him in his sights, though, and he wouldn't let him get away this time. He leaned forward over the horse's neck and pushed the animal beyond his limits.

The stream was just ahead, and Snooks raced along the bank, Ram closing the distance between them. At a shallow spot the man suddenly turned the wagon and splashed into the water. Ram cut through the brush at the water's edge and drove his horse into the icy stream. It was deeper here, and the animal cried out as he sank below the water, but he sprang up again and immediately began to swim at an angle toward the wagon.

Snooks kept looking over his shoulder as Ram closed in on him. The wagon was heavy, the stream bottom soft. He was slowing down, and Ram could see the fear and desperation in his eyes. But he was almost to the other side.

Ram felt his horse shift and lunge as his hooves touched bottom again. The animal charged forward, eager to be out of the stream. Ram urged him on.

But Snooks had reached the other side, and as he rolled onto the opposite bank, Ram saw him struggling with something heavy, trying to pull it up from behind his seat. A rock of fear lodged in Ram's throat. His legs suddenly felt weak and he almost lost his seat as he saw a tangle of red hair fall over the edge of the wagon bed.

Turning loose of the reins for a split second, Snooks grinned at Ram, then heaved Hannah's lifeless body out of the wagon and into the water.

Chapter Twenty-five

The distance to where Hannah disappeared beneath the water seemed to stretch into eternity for Ram. He felt the horse pounding the ground, but his vision tunneled and distorted and he felt as though he was being dragged farther away from her instead of drawing closer.

His heart pounded against his ribs, his blood raced through his veins. He couldn't breathe and didn't care. If Hannah was dead . . .

Finally, after what seemed like forever, he reached the spot where Snooks had dumped her. Jumping from the horse's back, he realized the current ran swifter than he'd first thought. It was only about thigh deep where he stood, but it dropped off sharply behind him and he couldn't see the bottom. He couldn't see Hannah.

He dove beneath the surface and swam in a wide circle, searching. He rose to suck great gulps of air into his frozen lungs. He looked around for some sign of her, the water running in his eyes making it hard to see.

Downstream about twenty yards a flash of red surfaced briefly and then disappeared again. He dove toward it.

With several swift strokes he reached Hannah before the current could carry her farther away. Cradling her, he carried her limp body toward shore. The group had caught up to them and Daniel, Martin and some of the others helped him out of the water. They tried to lift Hannah from his arms, but he refused to relinquish his hold.

He settled her gently on the soft grass near the bank, brushing the tangled mass of hair from her face. He saw the bruise on her temple, the gash that had opened and was bleeding again. His heart stopped beating. He couldn't breathe. A rock of fear lodged in his chest.

"Ram?" Martin's face loomed before him.

"She's going to be all right," Ram said, ignoring the drawn, sorrowful expressions surrounding him. He gripped her hand. Her fingers were stiff, her skin icy. She was cold, so cold.

"I need a blanket, or someone's jacket," he cried.

One of the men tossed him a duster, and he wrapped Hannah in it.

"Ram," Martin said, softly, kneeling beside him and touching his arm. "Ram, I'm sorry, but . . ."

"No. No, she isn't. She can't be."

But Ram couldn't ignore Hannah's stillness. He could feel no breath coming from her, and her chest didn't move as he watched closely for signs of life. He touched her cold cheek and drew the duster closer about her small body.

"No," he repeated. "No, no, no."

He set her head gently on the ground and looked up. Martin was frowning, his expression dismal. Ram's eyes went to Daniel, and he saw the tears rolling unabashedly down the kid's face.

"I'll kill the bastard," he said. "Where's my horse?"

He glanced around as Martin tried to grasp his arm.

Spotting his mount, he shook off the man's hand and raced forward, leaping onto the horse and kicking him forward in one smooth movement.

"Ram, wait," he heard the saloon owner call out, but Ram was no longer listening. He couldn't think, couldn't hear. He could only feel, grief and anger like he'd never known. He saw the wagon racing off in the distance, a puff of dust trailing the cluster of men who had continued the chase.

Ram slapped the ends of his reins against the horse's flank, over and over again. Mercilessly he drove the animal forward, only one thought on his mind. Snooks, that cold-hearted bastard, would not live one hour past the time Hannah had lived.

He saw Snooks drive the wagon toward the canyon wall. The man was trapped; there was no way out without going back the way he'd come. Through the posse, and Ram.

Suddenly Snooks jerked the reins, swerving and turning the wagon sharply. It leaned precariously on two wheels, seeming to hang suspended for a moment, before crashing to its side and sliding to a halt. Ram saw Snooks leap from the seat before the wagon hit, rolling behind the cover of the overturned bed.

The wagon's team screamed in pain and twisted in terror, still attached to the hitch. Their legs flailing, they finally managed to break the crossbar. They sped away, dragging it behind them.

Ram passed up the band of men who'd continued to chase Snooks. He heard a shot ring out and ducked low over his mount's neck. Behind him a man cried out and Ram tensed, certain someone had taken the bullet intended for him.

He rode forward without hesitation, knowing he'd see Snooks dead if it was the last thing he did on this earth.

The man shot at him again and still Ram pushed forward, uncaring of his own fate.

Driving the horse toward the overturned wagon, he felt the spring as the animal prepared to hurdle the obstacle. As they cleared the wagon bed, Ram leaped from the horse's back and landed atop a startled Snooks.

He wrestled the man to the ground, took the rifle from his hands and used the butt to smash the man across the head. Snooks went down, blood splattering the ground and the front of Ram's clothes. The rifle slid out of his hands and he gripped Snooks by the shirt and pummeled his bloody face with his fists.

"Ram! Ram, stop it!" a voice cried out. Footsteps pounded in his ears, but Ram couldn't stop himself. Even when heavy hands dragged him backward, off Snooks, Ram struggled to fight off the restraining hold. Other hands soon joined in, and he finally released the man, letting Snooks drop to the ground, bloody and beaten.

"Why did you stop me?" he shouted, shoving through the group of men gathered around him. "Why didn't you let me kill him?" He drew his gun and aimed it at the man on the ground.

"Stop it, Ram." Ed Pearl gripped his hand and shoved it down, pointing the gun harmlessly at the ground. "Listen to me. Hannah's not dead," the man told him.

"What? What are you saying?" he repeated numbly, searching the faces of the group. "But I saw her, I held her. She was so cold."

"It gets awfully cold out here at night. Snooks must've had her in the bed of that wagon with no cover all night. She was near frozen before he tossed her in the drink, and that water's like ice. We just sat her up and forced some water out of her, and she coughed and started right up breathing again."

For a long moment Ram couldn't comprehend the words. "All that blood, at her house?"

"Head wound. Bleed like the dickens, even when they're not as bad as hers."

"Hannah," Ram whispered.

Ed nodded. "Is alive, yes."

Ram met the solemn gaze, saw something there. "What is it? Something's wrong."

"That shot Snooks took at you . . ." he said.

"Yeah?"

"It hit Sheriff Dobson. He wasn't so lucky," he told Ram grimly.

Ram struggled against the urge to rip Snooks's throat out right there on the spot. He knew that wasn't the answer, though. Right now he wanted—no, needed, to see Hannah.

"And for that, among other things, I'll see him hang," he told the other men. "Ed, tie him up. Good and tight."

Leaving the group trussing Snooks up like a Thanksgiving turkey, Ram started back toward the stream. He saw four or five men gathered around the still body of Sheriff Dobson and Ram went to them. The sheriff lay still, the front of his vest covered with blood.

Ram had liked Dobson the first time he'd met him. He was a good man, honest and dedicated as the day was long. He'd be missed, and for a second Ram wondered who could ever fill the man's shoes.

He patted Daniel on the shoulder. "Wrap him up and put him over his horse's back. We'll take him home and give him the hero's burial he deserves."

"Yes, sir," the kid muttered, his voice watery with emotion.

Ram hurried back to Hannah and found her lying by the water's edge where he'd left her. Martin Pollack and several of the other saloon owners were gathered around her. He felt fear choke him, and a cold finger of dread raced up his spine.

Had Ed Pearl been wrong about her being alive? Could the man have made a mistake?

She was still in the position in which he'd set her when he'd gone after Snooks. The only difference being, someone had rolled a jacket and placed it beneath her head.

"Martin?"

"She's alive, Ram. Breathing is still shallow," he admitted, "but she's definitely alive."

Ram knelt by her side and took her hand. It did indeed feel softer, warmer, than when he'd pulled her from the stream. He stroked her hair back and saw the gash on her forehead drip blood.

She *was* alive, he thought, awash with relief. If her heart hadn't been beating, there wouldn't have been blood coming from the wound on her head. He felt foolish for missing that the first time.

"Let's see if we can get that wagon set right," he called over his shoulder. "We need it to get her back to town, as soon as possible."

Hannah woke, swimming up from a deep blackness. Her head throbbed, her body ached and her eyes felt gritty and heavy-lidded.

"Morning, Hannah, honey," a deep, husky voice spoke close to her ear. She struggled through a fog, trying to find that voice and the man she knew it belonged to.

"Ram?"

"Right here, darling," he said. "Just open those beautiful green eyes and have a look for yourself."

She did as he suggested and smiled as his familiar features came into focus before her. Then she glanced around at the room she was in and frowned.

"Where am I?"

He looked sheepishly around at the bare walls, the single modest chest of drawers and bedside table.

"My room, at the saloon," he said, eyeing her with unease. She opened her mouth in shock and tried to sit up.

Ram pushed her back down on the bed and rushed on. "The doctor's place is full of kids with chicken pox, and no one knew if you'd ever had them. Your place is something of a mess, and I haven't had a chance to get over there and straighten it up, what with you being out all this time. Besides, I didn't think it would be proper for me to stay there with you, and I wanted you close by, just in case."

"In case of what?" she asked, arching one eyebrow. She winced at the stiffness in her forehead.

"In case I felt the need to look at you and assure myself you were really safe," he told her, his words rippling over her like a soft caress. He took her hand and pressed it to his cheek.

How could Hannah argue with logic like that?

"You need a shave," she said, smiling softly. Just the touch of his hand made her feel better.

He laughed lightly and stroked his jaw. "Yeah, I've been kind of busy the last couple of days."

"Couple of days?"

He nodded. "Brought you back Monday night. This is Wednesday."

"I've been unconscious for three days?"

"Near about that, best we can figure. We can fill in the details later, when you're up to it."

"There's a lot you'll have to fill in for me," she told him. "I don't remember anything after that man grabbed me in my bedroom."

Ram nodded, his mouth forming a grim line as he thought back over the hours since he'd discovered Hannah missing Sunday night. "That's probably a good thing," he said. "How do you feel other than the hole in your memory?"

"My head hurts."

Again he nodded, not trusting his voice to sound steady. He cleared his throat. "That's only natural. Doc Collier put twenty stitches in your head where Snooks beaned you with the whiskey bottle."

"Doc Collier. What's he doing here?"

"I wired him Monday evening when we brought you back. That other young doctor said you had a crack in your skull and might never wake up. Collier rode all night to get here, stitched you up real good so there'd be less chance of a bad scar and has been here ever since, waiting for you to wake up. He never had any doubt you'd be fine. He's just outside. Do you want me to fetch him?"

"In a minute," she said. Her eyes sought his gaze and held it, heat and something else reaching out to him. Could it be love? he thought.

"You saved my life, though, didn't you? You rescued me again." It wasn't a question; it was a statement made with certainty.

"With a little help from your friends."

"My friends?"

"Martin Pollack, Dewey Miles and Frank Long, among others."

"The saloon owners?" She gasped.

Ram grinned. "Every one of them. Plus Daniel Dowd, Ed Pearl and most of the men in town. Rupert Gray wanted to go along, but what with his broken leg, he knew he'd just slow us down."

Hannah leaned back against the snowy pillow and sighed. "I can't believe it. They all came to my rescue. Even the ones who hated me so?"

"No one hated you, Hannah. Except maybe Snooks."

"The whiskey-seller?"

"One and the same."

"He was the one responsible for the threats? The broken window, the bucket of blood, all of it?"

"Every last trick," he told her.

Hannah shivered as she remembered the struggle in her kitchen. Pieces were coming back to her now.

"Where is he? Did you . . . ?"

"Kill him? No, but I would have if Martin hadn't stopped me."

"I have something else to thank Martin Pollack for," she said, sounding less than enthusiastic about the prospect. It would be difficult for Hannah to continue her efforts to destroy these men's livelihoods when they'd risked their lives to save her.

"I reckon. Snooks is awaiting the federal marshals, who're right happy that he's finally been found and captured. Apparently our Mr. Snooks has been hiding out from the law for some time. Which explains his shyness, and the fact that he's been living in seclusion north of here, happily making whiskey and remaining anonymous."

"You mean he's a wanted criminal?"

"Wanted from Carolina to Texas on every sort of warrant, from crimes committed following the War between the States, when he rode with a band of marauders, to a train robbery just a few years back led by a most unsavory character named John Wesley Hardin."

"My word," Hannah breathed, a shiver running down her spine. She trembled. "But why did he kidnap me? Why not just kill me when he had the chance?"

Ram looked uncomfortable, and Hannah knew he didn't want to answer her. She hadn't really thought about it; the question had just popped into her mind. Now she was desperate for an explanation.

"Ram, tell me. I have a right to know."

"He felt you owed him, Hannah. You'd cost him a bit in sales, not to mention the whiskey you destroyed in the alley that day. He wasn't a nice man, honey. And he had some pretty unsavory friends, whom the Pinkertons should be closing in on right about now. He planned to sell you to the highest bidder to recoup what he felt you owed him. That is, after he was finished with you."

Another icy shiver racked her body, and she closed her eyes as she thought how close she'd come to that fate. Ram had truly saved her, once again.

"All that business about being gone a month to try and sell his whiskey was just a ruse. He never planned to come back here. He sold his entire stock to the saloons. With that money, and what he planned to get from selling you, he and his friends figured they could get far enough away that they'd never have to worry about being caught."

"That's incredible," Hannah said when she could finally find her voice. "And yet you were able to catch him."

"Well, not me alone. In fact, Daniel Dowd will be getting the reward money the marshals had posted on Snooks's head."

"Daniel? That's wonderful. But how."

"He was the one who tracked Snooks after he left town with you."

"Sure," she said, a knowing smile on her pale lips. "Daniel can track better than most hunting dogs. But rewards usually go to the sheriff. How'd he beat Sheriff Dobson out of a prize like that?"

Ram glanced down at his hands, clasped between his knees. He'd dreaded this moment, telling Hannah about the one friend she'd had who'd given everything to get her back safely. He looked into her bright green eyes and shook his head. He saw her swallow hard, the emerald orbs obscured by a sudden flood of tears.

"Oh, no," she cried, pressing her hand to the bandage

covering her forehead. Pain radiated out from behind her eyes as she tried to hold back her sobs. "How?"

"Snooks took a shot at me. I ducked; Dobson didn't," he said with grim finality.

Hannah could only shake her head and cry silently. She'd had a run-in or two with the sheriff because of her protests, but he'd always been a decent, fair man who loved this town and watched over its people like they were family.

Hannah wasn't surprised he'd given his life for her. But she was desperately sorry he'd had to.

"He cared for you a great deal," Ram said. "Everyone in this town does, Hannah. You would have been proud of the way they stood up for you, every last one of them."

Except the preacher, he thought, remembering Francis's cowardice with a barely suppressed sneer. The man had lost a lot of points with the people of Fortune when they found out he'd been unwilling to join the search for Hannah.

Somehow, Ram thought, the Reverend Healy probably wouldn't be around much longer.

"He was the best sheriff," Hannah sniffed, wiping at the tears on her cheeks. "I don't know who we'll get to replace him."

Ram cleared his throat, clasped his hands and let his eyes wander back to the floor.

"The town has already taken a vote on that," he told her. She saw him reach up and flip the lapel of his jacket back. A bright silver star surrounded by a circle was pinned to his chest.

Chapter Twenty-six

Hannah gasped and pressed her hand over her mouth. She couldn't help the small chuckle that escaped.

"You?" she cried. "They made you the sheriff?"

"Well, don't act so surprised," he said, feeling slightly offended by her shock. "I think I'll make a fine sheriff. Besides, you're not the only one who cares about the people of this town."

"Do you mean that, Ram?" she breathed, touched to the very core of her heart.

"Sure, I mean it. I wouldn't have agreed to wear this thing if I didn't. It isn't like I set out to wind up the sheriff of a little hole like Fortune, Oklahoma. But I can see when something is just meant to be."

"You were meant to be sheriff?"

"I was meant to stay here," he said, holding her gaze.

"And why is that?" she asked, breathless now for another reason.

He leaned forward and took her hand. "Because this is

your home, Hannah. And I would never ask you to leave it."

"What are you saying?"

He placed a kiss on her knuckles, still showing signs of the fight she'd given Snooks in her kitchen. No doubt a few drops of the blood on her floor belonged to him.

"That I want to stay here with you."

A warm sense of peace and contentment flowed through Hannah. She hadn't expected a proposal of any kind from Ram. The differences between them were vast.

But, she saw now, this moment had been inevitable since the first time he kissed her in the alley. She'd known at that moment that no one else ever had, or ever would, make her feel so alive.

"What about the saloons?"

"I don't work for them anymore."

"What about your taste for alcohol? You know better than anyone why I can't—I won't—live that sort of life again."

He took her hand in his and gazed into her eyes, his expression grave. "I can promise you this, Hannah, honey. You will never see me drunk. Not in our home, not on the street, not in a saloon. Never. If," he added, a mischievous gleam in his eye, "you promise not to nag me when I occasionally want a whiskey after dinner in the evenings."

Hannah quirked one eye, winced when it pulled at her wound and then forced a half smile. "I suppose I could live with a compromise like that."

"Then it's settled? You'll marry me?"

She lowered her eyes to their clasped hands and a single tear rolled down her cheek. "Just one more thing, Ram," she said, looking up at him through her lashes the way he loved so much.

"Anything, darling."

"Tell me about your wife."

He sucked in a gasp and instinctively pulled his hand away. Hannah reached for it and closed it between both of hers. "I want you to be able to share everything with me, Ram—the good and the bad. The same way I've shared everything about my past with you."

He stared into her eyes and felt the knot of tension in his stomach uncoil. It was something he never wanted to think about, much less speak about. But somehow, here with Hannah, it didn't seem so hard anymore.

He eased himself onto the bed alongside Hannah, stretching out his legs along the length of hers and putting his arm around her shoulders. He settled her head on his chest, just the way she liked.

"I suppose that's only fair," he said finally. "Her name was Doreen, and I met her when I was nineteen."

Ram talked about their first meeting at one of his father's tent revivals. Doreen had come with a friend of hers, and they sat in the front row, enthralled by the whole event. Afterward she'd tried to sneak into his father's tent to meet him. Ram had caught her, and they'd gone to his tent instead, where they stayed up all night, talking.

"I knew she was high-strung," he said sadly. "But at the time I thought my own levelheadedness would balance the scales."

It hadn't. They'd been inseparable for the three days the revival had been in her town. When they left, she went with them as Ram's new wife.

"In three days? You must have loved her very much." She must have been something wondrous, indeed, Hannah thought jealously.

"I was on the edge of manhood, desires raging. She was very pretty, and her vulnerability made me feel strong and needed. I was totally infatuated with her, but that wasn't love. Not real love.

"The first time we made love wasn't easy for Doreen,"

he told her. "I thought it would get better between us with time."

Hannah frowned, confused. "Do you mean it wasn't . . ." She couldn't go on.

"Wasn't good? That's exactly what I mean."

"But how could that be?" she asked. Then she realized what she'd said and flushed with embarrassment. "I just thought it was always like . . ."

"Like it was for you and me?"

"Yes."

"It isn't. What we share, Hannah, is something special. People dream of having what we have. I dreamed of having that with Doreen. But it never happened. She hated making love. The more we did it, the deeper she sank into her Bible and her prayers and her sackcloth and ashes. I would find her, afterward, kneeling on the hard ground, praying for forgiveness. It just about killed me. It finally killed her."

"Ram! Don't say that."

"It's the truth, Hannah. She would rail at me, screaming and saying sex was the devil's deed. Her tears made me feel barbaric. She hated it so, I finally quit going to her at night. For almost a year I lived celibate. And then one night we argued. I told her it was her duty as my wife, and she submitted. It was horrible. I felt sick. She just lay there and cried. That was the last time."

Hannah bit her lip and tried not to cry. She could hear the pain in Ram's voice, feel the tenseness in his body beside hers. She considered herself a religious person, but she couldn't imagine anyone being this close to Ram and not wanting to make love with him. Lord knew, she did.

It wasn't a sin, she thought. Love like that was a gift.

"I thought that was the worst night of my life," he said, the flat tone making her stiffen in fear of what he was about to say. "But then she learned she was pregnant. I was both happy and horrified, not certain what she would do. She worsened quickly, turning into some sort of fanatical zealot. She lost weight, a lot of weight. Her hair was limp and thin, her eyes always tinged with purple shadows. She looked like death. I knew something was brewing, that it would all come to a head before long. It happened when she went into labor."

He took a deep breath, and Hannah heard the raggedness of it as it trembled through his lungs. As though the simple act of breathing was now painful to him.

"She went berserk, threw herself down the stairs, screaming about the baby being the spawn of Satan. She was trying to kill my child, I suppose, and herself. I went to her, trying to calm her, but she struck out at me, clawing my face and cursing me. I sent for a doctor, and he strapped her to the bed to keep her from hurting herself or anyone else. I listened to her scream like that for nearly nine hours before her labor became too intense for such histrionics. She gave birth to my son, who lived only three hours. Doreen didn't live that long; she died cursing my name with her last breath."

Hannah didn't try to stop the flow of tears coursing down her cheeks. How could a mind be so terribly twisted? she wondered. A woman so mad?

"She said God would punish me for what I'd done to her," he said at last. "And she was right. He's been punishing me ever since by letting me live with the memory."

"Oh, Ram, God isn't punishing you. Your wife was ill. She wasn't right."

"I understand she wasn't responsible for her words or her actions. But she didn't deserve to die that way, and I *was* responsible for it. I caused that, and my guilt is the hell I've lived with."

Hannah pressed a warm kiss to his chest and wrapped her arms tightly around his waist. "Sometimes terrible things happen, and there is no underlying message or lesson. I don't pretend to have all the answers. Lord knows, there have been times I wanted to rail at Him for some of the awful things in my own life. But I finally came to understand that He isn't responsible for everything we face in our lives. The Bible says He will never forsake us, and that I do believe. He has gotten me through the worst times imaginable."

"You got yourself through them, Hannah. Your strength and your fortitude."

"Yes, and where did I get those things?"

"From inside yourself."

"No, silly, from faith. *Faith is the substance of things hoped for.*"

"You truly believe that?"

"I do."

He hugged her close and pressed a kiss to the top of her head, mindful of the bandage and the wound beneath.

"You are an amazing lady, Hannah Sullivan. And you still haven't answered my question," he reminded her, deciding it was time to change the subject and continue the discussion they'd been having prior to this unpleasant trip through his past.

He held his breath as he waited for her answer. What had Hannah said that other time, in her room after they'd made love? God answers all prayer; sometimes the answer is no.

"And you have yet to ask it. Properly," she added with a smile.

"Hannah Sullivan," he whispered, his lips close to her ear, his arms embracing her, "more than anything in this world I wish for you to be my wife."

She turned to face him, holding his gaze with tear-filled eyes. "Ramsey Kellogg, it would be my honor and my pleasure," she said, closing the distance between them and placing her lips over his.

And sometimes, Ram thought with a smile, *the answer is yes.*

Ram rolled her gently onto her back and deepened the kiss, his hands touching her body, memorizing every curve. He cupped her face and let his tongue search for the sweetness he'd craved since first kissing her.

She drew back slightly and let her hands roam over his back. "You know," she said softly, a wicked gleam in her eye, "I'll want to be married in church."

"And you know I have vowed never to set foot in one again," he told her, meeting her intense gaze with one of his own. One filled with longing, but also with steadfast resolve.

She let her hand trail lightly over his side, his ribs, his chest. She found the hard, round medallion of his nipple and circled it with one smooth finger. Ram sucked in his breath and tensed.

"I think it's time for another negotiation," she said. "I'm sure if we put our heads together, we can settle this dilemma as we have all the others."

"I don't think it's our heads we've used to overcome the obstacles between us, Hannah, honey. I think the solution can be found considerably south of there."

Hannah lowered her hand and found just the right tool she needed for the process to begin.

Chapter Twenty-seven

Hannah twisted the ribbons trailing from the bow on the bodice of her new blue dress and tugged impatiently at the waistband.

"Hannah, honey," Ram whispered, leaning over in the pew, "stop fidgeting."

"I can't help it," she said, blowing the stray hairs off her forehead with a tired sigh. "Who would have thought a man like Rupert Gray would turn out to be such a long-winded preacher?"

Ram held the hymn book higher, muffling their voices. "You are the one who nominated him for the job, darling," he needlessly reminded her.

"What choice did we have after Francis Healy ran out on us? I blame whoever gave him that little tip about tent revivals being so profitable."

"Is it my fault the man inquired into my past? I only mentioned how a good preacher might earn a few just rewards here on earth."

"And what about poor Daniel? What do you have to say for yourself there, husband dear?"

"Now you certainly can't blame that on me. You knew Tabby Reid had been keeping company with the rev ever since the night of the vigil."

"I thought she'd found the Lord. How was I supposed to know she'd decide to run off with him like that?"

"Well, I still say Daniel is better off. A girl like that would never have been happy living in Fortune the rest of her life. Besides, I have it on good authority that a certain vice-president of the Pinkerton Agency is interested in interviewing that young man for a job when he passes through this way next month."

Hannah's eyes lit with excitement. "Ram, do you mean it? You managed to get him the job?"

He pressed a finger over her lips to silence her and smiled at the older lady glaring daggers at them across the aisle.

"I got him an interview," he said. Then he grinned. "But I'm sure the position will be offered to him. They'd be fools not to take him on, even though he is a little young."

"That will put the sparkle back in his eye for sure," she breathed. "Imagine, our Daniel, a Pinkerton man." Her sigh was soft and seductive, and Ram gazed down into her half-closed eyes.

"Had I known you were so besotted by the title, I would have continued my affiliation with them," he teased.

"Oh, no," she said, her eyes going wide. "You are needed here in Fortune. Doing exactly what you've been doing these last six months."

"And what is that?"

"Protecting this town and its citizens. And coming home every night to make love to your wife."

Ram turned away from the heat in her gaze, tugging at his collar.

"Damn, Rupert Gray," he mumbled, a strained look on his face as he turned toward the pulpit. "Is he ever going to run out of wind?"

Hannah stifled a giggle and lifted her hymn book higher.

When the service was finally over she filed out into the aisle with the rest of the townsfolk, Ram close behind her. They slowly made their way to the back of the church, where Rupert and Mary Beth stood shaking hands with the congregation as they passed.

The minister glanced up and saw Hannah and Ram, and the smile momentarily left his face.

"Rupert," Hannah greeted him, shaking his hand. "I mean Reverend Gray. That was a fine sermon today. Most inspiring."

"Do tell," he said, holding her hand when she would have drawn it away.

Hannah frowned and tugged gently, but she was well and truly caught.

"And how about you, Mr. Kellogg? What did you think of my sermon?"

Ram rubbed his jaw and tried to cover his grin. "As lengthy a dissertation on the Commandments as I can ever remember hearing," he said, a bit too honestly.

Rupert shook his head. "I do believe your husband is having a negative influence on your participation in weekly services, Hannah. I kept hearing the most annoying chatter coming from that second pew."

Hannah's smile faded. "I'm sorry, Rupert," she said, nudging Ram in the ribs as he prodded her toward the door. "I'll try to be more attentive next Sunday."

She and Ram hurried for the door, making their escape. They clasped hands and sped across the churchyard, racing eagerly for home.

Once inside, Ram immediately reached for the buttons lining the front of Hannah's bodice. She tugged at the fastening on his trousers and slid his arms out of his black frock coat.

They were both nude before they reached the bedroom, and they fell across the bed, kissing and clutching and making love with the abundant passion that never seemed to decrease in intensity.

It was nearly an hour later when Hannah's breathing calmed enough for her to speak.

"Rupert thinks you've corrupted me, Ram. He as good as said so today."

"Does that bother you, Hannah, honey?"

"Well, I have all but given up on closing the saloons. But that has a lot to do with not wanting to hurt the men who saved my life. Besides, I've kind of lost my zeal for the cause since we married, and I can see now that everyone who drinks isn't necessarily an abusive drunk. Besides," she added, "he could have at least acknowledged the fact that you've been by my side throughout his extensive sermons for the last four Sundays in a row."

"That's true."

"And that's no small victory, either," she declared, propping herself on one elbow as she turned to face him, her breasts pressing against his chest and her legs still entwined with his. "I don't have time to save the whole town. I have my hands full just trying to save you."

"I am a handful," he admitted. "And your little triumphs have been hard won," he said with a wicked grin.

Hannah slapped playfully at his chest. "That's not funny, Ram. Is it my fault I had to compromise just to get you into church?"

"Nope, but may I just say again that I think it's a fine solution for everybody involved."

"The ladies might disagree with you there," she said.

"They've been asking why I haven't stayed for a single supper on the grounds in over a month."

"And did you tell them why?"

"Certainly not," she gasped. "What would they think? A wife making a deal with her husband like that. Exchanging your attendance at Sunday services for my agreeing to spend the rest of the day in bed with you."

"It's a bargain I'll have no trouble living with, I can tell you that," he said, placing kisses on her bare breasts as his hand slid over her hip to cup her bottom seductively.

"You agreed to be a little more reverent in public," she reminded him.

"And you agreed to be a lot more sinful in private," he finished, rolling her onto her back. "Here, with me, like this."

"Amen," she whispered, just before he covered her mouth and silenced her with a very wicked kiss.

Dear Readers,

As I celebrate the release of my seventh book, *Sinful*, I'm proud and excited to now be a part of the Kensington family. I appreciate all the cards and letters over the last three years and hope you found *Sinful* to be worth the wait.

As with all my books, *Sinful* contains actual historical facts and individuals, along with my fictional characters and setting. I've taken a few liberties with the dates of Carrie Nation's renowned battles against the saloons, but otherwise the information on her, William Demorest, and Frances Willard is accurate.

I love to hear from readers and you can write me at P.O. Box 63021, Pensacola FL 32526.

Best Wishes Always,
Marti Jones

Put a Little Romance in Your Life With
Betina Krahn